CLOUD OF DEATH

TERROR IN LOS ALAMOS

A NOVEL

DONALD HOUSER

DEDICATION

I dedicate this book to all concerned about runaway militarism and the survival of the Planet.

ACKNOWLEDGMENTS

Although this book is based on contemporary circumstances and issues, any resemblance to real people or places in this book is purely coincidental.

I want to thank my editors Ioanna Carlsen, John Voorhees, and Marianna Versteeg for all their help.

CHAPTER 1

Abdul finally decided to leave Chicago, but wasn't sure where he should go. He knew the San Francisco area reasonably well after four years of college at Berkeley and wondered if Cindy Clayton would still be in the area. She undoubtedly had graduated last May with her pre-med degree and may have left the area. He would relish seeing her again. Even just catching a glimpse of her would be rewarding. He recalled the wonderful times he had spent with her— her mesmerizing face and laugh, her beautiful body next to his.

As he pondered where he could go and what he should do, thoughts about Cindy grew like an entwining vine that Abdul could not ignore. When he searched the internet for her address, he found her address in Albuquerque. She was either in medical school or taking time off, living with her parents. But her parents lived in Santa Fe.

He doubted that Cindy ever expected or wanted to see him again. She could easily be in another relationship, attracting men and captivating them with her wit and beauty wherever she went. He had been so enamored of her. His decision to ignore her the end of the last semester washed over him like a douse of putrid water. Seeking her out from a security standpoint could be dangerous. In the end, his desire to see Cindy again became a towering obsession that overcame his doubts and fears.

On August 10, 2018, he bought his bus ticket for Albuquerque, ignoring all the reasons why contacting Cindy was ill-advised. Upon his arrival in Albuquerque, he went first to the University of New Mexico and lifted a student's wallet, taking the student's ID. He substituted his picture on the ID and rented a room in the area. Once settled, he went to an internet café and looked at Google maps for Cindy's location. She was residing in a residential area near the University. He decided to clandestinely surveil her house to learn her daily activities.

Abdul drove the stolen Yamaha motorcycle past Cindy's house, his identity hidden by the helmet and visor. The morning was warm, but hadn't reached the hot summer temperatures that the city regularly experienced. He loved the clear blue skies with only a few wispy clouds that were so common in New Mexico. Cindy's house was a large, gabled-roof, two story house with a sizable oak tree in the front of the grassed yard. The neighborhood seemed upscale and inviting with many different style houses, most with lawns and pleasant landscaping.

Was he making a stupid mistake wanting to contact Cindy? Maybe instead he needed to go to San Diego and meet with Zahra, his contact of last resort and leave the US. No, he wasn't yet at a last resort. He had money and guile. He just needed to calm his errant mind and find some semblance of normality. Cindy could always draw him out of his shell. She was a pacifist and would be against any violent act. He thought many of her views were naïve, but loved her commitment to peace. He wouldn't be able to discuss any possible plans with her and would have to repeatedly lie. Such subterfuge did not appeal to him, but would be a necessity.

Meeting her in a neutral setting as if he just ran into her, he resolved would be the best approach in order to gauge her reaction upon seeing him again. In the morning after removing his false mustache and dying his hair back to its original color, he waited near her house for her to emerge. When she left her house walking toward the University, he followed her. She entered a coffee house and took a seat by herself. He surveyed the coffee house for cameras and located only one. He kept his face down, entered, bought a coffee at the register, and walked toward her table. The alluring aroma of the roasting coffee reminded him of the many times he and Cindy had enjoyed coffee together.

He stopped at her table and waited for her to look up. "Cindy, is that you?" he asked, feigning surprise with a stretched face.

Cindy dropped her phone and looked at him with a double take. "Abdul!" she exclaimed, leaping up to give him a hug and kiss on the cheek. "What are you doing in Albuquerque?"

Her familiar perfume, intimate hug, and kiss made him swoon. "Checking out graduate schools," Abdul answered after recovering his breath.

"Sit down," she said pointing to the chair opposite. "I'm at the University Medical School." She paused to scrutinize him. "You look great, you've gained some weight."

"You look great yourself," Abdul replied. "I am so pleased to see you."

Cindy was wearing black jeans and a short sleeved mauve shirt. Her scintillating deep blue eyes and golden hair, hanging loosely, enchanted him. He felt so tranquil in her presence and was glad he had decided to contact her.

"How long are you here?" she asked with enthusiasm.

"I'm not sure. At least a few days. I need to be back at Berkeley before the end of August to finish my last year."

"I looked for you at the graduation ceremonies last semester. When you never returned my calls, I thought I had offended you, or you had found another friend."

"I'm sorry I ignored your calls. There was never anyone else. The news of what was happening in Yemen drove me into such agonizing despair and worry for my family that I couldn't think straight."

"You don't need to explain. I can't imagine the worry the situation in Yemen caused you. It's horrible and criminal what is happening there." She gazed lovingly at him, and he felt buoyed by her gaze. She looked even more beautiful than the last time he saw her.

"It's so good to see you," she said as she placed her hands on the table and leaned in. "I thought I'd never see you again." She looked down in embarrassment, her smooth cheeks rosy. Looking up with a brilliant smile her eyes wide, she announced, "Hey, I was planning on going to a party tonight." She reached across the table and grasped his hand.

Her touch created the warm excitement that it always did. He felt his blood coursing and wanted to embrace her.

"Would you like to go with me?" Cindy asked. She didn't wait for his answer. "The party should be fun. Why don't you come by my house around eight? I share the house with a few other female students." She glanced at her phone. "I'm sorry I can't stay and talk more. I've got a class." She hastily wrote down her address and phone number on a paper and handed it to

Abdul, then stood. "I'll see you tonight then. I won't take no for an answer. This is wonderful."

Abdul stood with Cindy. She quickly hugged and kissed him on the cheek before holding him at arm's length. "See you tonight," she said as she swiveled away, striding from the shop.

He watched her leave, astonished by her happiness at seeing him again. He felt so tranquil— as if a stifling hood had been lifted from his head.

At the party in a student shared house attended by mostly medical students, Cindy was rushed by young men wishing to talk to her. She looked spectacular in a sleek blue dress and turquoise squash blossom necklace. She introduced Abdul to all, but fortunately did not reveal he was from Yemen. He enjoyed the party and its atmosphere of normality. His training in Sana'a and his travels from Yemen for revenge seemed so foreign in this jovial company.

After leaving Cindy to obtain another soft drink, he rejoined her as she was engaged in a heated conversation with another student. "Trump has done the opposite of his campaign pledges to get us out of these foreign wars," Cindy vehemently declared in reply to the student's statement that Trump was a good President and was keeping the US safe. "He has increased military involvement in Afghanistan and Syria and ramped up support for Saudi Arabia's criminal bombing of Yemen. He's one of the best terrorist recruiters we've ever had."

The student was cowered by Cindy's retort. "I don't know much about that," he replied. "I think Trump's a lot better than Hilary would have been."

Cindy stared with disgust at the student before turning away and grabbing Abdul's arm. After they moved away a short distance, Cindy turned to Abdul. "The ignorance of Trump supporters makes me so angry. How can a graduate student studying medicine be so easily duped by the crap Trump says?"

Abdul kissed her cheek. "Some people just need an authoritarian figure."

"Oh, Abdul I'm so happy you are back." She hugged him tightly. "Let's go back to my place. I can't take anymore idiots."

When Cindy escorted Abdul into her house, he was so keyed up that he felt light headed. He told himself he should leave, but knew he wouldn't. Cindy shouldn't have to endure his duplicity. She was so trusting of him. Sadly, he was already betraying her trust. They stood looking at each other in the entrance way in front of the stairs as if they'd just met for the first time. Abdul wanted to grab her and kiss her passionately, but his compunction about deceiving her kept him rooted to the spot.

"Let's go upstairs to my room and get comfortable." Cindy finally said, seizing his hand.

He allowed her to pull him up the stairs, his anticipation building like a storm cloud. Her spacious room had a large window with purple curtains that matched the bedspread, a bookcase loaded with books, and a small oak desk. She left the light off, letting the moonlight shining in the window illuminate the room, giving the room an ambience of intimacy. After an energetic sexual romp, Abdul laid back, clutching Cindy to him, cherishing the warmth that infused his body and mind.

"It's so lovely to be in your arms again," Cindy said "I've missed you, Abdul, more than I realized. I feel so happy." She placed her hand on his sculptured chest. "What did you do over the summer?" Her soft voice and loving gaze struck deep into his heart.

He stared at her in silence a few seconds, his thoughts whirling like a dust devil. He knew it was unwise to tell her about his family, but the urge to unburden himself was too great. "I went back to Yemen," he said, trying to hold back the tears.

She sat up. "How was your family? How did you manage to get there?" Her questions weakened him, and he could feel the overwhelming sorrow rearing its ugly head. "From what I understand it is hard for even journalist to get into the Houthi controlled areas."

The damn broke and he started weeping uncontrollably, covering his face with his hands.

"Abdul, what happened? Tell me." She hugged him to her. "Oh, Darling, it must have been horrible there."

He closed his eyes as his tears continued. It felt so good to be hugged and comforted. He would never ever again experience his mother's soothing caress. "I witnessed my home being bombed and my family killed," he blurted out.

"What!" She shoved him apart to look into his tear filled eyes, then grasped him to her even tighter. "No... Abdul, how horrible. My God, I am so sorry." She kissed the top of his head and rocked him as she wept with him.

He cried for what seemed like an eternity. He couldn't seem to stop. When he softly lifted himself away from her, her chest was covered with tears and mucous. He touched her tear-covered face. "Thank you.

I've never told anyone about what happened. I'm sorry for breaking down." He took a deep breath, slipped from the bed and walked into the bathroom to splash water on his face. He felt a profound lightening of the burden he had been keeping to himself.

"I feel so helpless and forlorn," Abdul said when he returned from the bathroom. "I have no family anymore. I feel like a tree that has been uprooted. I have no home. Sometimes I hate the Americans so much I want to strike back at this crazy country."

"Oh Abdul, I understand your anger. We must protest and organize to stop the murder the Saudis are raining down on Yemen."

Abdul accepted Cindy's comment in silence. No—protesting and organizing would not be his course of action. He would strike back at the Americans despite what Cindy would think of him. America was waging war on Yemen. They were as guilty as the Saudis for killing his family, and he would make them pay somehow.

CHAPTER 2

Abdul was forlorn and miserable when he first came to the United States to attend the University of California at Berkeley in 2014. He had never been away from home and family for any extended time and worried about being able to adapt to such an unfamiliar situation. He had applied to the University at his father's insistence. His father told him it was considered the best public university in America. Only the best for his son. When he was accepted, he couldn't believe it.

He didn't want to be so far away from his family, but the package they offered him was one of the best of the colleges. Besides English, he was fairly fluent in German and French although both were not as good as his English. He thought his acceptance to the Paris Sciences et Lettres or the Humboldt Universitat zu Berlin were better choices since they were closer to Yemen. His father and mother had told him it was his choice, although his father favored Berkeley. His father was excited that Barack Obama was President of the US and believed Obama would lead the world to greater peace.

He remembered vividly the night his mother had joined him outside in the vineyard as he watched the moon and twinkling stars over the mountains and reminisced about the wonderful times he had had as a boy in his mountain village. She had placed her arm around him and kissed him on the cheek. She was beautiful in the moonlight, her reddish brown hair peaking from her head scarf and those gray eyes reflecting moonlight like rays of love.

"My beautiful and dutiful Son," his mother had said, "are you thinking of what university to attend?"

"Yes, Mama." He turned to face his mother. "I know Father wants me to go to Berkeley, but I worry about being so far from home. Maybe Europe is a better choice."

"I know you want to be near us, and I would love if you were close. I expect things to get worse here. The discontent with Hadi and his ties to Saudi Arabia is growing. I hope you will decide to accept one of the wonderful offers in America or Europe. The choice is yours, but I believe America will determine the future of Yemen. Perhaps going to university in the US will prepare you better for the future world and Yemen. I want you to be a leader and foresee a great future for you."

He had cried for the first time since he was a small child as soon as he left his father at the Sana'a Airport and stepped into the security line on August 20, 2014 at the age of 21. When he said goodbye to his mother, brother and sister outside their village home, he had hardened himself to keep his tears at bay; but, as he walked away from his father, the import of his schooling so far away hit him like a crashing wave, and he couldn't stop the cascade of tears.

When he was out of sight, he stopped, dropped his bag, and tried to compose himself. Wiping his eyes, he tried to focus on the opportunity college in the US would offer. He sighed, picked up his bag, and moved to the X-ray machine, placing his bag on the rollers. He passed through the security metal detector and walked toward his gate, feeling that he was embarking on a journey that would change his life forever.

He had always liked traveling and learning new things. He had travelled as a teenager all over Yemen, visited Oman, and a few places in Iran, but he had never been to Europe or North America. When he had asked to stay until the situation in Yemen improved, his father had been adamant that he couldn't pass up the opportunity he had been given. "You are the future of Yemen, you must go," his father had said.

As the plane touched down at the Frankfurt Airport, Abdul felt a rush of relief. Flying for the first time in his life from Sana'a to Frankfurt had been scary and exhilarating. He was amazed at the engineering feats that had gone into making these immense airplanes capable of traveling such long distances with so many passengers. While waiting patiently for his connecting flight, he couldn't believe the size of the Frankfurt Airport, and the swarm of people scurrying to their flights or waiting to board their planes. When he boarded his plane for San Francisco, he wondered what life in the US would be like. His only knowledge of the US was the international news and the few American TV programs he had seen. He felt like an avatar of himself, and the avatar was making this journey while his real self was still in his beautiful mountain village.

When he touched down in San Francisco, he thanked God for keeping him safe. The long passport control lines worried him. He had a student visa and anticipated he would be allowed entry. Even so he was still nervous that there could be a problem. If so what would he then do?

When it was his turn, he stepped up to the Immigration Officer and smiled. The man looked at him without smiling and perused his passport. He asked Abdul's destination. After Abdul told him he was a going to attend college at the University of California at Berkeley, the man asked to see his college admittance. Abdul nervously withdrew his admittance papers and handed it to the officer. When the officer stamped his passport and said 'welcome to the United States', Abdul almost fainted. He thanked the officer profusely. The officer nodded, motioned him onward, and called 'next'.

His bus ride to Berkeley across the immense Bay Bridge with the steady stream of vehicles astonished him. How could there be so many cars? He thought he saw more cars on his journey then there were in all of Yemen. When he went to the admission office after exiting the bus and taking a taxi to the University, he felt out of place in the cluster of large buildings and the many students rushing every which way.

The dormitory room at the University he would share with two other students was modern, functional, light, and airy. He was glad to settle back on the single bed exhausted by his trip. He was still shaking from the ordeal.

The other students in his room arrived in a few days and seemed friendly upon first meeting. He was on an all-male floor while other floors of the dormitory had both male and female occupants. He was glad he wouldn't have to adapt to being on the same floor as women. Just the fact that women were living in the same building would take some getting used to. Everything seemed so alien to him.

The other students in his room, both Americans, made fun of his unsophisticated manner and accent when they got to know him more. He didn't have a cellphone or a computer and soon realized he would need to acquire both. The travelling money his father had given him would not be enough for both. He was able to buy a used laptop and hoped his arranged job at the food commons would allow him to afford a simple cellphone.

His roommates began to call him the Arab openly, which made him mad. He didn't want to stand out. He cherished Yemen's rich history and believed Yemen to be the jewel of Arabia. He disliked the Saudis and their backward repressive monarchy that he believed was responsible for much of the turmoil Yemen had experienced.

He mostly ignored the spoiled roommates, who seemed more interested in their cell phones than their studies, often talking about posts on Facebook, or Twitter, or the women in their classes. He thought they were foolish and immature. He buckled down to his classes, finding them challenging and difficult. He was way behind in many of the skills the other students possessed. He had to study long and hard. Since he had always excelled at school, he expected with hard work he could do well in his classes even in the midst of such a strange environment.

He hoped his understanding of English, which he had learned at a young age from his mother, Adelina, who spoke fluent English, French, German, Farsi and of course Arabic, and had an uncanny ability to mimic the voices of others, would be an essential asset for his studies. He owed so much to his amazing mother. They often played a game mimicking the voices of people they knew, who the other would have to guess.

Adelina had graduated from the University of Dhamar, one of the first female graduates, where she met Abdul's father, Kasim. She encouraged Abdul's learning and inspired his interest in literature, science, art, and philosophy. Although she was a Moslem, she urged Abdul to learn about other religions. He felt that her religious proclivity was for a universal religion where all people were respected and honored. She forbade him to use the world infidel.

His father was in contrast a practicing Sunni Moslem, who often didn't agree with the eclectic view of his wife and had encouraged his son to follow the precepts of Islam. Kasim's job with the government made their life relatively prosperous compared to the other families in the village. Kasim wore a turban, traditional white thoob with a western style sports jacket, and his jambiya dagger to work as many prominent Yemen men did.

Most of his youth Abdul wore the thoob and was given his jambiya when he was ten. He had been so proud of the jewel encrusted dagger, symbolizing his entrance into manhood. He was happy in his youth, living in the secluded village high in the mountains.

In 2010 Abdul discarded the traditional thoob for trousers and a shirt much to his father's displeasure. His father believed tradition was to be cherished, but knew Yemen needed to modernize. He often complained of the corruption and tribalism that affected the government. His father's greatest delight was their beautiful property with its productive terraced vineyard handed down from his father's grandfather and his father before him.

CHAPTER 3

Abdul settled into a routine at Berkeley and was soon able to afford a simple cell phone and its monthly fee, although he rarely used it. He had no real friends to call. His scholarship grant included books, food plan, tuition, and payment for his work at the Food Commons.

He had left Yemen for the US as rebels fighting Hadi's persecution of the Houthi were gaining control of towns in the north, taking advantage of Hadi's inept governance. Climate change and the resulting drought had affected crops and the availability of clean drinking water. Poverty was increasing and corruption was pervasive. President Hadi's removal of the fuel subsidies fostered additional discontent and further fueled increased Houthi's attacks on government troops.

When Abdul learned the Houthi had seized control of the capital, Sana'a, in September, he became worried about his family. He wrote his father and asked if he could return, doubting he could do well in this strange country. It was as if he was in an American movie that was nearly impossible to understand. He was disappointed when he received his father's response, mandating that he remain in the United States until he graduated and the fighting in Yemen ceased.

In January 22, 2015 Hadi and his government resigned and Hadi fled to Aden. The Houthi had tried to institute a power sharing agreement with the Hadi government, but Hadi and the international community rejected their efforts. In March the Saudis and Emirates started their bombing campaign with the help of the US and Great Britain to unseat the Houthi's control. The bombing caused the closure of the Sana'a Airport, ruined any chance of Abdul returning to Yemen without great difficulty, and ended any correspondence from his family.

Abdul, devastated by the news coming out of Yemen, had a hard time with his studies. He reduced the number of classes, so he could concentrate more on his courses and improve his skills enough so that he could compete with the other students, determined to make excellent grades and make his father proud. He took classes in the summer to make up for some of the classes he dropped. He wanted to complete his degree as fast as possible to hasten his return to his family. Even with summer classes, the number of courses that he would need to carry to graduate in four years in electrical engineering he found daunting. He came to the realization that he would need five years to complete his degree. His first year he earned almost all A's except for his English composition class for which he earned a B. He vowed that the B would be his last. He would get nothing but 'A's.

To Abdul's dismay, his Arabic accent when speaking English made him stand out in his classes and his work at the Food Commons, subjecting him to obvious discrimination. He longed to blend in and be accepted as just another student. Other Muslim students sought him out, but most seemed brain washed by their religion, and he avoided their company. He felt so alone and cut off.

To alleviate the discrimination and better integrate into the student population, Abdul believed he needed to get rid of his accent. With his light skin, light brown hair, and gray eyes, he expected he could pass as an American if he had no recognizable accent. After months of practice, mimicking the speech of American students, he believed he had successfully eradicated his Arabic accent. No one would know he was from Yemen unless he told them. He felt much better being accepted as another American. He enjoyed telling people, whom he met in town, he was from LA. When they believed him, he felt triumphant, which helped to distract from his loneliness.

He took a second job in town to make up for the money he no longer received from his father. With two jobs, it seemed that almost all of his time was spent studying or working, which although exhausting seemed to moderate his loneliness by keeping him engaged. During nights of deep despair, he often thought of just giving up and returning to Yemen. Other nights, he considered himself honor bound to complete his studies.

He sought out news about Yemen with a passion. The news was horrible and added to his uneasiness at being in college in a totally alien environment in a country that was the chief supporter of the Saudis. The relentless bombing campaign was wreaking havoc on the Houthi controlled areas of Yemen, killing large numbers of civilians. Famine and cholera were spreading. The world health organization called Yemen the worst humanitarian crisis on the planet. His only consolation was that the isolated nature of his village in the mountains had no military significance, and his family home would probably be safe from the bombs. However, his father's daily travel to and from work and his office in the government building in Dhamar exposed his father to the bombing. He wasn't sure his father even still had his job as an accountant or for that matter was even alive.

He thought of possibly transferring to a University in Germany, but even Germany sold arms to the Emirates, who were bombing and fighting the Houthi rebels as well as the Saudis. Besides, he doubted, given the Yemen situation, he had any chance of admittance at a college in Europe. His depression was like a monkey on his back, driving him into even greater hopelessness. America was not the country he and his family had imagined. The Government official poverty rate was fourteen percent of the population, although he suspected the parameters for calculating the poverty rate were grossly conservative and did not include the burgeoning homeless population.

Remembering the beach along the Red Sea he enjoyed with his family, Abdul visited the beaches in San Francisco to find some semblance of enjoyment. On his travels across the city, he was dismayed by the extent of homeless people he saw. How could the supposed richest country in the world allow the poor and troubled to be abandoned? America was essentially in the control of large corporations and wealthy families, who appeared to disdain the poor. A government for and by the people was a joke.

Maybe the corruption wasn't as blatant as that in Yemen, but existed just the same. People had the right to speak out without fear of being put in jail, but their lives unless they were privileged in some way were a struggle, especially for minorities. The wealthy in the US lived in splendor like the wealthy in Yemen.

Repression of the poor by the police was staggering. The per capita prison population was the highest in the world, unless one considered North Korea, which did not disclose their prison population numbers. Private prisons had turned incarceration into a lucrative business.

He seldom went out at night and never dated, although many attractive young women flirted with him in the cafeteria and in his liberal arts classes. When he was in secondary school in Yemen, he had many female friends, but the norms of Yemen society prohibited any intimacy, and he had never been alone with a woman, other than his mother or sister. A part of him missed female friendship, but he paid women little mind, until the day near the end of his second year, when a young woman in the library bumped into him, sending her books to the ground.

"I am so sorry," he said as he crouched down and helped pick up her books. The women's sapphire blue eyes, stunning face, and long blond hair captivated him.

"Don't worry… it's my fault," she said. "I wasn't looking where I was going." Her sweet honeyed voice reminded him of his mother's voice. "I've seen you around campus. You work at the Food Common. I've heard you're from Yemen."

Abdul stunned by her statement and smile, looked away briefly before he could manage to reply. "Yes."

"My name's Cindy," she said extending her hand.

"Mine is Abdul." He grasped her hand and shook it gently. Her warm hand felt marvelous and he was reluctant to let it go.

"I'm so sorry that the United States is supporting Saudi Arabia. I think the bombing in Yemen is criminal." Standing, she was nearly as tall as Abdul. She was wearing an unbuttoned royal blue shirt on top of a light blue tank top, and tight blue jeans. Turquoise tear-drop, silver earrings, hanging from her delicately shaped ears, were revealed when she pushed he hair behind her shoulders, her face flushed in embarrassment. She had a lithe, shapely, model's body. Her nearness and beauty made his mouth dry and his breath difficult.

"I agree." Abdul said. He felt extremely warm and wanted to flee, but could not stop gazing at the woman.

"I'm glad I ran into you." She laughed. "Not literally." She studied him looking like she was working out a puzzle before continuing. "There's a meeting tonight of the War Resisters League. I go to most of the meetings. I think it's an important organization, which you might be interested in learning more about. Would you like to go with me?"

Her invitation startled him. Why would this striking American woman be inviting him to accompany her anywhere? He stared at her in silence, trying to decide what he should say. "Could I get in trouble for attending?"

"No. Why do you say that?" She placed her hand on his shoulder.

"In my country such activity would be very dangerous." He felt as if he was melting with her touch. He had never been touched by a woman so tenderly except his mother.

"Don't worry it is perfectly safe. I think you'll find it interesting." She stepped closer. "What do you say?"

He didn't think getting involved with an American woman or going to such an organization was wise. He had heard that Moslem students were often under surveillance. He didn't want to do anything that would jeopardize his scholarship. "Yes, I would like to go." He was surprised by the answer he had blurted out. He didn't understand why he felt he needed to go with this friendly women. Maybe it was because if he didn't go he might never see her again. And he definitely wanted to see her again.

"Great, I'll meet you in front of the library at 7:30," she announced. She smiled brightly. "See you later." She turned and walked away, her long legs moving with alacrity as Abdul stared at her disappearing form.

CHAPTER 4

Abdul enjoyed the meeting of the War Resisters League. He had read about the immense US military budget, and the meeting brought to light the vast armaments and nuclear weapons the US produced. The size of the US military spending seemed absurdly large given the percent of the national budget, and how it dwarfed military spending in the rest of the world. He learned about President Eisenhower's farewell speech warning about the danger of the military industrial complex to democracy. After the meeting, he wasn't prepared for the interest the members paid him when they learned he was from Yemen. He was relieved when Cindy interrupted the group gathered around him and pulled him from the meeting.

"I could tell all the interest from the members was causing you discomfort," Cindy said, rubbing his shoulder. "I'm sorry that I announced you were from Yemen. I should have known everyone would want to harangue you."

"Thank you. It was a little overwhelming."

She took him to a small café, and they had coffee. Most of the others at the meeting were going to a bar to continue their discussion. Abdul told her that coffee originally came from Yemen, and in ancient times Yemen was the leading producer of coffee. Coffee was still grown in the mountains of Yemen for export and was the favored Yemen drink. Being with Cindy felt wonderful, and he was glad he had accompanied her. He wanted to ask if he could see her again and was formulating his request in his mind.

"Tomorrow, a friend of mine is playing at a local bar and restaurant in the evening," she announced. "I know as a Moslem you do not drink alcohol. Is it forbidden to go to places that serve alcohol?"

"No. I do not drink alcohol, but I have nothing against being in a place where it is served. I like music. I played the oud in Yemen." He didn't want to admit he had tried alcohol and enjoyed the taste of beer.

"When you finish work I could meet you outside the Commons, and we could go if you like."

"I would like that very much."

The following evening, Abdul accompanied her to the bar that was already crowded when they entered. The noise level in the small space seemed deafening to Abdul, and he wondered how someone could play over the din, but once the guitar player took the stage the crowd became surprisingly quiet. Abdul enjoyed the guitar playing and singing of her friend. He liked music and missed the haunting sounds of the homayni folk music his mother loved. He wished he had brought his oud with him to the US. His mother often had sung along as he played his oud, her lyrical voice sweet and uplifting. Oh, how he missed his family. He had given his oud to his sister when he left. He knew his mother would teach his sister to play the instrument as she had taught him.

Cindy and he began to meet often after his work for coffee or to attend music events. He came out of his shell gradually. Cindy's attention was like a poultice drawing out his shy personality. He grew to like hearing American folk music especially the music of Bob Dylan.

Cindy's favorite Bob Dylan song was *Masters of War*. A song she claimed the Americans needed to take to heart.

Cindy seemed genuinely interested in him as a person and not just because he was from Yemen. He knew that his uniqueness as a Yemeni had drawn her to him, but he sensed she grew to like him as a person. She asked about his life growing up, his parents, and siblings. She was a breath of fresh air.

Abdul had had a happy childhood. He was the first born and enjoyed being the only child and the lavish love his mother nearly suffocated him with. When his sister was born when he was eight, he was a little jealous, but soon grew to enjoy having a baby sister. He became very protective of her and would not allow anyone to tease her. She was a jolly child, who loved to laugh. When he was fourteen, his baby brother was born, and he delighted in playing with the rambunctious child. He taught his sister how to swim on the many family excursions across the mountains to the Red Sea and loved to skim his little brother over the water to the child's throaty laughs. His neighbor friend, Mohammed, would often accompany them. He didn't mind when his sister followed Mohammed and him on their many hikes into the majestic mountains. He had loved his family so much and their life in the mountains. He wished he was able, like the many other students, to visit his family for the summers and the holidays.

Cindy took him to movies, plays, and demonstrations. She told him her parents were both lawyers and insisted on paying her share. They often argued about who would pay. He felt as a man he was required to pay, but grew to like her sense of independence. She was a strong woman like his mom.

She was from Santa Fe, New Mexico, a town high in the mountains like his village in Yemen. She told him it was a unique and beautiful town like no other in the United States. It had three cultures, Native American, Hispanic, and Anglo. It sounded very interesting.

At the end of the semester, Cindy left for the summer to travel with her family to Europe, and he missed her company immensely. He mostly moped through the summer, going to class and working. He hoped he could save enough money to buy an oud so he could play Yemeni music for Cindy. He did go to one meeting of the War Resisters League that summer, but was inundated with questions about the situation in Yemen, which he only knew about through the articles he read in the papers and online. Unless a hospital was blown up or some other bombing of civilians occurred, there was little mainstream news about the war. He relied on reading news of Yemen mostly on the Aljazeera and BBC web sites.

When Cindy returned at the end of summer, he was delighted to see her. His student life was so much more enjoyable and fulfilling when she was around. They became even closer. They studied together and went almost everywhere together when he wasn't attending classes or working. She helped with his computer skills and opened his eyes to what global warming was doing to the planet.

She was a staunch vegan. A concept he had never heard of before. Meat was a luxury for most in Yemen. She believed meat and dairy production needed to be drastically curbed if global warming had any chance to be mitigated. Global warming was already wreaking havoc and would get catastrophically worse. Exploitive capitalism needed to be reined in if the world had any chance. Global temperatures were already reaching new highs and were projected to get worse.

The soaring summer temperatures and drought in Yemen had been causing problems even before he left. Cindy purported that if significant actions were not taken the world seemed on a course to deadly warming that would cause incredible chaos and could destroy humankind.

He was intrigued by Cindy's world views, but thought her views were unrealistic. People in Yemen would welcome growth and a less chaotic society. She introduced him to smoking marijuana. He liked the effect much better than qat, which was extremely popular in Yemen. Qat was made from the leaves of a flowering shrub native to the Arabian Peninsula. Chewing qat induced a feeling of euphoria and stimulation similar to the use of amphetamines. He had often shared qat with his father and other men in the village. It was a Yemini tradition that he thought was much too pervasive. Much of the agricultural area in Yemen had been converted from growing food to qat, which required large amounts of water, a dwindling resource in Yemen.

Abdul attended the Woman's March in San Francisco with Cindy in January 2017. The size and peacefulness of the demonstration against President Trump amazed him. The Arab Spring uprising demonstrations in Yemen in 2011 were brutally attacked by the military, resulting in the death of 200 demonstrators. He wondered how such an unpopular person like Trump had been elected President. Cindy said it was because too many voters didn't bother to vote and the antiquated electoral system that allowed a candidate, who lost the real vote, to win the electoral vote.

He was surprised that Americans would not exercise their right to vote. Almost everyone he knew in Yemen felt voting was important. Cindy said voter suppression was used by the Republicans to reduce the number of minorities voting. People were taken off the voter rolls because they had the same last name as people in other States or other spurious reasons. She believed Michigan and Wisconsin, both controlled by Republican Governors, cheated in counting the votes so Trump would win the Electoral College. She believed Hilary Clinton had actually won even the Electoral vote and should be President. Trump was an illegitimate President as far as she was concerned. It seemed the US was not that much different than Yemen where the elite in power thought they could get away with such actions.

Several months after the Women's March, Cindy invited him to stay over at her off-campus apartment she shared with another woman. He was so nervous he had trouble breathing and his heart sounded like it was pounding in his head. When they finished watching the news, she took his hand and pulled him gently into her bedroom. She had him sit on the bed while she disrobed in front of him.

His stiffness was soon like a crowbar as he watched her with rising anticipation. Naked, she pulled him up from the bed, kissed him passionately and began unbuttoning his shirt. He frantically helped her remove his clothes, and they fell together in bed. Their love making was energetic, causing him to almost pass out when he climaxed. The warmth that enveloped his body was so enjoyable. He understood for the first time why romantic love was so universally esteemed in literature around the world.

CHAPTER 5

Abdul's fourth year at Berkeley was split between the joy of being with Cindy and the distress with the continuing humanitarian crisis in Yemen. The constant news about the demented American President didn't help. Cindy hoped the Mueller investigation would eventually cause President Trump to resign. He, however, thought the President would never resign. Trump's rally speeches and actions, he thought were a prelude to him seizing complete fascist control. Dictator wannabes seldom relinquished power without being forced to. He was amazed that the Republicans were supportive of such a dangerous liar. He often wondered why he continued to study in this crazy country.

He had a brief respite from the distressing news when he accompanied Cindy to visit her parents in Santa Fe for Christmas. The spectacular walk down Acequia Madre and Canyon Road on Christmas eve to view the soft light of thousands of farolitos, paper sacks with candles, along the roads, on walls, and on the parapets of houses, and luminarias, small fires to warm the viewers and act as stations to sing carols, had been a joy. When she took him to the Native American ruins at Bandelier National Monument where Puebloan ancestors lived from the 1150 to 1350, he had been fascinated by the settlement and their primitive dwellings. Yemen during this same time period was ruled by the Ayyubid Dynasty that fought the Zaydis Shia and conquered Sana'a and Dhamar in 1198, putting the Zaydis and most of Yemen under Sunni control. Quite a different history of turmoil and war from the peaceful Puebloan communities.

After Bandelier they went into Los Alamos. He didn't really like their visit to the secluded city on the mesas, where the first atomic bomb was made. Something about the town gave him an eerie feeling that was compounded when they visited the Bradbury Science Museum. He had been appalled by the history of the National Laboratory and its destructive nuclear research.

Once back at school the beautiful trip to Santa Fe and the disturbing trip to Los Alamos faded to a distant memory like so many memories that crowded his brain. His courses became more exacting, and he had to study longer and harder. His growing moroseness with the news from Yemen didn't help his studies. He often found an excuse that he needed to study to beg off going with Cindy to some event. It seemed crazy to be involved with an American woman no matter how supportive she was of him. Toward the end of the semester, he broke off contact with Cindy and didn't return her calls. The few times he encountered her from a distance on campus he would turn and go the other way. He just couldn't face being near her and rationalized that it would be better if she forgot about him.

When his semester ended in May of 2018, he was determined to see his family for the summer and see for himself what the Saudi led bombing was doing to Yemen. The so-called Muslim ban by Trump had been stayed by the courts, but was going to the Supreme Court. It was possible he would not be able to return to the US and complete his degree if he left, but this gave him little pause. He had to see his family.

He understood that travel to Yemen would be fraught with difficulties. He didn't think it was safe to fly to Aden where periodic fighting was common and his home in the Houthi controlled area of Yemen might be a problem with passport control. He had never liked Aden, a port city of lawlessness. He certainly wasn't going to travel to Saudi Arabia and cross into Yemen.

Discounting all the problems that he would face traveling back home, he decided he had to go. On May 15, 2018, he boarded a plane at San Francisco Airport for Frankfurt, Germany. From Frankfurt, he took a bus to Berlin. He was worried that he might be tracked as he suspected many Arabs were and thought leaving Germany from a different airport might be wise. Also, the flights from Berlin were less expensive. He had saved quite a bit of money, but worried about retaining enough money to be able to make his return journey to the US.

In Berlin, he purchased a ticket for a flight to Istanbul, Turkey. Direct flights from Europe to Tehran were banned. He arrived in Istanbul the day after Ramadan began. From Istanbul, he flew to Tehran. He stayed overnight in Tehran at a pleasant hotel, and, in the morning, he purchased a bus ticket to the port city of Bandar Abbas, sleeping in bus stations, awaiting the onward buses. In Bandar Abbas he caught a ferry to Muscat, Oman.

Upon arrival at Oman, his Yemen passport was scrutinized carefully and his bag searched. Oman had not joined the Emirates in support of the bombing campaign against Yemen, but did not support the Houthi rebels. He thought they were a backward country much like Saudi Arabia with their Sultan and repressive government. He was glad when he left the passport and customs office and their stupid questions.

The bus rides across Oman were tedious and exhausting. At the Yemen border, he was questioned rigorously about his reason for entering Yemen from Oman. He had told them he had visited a friend in Tehran, who also went to University in the US. After being kept in a room for several hours of questioning where he had answered repeatedly that he was not political and knew little about the war between the Houthi and Hadi loyalists, he wondered if they would ever let him go. He had explained that he knew Hadi had won the presidential election, and consequently, he believed that Hadi must be the legitimate president. He just wanted to visit his family for the summer and would return to the US to complete his college degree. Eventually, he was allowed to enter Yemen. The whole episode had been draining.

His journey across the desert of Eastern Yemen took longer than expected even though there was little fighting or bombing in what was referred to as the Empty Quarter. He had forgotten how hot it got in this part of Yemen. The midday heat was unbearable and most travel accommodations were only available in the early morning or evening. The oil towns to the south were full of foreigners, whom he occasionally encountered as he travelled across the desolate desert to the north. He sought out the Bedouin tribes, who were a law unto themselves, on his overnight stops. He had traveled among the Bedouins when he was a teenager and knew their code required giving sustenance to visitors. Even though the Bedouins lived a rather primitive life, he admired them and their toughness. Their hospitality and rugged friendliness was gratifying, and he was glad to be in Yemen again. Transportation across the Eastern Quarter was irregular, and he often had to wait most of the day for the minibus taxis to have enough passengers to take him to the next city.

As he got closer to the Houthi controlled area, he knew crossing the front line would be difficult. He went north of Ma'rib, another oil town, and waited at night to sneak into the Houthi area. He was apprehended by Houthi fighters. After a lengthy interrogation, they accepted that he lived in the mountains east of Sana'a, posed no threat, and let him go.

When he entered Sana'a, he expected to see the results of the Saudi bombing campaign, but was unprepared for the devastation. Vast destroyed areas of the city were everywhere. The dust from the building debris, kicked up by the wind, soon coated his face. Emaciated and forlorn people roamed the streets like zombies. He wondered if Dhamar was as devastated. Had his father's government office been bombed? He fretted as he joined the minibus that would rise from Sana'a into the mountains. He would soon know what the war had cost his family.

When he embarked from the minibus, he was excited and anxious. He had heard that the Saudis even bombed mountain villages. He left the road and hurried up the dirt path that would take him to the tiny village of his birth. As he crested the hill, he felt a great relief— the scattered houses were untouched by bombing. He nearly ran to his home with abundant anticipation at seeing his family after four long years.

When he entered the house, his mother, Adelina, turned with surprise and dropped her embroidery. Jumping up, she seized him with joy and wept with happiness. "My son how wonderful to see and hold you, but why have you come? Have you graduated?"

"No Mama, I had to come to see my family. I was so distraught not knowing how you all were. I need another year to graduate with my degree." Abdul held his mother, feeling the warmth her nearness gave his soul. He felt positively overjoyed.

"You shouldn't have come. I don't know how you were even able to get here. Going back may be even more difficult." She shook her head, but seized him tight. "Oh, how wonderful it feels to have you in my arms. You have gotten taller, I think, and even more handsome." She kissed him repeatedly on his cheeks. "Thanks be to God that you have arrived safely." She looked beautiful in her blue and red flowered dress, her long reddish brown hair hanging loosely along her shoulders. Her gray eyes, highlighted by the kohl around them, shone brightly despite the tears.

When his brother came into the house, he stood dumbfounded, staring at Abdul. "Abdul... how can this be?" He rushed up and hugged his brother. "Where did you come from? How did you get here?"

"Oh, Jabir, you have grown so tall," Abdul said as he hugged his brother to him, tears running down his cheeks. "Where is Raufa?"

"At a neighbors," his mother said.

Jabir extricated himself from his brother's arms. "I will go get her. She will be amazed." Without waiting for comment, off he ran.

When Raufa, his sister, came running into the house, Abdul hardly recognized her. She plowed into him at full speed, knocking him back. "Abdul, how wonderful."

Abdul, held her at arm's length. "Raufa, you too have grown so much. You have turned into a beautiful young woman. I bet the boys follow you like bees to flowers."

Raufa blushed and shoved Abdul playfully. "Did you finish college?" Raufa asked.

"No, I have come to visit. The news of what was happening to Yemen made me want to see my family."

His stern father when he returned from work was initially upset. "Abdul, what have you done? You shouldn't be here."

"I was so worried. I needed to make sure you were all alive and well."

"Are you stupid? There is a war on. How did you get here? Has something happened at school? Have you been thrown out?"

"No, Father, I am doing well at school. One more year and I will graduate. I have made straight 'A's."

"Then why have you come? What is wrong with you? You have ignored my wishes. I told you in my last letter that you should not return until the war is over."

"I was so worried. I had trouble studying. I had to know if my family was safe."

"As you can see, we are all safe." His father's screwed-up, angered face relaxed. "Come, my son, embrace me," he said as he held his arms wide.

Abdul rushed to his father and hugged him. His father kissed his cheeks and released Abdul. "I see the

American food has agreed with you. You look well, and I feel the strength of you. I am angry that you have disobeyed me, but overjoyed to see you."

In the evening to break the Ramadan fast, his mother made him his favorite lamb Saltah, a brown stew with fenugreek and chilies, which he devoured with joy. She had recently butchered their last lamb as if somehow she had been expecting him. She couldn't stop kissing him on the cheeks, embarrassing him, but also warming his heart. She was a jovial, tall woman, who tended her family and garden in the highlands and was loved by the entire village.

The whole family was so proud that he was attending an American University and would graduate, if all went well, next year as an electrical engineer, despite their hatred of the US's support of the Saudis. His eleven year old brother, Jabir, and seventeen year old sister, Raufa, hung on his every word. It seemed so long since he had seen them. Raufa was turning into a beautiful gangly young woman. The village boys were often over at their house to catch a glimpse of her. He was so glad to be home and in the bosom of his family.

They were a modest family. His father was the unofficial headman of their small village, more a cluster of houses in the mountains. Their four room house that he had helped his father expand was the largest in the village. Its white washed walls shone in the mountain sun, and the terraced vineyards rose up the descending slope in front of the house. The living room floor was covered with a large red and green, floral-pattern rug that had come from his mom's family and had a luxurious pile. A small table sat to one side near the kitchen where the family ate, sitting on embroidered cushions his mom had made. One wall was covered with his mom's red applique cloth with its yellow and green Islamic, geometric patterns that Abdul remembered staring at for hours, following their convoluted patterns.

His brother tended a few sheep after school and his father still worked at a government office in Dhamar. Abdul was surprised that with the war there was still a school in the mountains and his father still had his job. Most of the schools in the city had closed. A dedicated teacher kept the school open in the nearby village. His family was the only family in the village with a car, which his father, Kasim, drove the many miles to work and tended with loving care. Kasim often brought supplies from Dhamar for the whole village, but admitted that recently finding any food to buy was extremely difficult and incredibly expensive.

Although Kasim worked for the government, he was not political. He followed the Pillars of Islam: faith, prayer, charity, fasting, and pilgrimage. He prayed five times a day, gave alms, did not drink alcohol, or eat pork. He did chew qat as most men in Yemen did. As a young man, he had made his pilgrimage to Mecca. He had worked as a low level accountant for the Saleh government and now for the Houthi.

Kasim had been brought up as a Sunni Arab, but had no animosity for the Zaydi Shia. Adelina was a Zaydi Shia Moslem, but many of her ancestors were Christian. Kasim's family had been against the marriage and threatened to disown him, but he ignored them and they eventually dropped their objections. Adelina was a beautiful intelligent woman, who charmed them and played the dutiful wife. When Kasim's parents died, his father's property passed to him as the eldest of two brothers.

Abdul received religious instruction at school and his family attended the Mosque in Dhamar only occasionally, preferring a smaller, nearby Mosque in the mountains. When his father was not home his mother did not reprimand Abdul for not praying as often as the faith required. He had often questioned his mom about the rigid precepts of the Islamic faith.

The first evening back, Abdul and his father went out to the vineyard to smoke, sitting on one of the terrace walls. Abdul had given up smoking, but was happy to smoke with his father. "I couldn't believe the destruction I saw passing through Sana'a," Abdul said. "Is Dhamar as bombed out?"

"No, Dhamar has been bombed repeatedly, but not nearly as bad as Sana'a or Saana. My building has not been bombed, but other government buildings have." He rubbed his son's back. "Most of the Saudi targets are military installations, but they purposely target hospitals and markets to break our will to fight. They bombed the museum in Dhamar, destroying the artifacts of our history. It is criminal the way the Saudis drop their bombs. Even villages in the mountains with no strategic purpose have been bombed."

"I am worried about you in Dhamar."

"Yes, it is dangerous, but a necessity. The Houthi pay me for my work. Not regularly, but enough to keep the family and the village from starving as many in the cities are. I can't understand why the US supplies the bombs and assists the Saudis with refueling and targeting. The

Saudis bombed and blockaded our only port, Hodeida, which could provide international aid to the starving masses. I expect this kind of cruelty from the Saudis, but cannot imagine how the US condones this."

"The US President Trump is an evil force. He cares nothing for people, only money and power."

"Yes, I see. He is like the Saudi crown prince, Mohammad bin Salman, a despotic madman. Mohammad has taken complete control. He has arrested the others in the royal family that could challenge his power. His father, King Salman, is old and has left the running of Saudi Arabia to his son, who wants to expand his power and control over the entire Middle East. Mohammad wants to restore Hadi or some other puppet leader to power in Yemen, who he will be able to control. He is even working with the Israelis. I think he is using the war with Yemen as a prelude to a war with Iran, practicing his war making skills. Cannot the Americans understand what the Saudis are doing to Yemen?"

"Father, the news of what is happening in Yemen is rarely reported in the US and, even when it is, it garners little interest. The US is not the country we had thought. Its militarism is out of control. The people have become inured to the atrocities the US condones and propagates."

"Yes, my Son, I think you are right. It is sad what has happened to the United States. When Obama was elected I thought the US would finally emerge from their obsession with oil, the Middle East, and lead the world to greater peace. It was not to be."

"The US has military installations in over a hundred countries, supposedly to stop terrorist activities.

However, in reality this militarism creates even greater terrorism."

"It is unfortunate that the US is led by such an evil man. I sincerely hope the people of the US will come to realize what the Saudis are doing to Yemen and stop this madness."

"Father, I want to stay and help the family. After seeing what the US support of the Saudis is doing to Yemen, how can I continue with my studies in the US? I am needed here."

"No," his father shouted. "This cannot be. You must return and complete your degree in electrical engineering. Yemen will need your expertise after the war is over. What could you do by staying here? Are you going to fight with the Houthis? No, of course not. What would your death gain? Nothing... as would any of our deaths."

"I could help with the farm. Perhaps get a job."

"Adelina, your sister, and brother help with the farm. We manage." He looked sternly at his son. "There are no jobs to find." He relaxed his face and placed his hand on Abdul's shoulder. "I cannot conceive that the war can last much longer. The Saudis will not be able to dislodge the Houthis from power with their bombing. Hadi's supporters in the south with the help of American Special Forces, who we know are there, will not drive the Houthis out either. The Saudis are scared of invading, knowing they would be no match for the Houthi, who are seasoned and intense fighters. Dropping bombs from aerial warplanes requires no courage. The Saudis are cowards."

Kasim grabbed his son's arm and turned Abdul to face him. "Please return to the US and complete your degree. I will then welcome you home with open arms of a proud father. You were foolish to return, but I am so glad to be able to see you after so many years." Kasim turned away to hide his tears. "God willing, the family will be safe. I can't conceive why the Saudis would bomb this tiny cluster of houses. In a few weeks you must go and make your return to the United States."

Abdul hugged his father. "I will do as you wish. The family may be safe here in the mountains, but I worry about you in Dhamar."

"Staying here would not prevent my death. If I die in the bombing, it will be God's will."

Abdul didn't believe in God's will anymore, but he would not tell his father this.

"The Saudis can bomb and starve northern Yemen to no avail," his father continued. "A peace settlement is the only solution, and the world will eventually stop the criminal Saudis. Perhaps we should go back to two Yemens. Northern Yemen will never be a part or vassal of Saudi Arabia."

He hoped his father was right.

CHAPTER 6

As Abdul wandered through the vineyard in the early evening of May 29, 2018, the fourth night of his return, while the rest of the family was preparing for dinner, his happiness brimming over despite the devastation he had witnessed in Sana'a, he reminisced about the many hours he spent picking grapes as a boy and playing in the mountains. Life was so simple back then. The last grape harvest his mother told him had been very poor— not enough rain. Their water well had dropped many feet and was only used for the house and watering the vegetable garden. The rise in average temperatures and depletion of fresh water in Yemen, had contributed to the conflict between the South and North Yemen. Global warming was a definite threat. The countries of the world especially the historic polluters like America needed to show by example the need to eliminate the spewing of carbon dioxide and methane and make the transition to clean energy.

He would respect his father's wishes and complete his degree. He had spent four years toward that endeavor. What was one more year? He was glad he had made the journey home. His family was safe and would remain safe. He could resume his studies, knowing his family was alive and well. His father was at daily risk in Dhamar, but he couldn't do anything about that even if he stayed.

When he heard the plane overhead, he stopped and turned his face upwards to watch the Saudi bomber, apparently heading toward Sana'a. He shook his head in dismay— another sortie to kill and maim. His anger rose, and he kicked the dirt of the terrace. "You bastard, Saudi war criminals will pay someday."

When he heard a whistling descent, he twisted back toward his house as a bomb landed, exploding, spurting rubble, fire, and smoke high into the air. For a second of disbelief, he stood unmoving before rushing back up the hill, ignoring the acrid smell and smoke. His family home was nothing but rubble in an immense pit. He frantically began removing the debris, looking for any survivors. Several other men joined him and helped search the rubble. He tore at the chucks of concrete and rocks like a crazed madman, ignoring the sharp rubble that tore at his hands. After what seemed like hours of toil, he found his mother clutching her other son and daughter in the area of the kitchen. He dropped to his knees and caressed their lifeless, torn bodies as his tears erupted. Raising his head, he bellowed at the sky, "No...no. Why... why?"

He continued digging in the rubble, despite the neighbors trying to pull him away. When he found his father in what was the living room, he threw up at the ghastly sight. He pulled what was left of his families' bodies from the rubble and laid them out in a row— Kasim, Adelina, Raufa and Jabir. He stood in a stupor, starring at the mangled bodies until he collapsed next to them. He should be with them. Without a family, he was nothing. His life was essentially over.

After hours of lying next to his family, crying uncontrollably, his neighbors encouraged him to begin the preparation of the bodies for burial. The mangled bodies were washed as best they could three times in accordance with Islamic tradition. Abdul found it extremely hard to participate in the washing as his tears continued unabated, but felt it was his duty. He helped wrap each of the bodies in three white sheets that the neighbors furnished. Others dug the graves in the vineyard, facing north toward Mecca.

In the morning since no caskets were available, Abdul helped lower the bodies in the four raw graves. He tossed the first hand of dirt over each body repeating the prayer, "We created you from it, and return you to it, and from it, we raise you a second time."

The others in the village did the same. Then the bodies were covered with dirt. Abdul with the help of a neighbor fashioned small wooden markers for each grave. In the evening after the burials were finished, Abdul slept at a neighbor's house although little sleep was had. He felt numb and completely hopeless.

He visited the graves in the morning before leaving the village, thanking all his neighbors for their help. To the questions of where he was going and what he was planning to do, he had no answers. In a daze, he followed the trail to the main road and shuffled down the road toward Sana'a. He had to get away as if putting distance from the horrendous scene of his family's death would offer some relief. He caught a minivan to Sana'a and obtained a room in a boarding house. After days spent mostly in bed or roaming around the devastated city often in tears, he decided he was honor bound to revenge the killing of his family. He went to the Houthi government office and asked to join the fight against Hadi and the Saudis.

He was directed to a Houthi rebel commander and joined their ranks, forgetting about ever going back to college. He wanted revenge against the Saudis and their enabler and helper the United States. He had little real interest in fighting the Al-Qaeda and Hadi loyalist in the south, but what else could he do?

CHAPTER 7

Abdul watched the line crossing the border July 9, 2018, wondering how long he would have to wait. The air was still without a whisper of a breeze as the sun beat down on the old gray Mercedes. Flies accumulated on the interior windshield, their buzzing an irritating distraction. The drive from Tabriz, Iran in the early morning had been hot and dusty. Abdul felt as if he was coated in a thin layer of dust and longed for a shower. He had been spoiled by his time in the States.

After arriving in Tabriz the previous evening, Abdul had met his driver, Mohammed, at a popular cafe where qalyan water pipes were plentiful. He had asked his waiter about hiring a car to take him to Turkey, hinting he did not want any undue hassle at the border. The waiter brought to Abdul's table a shuffling Mohammed, so overweight that it was an ordeal for him to sit. Mohammed spoke no German, but uttered a semblance of English. After some haggling, they had agreed on a price for Mohammed to drive Abdul all the way to Erzurum, Turkey.

The interior of the car was stifling even with the windows down as Abdul stared out at the stark, barren plain. He had traveled through Iran by buses on a counterfeit German passport under the name of Hans Zimmer after landing in Bandar Abbas, Iran on the ferry from Oman. He had purchased a bus ticket to Shiraz, staying overnight, keeping to himself and leaving his hotel only to eat. In the morning, he continued on to Esfahan with a new bus, where he maintained the same seclusion, staying in a hotel most of the time, and caught a bus to Tehran in the morning. After overnighting in Tehran, he felt more relaxed and anonymous in the cosmopolitan city. He decided hiding out was silly and ventured out, walking around the bazaar for hours, talking to vendors and eating kebabs and sweets from the myriad small kiosks. When he caught the bus to Tabriz early afternoon, his mood had improved, but he still harbored many conflicting emotions.

The slow movement of the line waiting to cross the border was a concern. If he was caught with a fake passport, it would end his quest for revenge. He thought the counterfeit passport was of high quality, and he expected the passport would be readily accepted as it had been at the Oman and Iranian borders, but one never knew what could induce a border agent to interrogate a traveler further. Border stations had always given him qualms even when he had nothing to hide. The real test would be when he flew to the United States.

As the line moved forward Mohammed showed signs of nervousness. He wondered if using the stranger to take him to Erzurum had been a mistake. The driver's perspiration was much heavier than warranted as the rivulets of sweat rolled over the folds of fat at the back of his neck. Getting out of the line of cars and trucks waiting to cross would draw undue attention to them.

"Mohammed are you feeling okay?" Abdul asked.

"No. My lunch... no good," Mohammed answered.

Perhaps Mohammed was telling the truth. The lunch in the village of Maku had been disappointing. Abdul had not finished his plate and drank many glasses of tea to mask the insipid taste. Mohammed had wiped his plate clean with Iranian Sangak bread. Abdul had little sympathy for people with little self-control. He hoped Mohammed had told the truth when he declared that he had crossed the border many times and knew all the border guards. Abdul took a deep breath and closed his eyes to center himself.

As they pulled up to the border guard, Mohammed presented the passports. The border guard recognized Mohammed and nodded. He gave a cursory look at the passports and Abdul. After stamping the passports, he waved the car through without searching or questioning them. Abdul breathed a sigh of relief. Two more border passport controls to negotiate.

They drove through the day and reached Erzurum just after dark. Abdul paid Mohammed handsomely, thanked him for his help, and walked away. He stopped to gaze at the tall tower on the Medrese Seminary, the largest building in the town, before continuing on the few blocks to the main hotel. It felt good to stretch his legs, and he breathed in the cool evening air. He recognized his nervousness at the border had been a little excessive. He needed to better calm his anxiety in such situations. His short, intensive training in Sana'a had been comprehensive, but he was fully aware that there would be a lot more to contend with on his mission than any training could have prepared him. He reminded himself that he had completed the journey so far with no real difficulties. Things were going well.

As he stepped into the hotel lobby, he was looking forward to a warm shower to wash away his tension and solidify his determination. The desk clerk scrutinized his passport before looking up with a big smile and greeting him in German, announcing he had lived in Hamburg, Germany for several years. Abdul returned the smile and described in German what he liked about Hamburg, despite never having been. He asked about a good restaurant as a means of ending the conversation and was given directions to a nearby restaurant that the clerk raved was the best in town.

Abdul smiled to himself as he took the stairs to his room. He had practiced his German and studied German geography and history in his spare time on the journey all through Iran when Wi-Fi was available for his laptop. He was delighted that the clerk was convinced he was German and had been to Hamburg.

After a quick shower that felt luxurious, he walked to the restaurant and had a tasty meal of mutton and onion skewers with flatbread and salad. After the meal and a Turkish coffee, he strolled in the cool night air, a welcoming change from the heat at the border in the old Mercedes. He felt restored, but knew the journey ahead would be considerably more difficult. Back at the hotel, he lay on the bed, reviewing his journey and the travel to come. He needed to sleep, but his nervous energy kept sleep at bay until his exhaustion took over.

In the middle of the night, he woke up in a sweat, tangled in the sheet. He recalled the nightmare of that fateful day and tried to force back the tears that erupted like a resurrected volcano, his many doubts contributing to his sorrow. Had he been coerced into this mission? His parents would be appalled at what he was planning. No... he was right to strike back. He was at war and attacking the enemy was what one did in war. He drank some water and laid back down, his tears continuing softly.

When he caught the bus in the morning toward Istanbul, he felt drained. He had lain awake from the dream the rest of the night. The bus was nearly full of mostly farmers with a few scattered business men in suits. The guttural sound of the Turkish language assaulted his ears and made him uneasy about the task ahead. He needed to drop his doubts and stiffen his resolve for he had a long journey. He had briefly contemplated asking Mohammed to drive him the entire way to Istanbul, but decided that changing his mode of transport would be wise even though he was confident no police or entity would be following his movements.

The bus ride from Erzurum seemed to take forever over the mountains, and he was unable to catch-up on any sleep with the constant turns and jerks of downshifting. Abdul stopped off in Trabzon, the huge port on the Black Sea, for the night, hoping he could at least catch a few hours of sleep. He'd pick up another bus in the morning. The sea port was noisy. He slept fitfully and woke up with the horrifying dream that plagued most of his nights. To his dismay, he expected the dream would be with him for years, but hoped to rise above its debilitating effect. To enliven himself, he recalled an enjoyable trip to the Red Sea that the whole family had taken when he was still in secondary school. He loved his family so much.

From Trabzon, he endured the two day journey to Istanbul without stopping overnight, catching snatches of sleep in between stops for meals, change in buses, and bus cleanings, determined to speed up his journey, afraid that dithering would weaken his determination to carry out his mission. The buses were air-conditioned and comfortable, but his unease rose with each mile.

The jovial chatter of the other passengers deepened his agitation.

Upon arrival at the Istanbul bus station, he splashed his face in the bathroom to perk himself up before hailing a taxi to take him to a hotel near the Hagia Sophia, the massive Byzantium church that was converted to a mosque and then to a museum. The three day journey had been tedious and he was apprehensive about flying out in the morning. Another day might help settle him some, but he decided he would not delay.

When he awoke to the call of the muezzin, he was disoriented. The nightmare of that fateful day had plagued him again. He sat up and wiped his tears. He decided to pray, something he had all but given up. His father's face from the dream had reminded him of his morning prayers with his father. He knelt on the rug and faced east, reciting in Arabic, "We have awoken, and all creation has awoken for Allah, Lord of the Worlds." He stopped and fell forward, crying profusely. What was he doing? He needed to get a grip on himself.

He took a quick shower and shaved, contemplating his face in the mirror. He was lucky that his features could easily pass for German. His skin was only a little darker than many Germanic people, but not enough to cause suspicion. He had his mother's Christian heritage to thank for his Western features. His rising anticipation was visible in his face. He told himself to seek calmness and recalled a pleasant memory of his childhood, playing in the vineyard with his friend Mohammed. He, like most kids growing up in a peaceful place, had wonderful memories to call on.

Yemen had a long history of internal conflict, but life in his village in the mountains had been removed from the strife. He hated the stupid schism between the Shiites and Sunnis that had led to the chaos that enveloped Yemen and much of the Middle East. Fighting over who was the rightful successor of the Prophet seemed absurd to him. Sunnis and Shiites had more in common than their few differences.

When the Saudis began their intrusion into Yemen by supporting Al-Qaeda in the south against the corrupt President Saleh in 2008, Abdul was in his first year of secondary school. He had worried that the al-Qaeda violence would spread from the south, and his worries came to fruition. In 2009 the Yemen affiliated Al-Qaeda attempted a failed bombing of a U.S. airliner leaving Amsterdam for Detroit. In response, the Yemen military attacked Al-Qaeda militants in Sana'a, Arhab, and Abyan, killing and arresting hundreds. A week later in Yemen, the US killed Anwar Al-Awlaki, a US citizen and radical cleric in a drone strike—the first time the US openly killed a US citizen without due process. Al-Awlaki had suspected ties to Al-Qaeda and preached jihadist rhetoric against the US.

Abdul became exceedingly worried for Yemen and took part in demonstrations in Sana'a in 2011 during the Arab Spring against the corruption and incompetence of the government. When President Saleh resigned and Vice President Hadi became President, he had hoped the corruption would diminish and Yemen would have a unifying government. Unfortunately, President Hadi proposed the government shift to a federal style of government with six autonomous regions, a government organization promoted by the Saudis. This was anathema to the Houthi Yemenis in the Northern Mountains, the most populous and poorest area of Yemen. Under this type of government, oil revenues of the eastern provinces would not go to the central government and the oil rich regions would reap all the benefits of Yemen's oil, 75% of the country's foreign exchange. In consequence, the Houthi militants increased their insurgency against the government.

In November 2012 his first year at Dhamar University, a Saudi Arabian diplomat was assassinated in Sana'a by Al-Qaeda. He didn't understand how the Saudis could support Al Qaeda in Yemen. He hated the Saudis with their repressive government and exportation of fundamental Islamic Wahhabism around the Middle East. In 2013 unrest continued with the Houthi rebels assisted by soldiers that had been Saleh supporters, clashing with the Hadi Army. His reservations about what was happening to Yemen and his dissatisfaction with his education at Dhamar became too much to bear, and he dropped out of college. Many of the better professors had left Yemen, and the number of students had dwindled. He considered transferring to the University of Science and Technology in Sana'a, but the situation in Sana'a was worse than Dhamar. He didn't know what to do.

His father was initially irate about him dropping out of college in Dhamar, but quickly grew to understand that attending college in Yemen under the worsening situation was pointless. He encouraged Abdul to apply to American and European Universities and ignore the worsening situation, believing it was essential that his son take advantage of his academic excellence— he was top of his class in Dhamar— and seek out colleges that would provide the best education. The family would be safe in their mountain village. His father encouraged him to pursue an engineering degree to take advantage of his skills in math and science, and then he could make a real difference when he returned to Yemen. It seemed so long ago.

After a light breakfast at a restaurant close to the Blue Mosque, he told himself despite his qualms what he was embarking on was necessary. He took a taxi to the airport and paid cash for his plane ticket. He could have used his Hans Zimmer, Visa Credit Card, but didn't want the transaction to appear. If someone reviewed the flight records, they would be able to follow him, but a credit card record would have made it much easier.

CHAPTER 8

Fred Sampson had been a distinguished FBI Agent for thirty years. He and his team had thwarted many terrorists both Muslims and white nationalists. They were currently following an organization of young Arabs, most of whom were from Yemen, who appeared to be led by Rasheed Malika, a naturalized American citizen, who came to the US as a teenage refugee from Syria, but professed to be a Yemeni. Rasheed had graduated from high school and worked part-time at a Queens's coffee shop. He seemed to have more money than his part-time job would supply, and often met with other Arabs at various apartments in the City. Fred and his team had put Rasheed and his group under surveillance after being alerted that Rasheed was suspected of terrorism links as a boy in Syria.

Fred, an only child, had grown up in New York City and loved living there. He enjoyed the diverse neighborhoods and the vast array of cultural activities available. He had been a good student and played football and basketball in high school. His senior year he was elected football team captain. His prowess as a fullback and outside linebacker was celebrated. He had dated a girl, who lived nearby, throughout high school and thought he was in love. When the girl moved away after graduation, he was distraught and pouted throughout the summer.

Fred had briefly contemplated going into the Army like his father after he graduated from high school, but his parents were adamant that he should go directly to college—the Vietnam War was over and the draft had essentially ended. His father had grown to see the folly of the Vietnam War and, although an entrenched patriot, felt that President Johnson had lied to the American people. What Nixon had subsequently done, had made his father sick. The War had accomplished nothing except a tremendous loss of life.

Fred enrolled at Columbia University and chose prelaw as his major. He thought as a lawyer he could help people. After graduation from Columbia, Fred went to Law School at Columbia. After a year of law school, he realized he didn't really want to be a lawyer. It seemed an adversarial occupation and the memorization required seemed daunting, so he applied to the FBI where he thought he could help innocent people by stopping the criminals that preyed on them. He was accepted into the program.

He liked protecting people and going after criminals. He developed a knack for his work and became a highly respected agent. He started off in the Criminal Investigation Division and after 9/11 transferred to the Counter Intelligence Division. He soon became a group leader. His intuition and success became legendary.

He had married Joan, his college sweetheart, a year after joining the FBI. Joan was a fiery redhead, who was not particularly beautiful, but had an air about her that was captivating. Fred was not handsome by any means, but had a bearing that was charming. He was tall and muscular, with thinning dark brown hair and brown eyes. He was not a man who stood out in a crowd— something he thought was an asset in his work. The first few years of their marriage, they were deeply in love and so happy to be together. When they learned, they weren't able to have children— Joan didn't ovulate properly— they both were devastated. After meeting with various doctors, Joan decided she didn't want to go through the hormone treatments or anything else. Fred accepted her decision, but it became a point of contention in their life together.

As the years passed, Joan grew to dislike the late nights and worry associated with Fred's work. She hated the thought that when Fred left in the morning he might not be returning. When he was badly wounded and almost died in a raid on a criminal sexual enslavement ring, she had had enough and asked for a divorce. Fred hadn't seen it coming and was devastated. After the divorce, he dedicated himself even more strongly to his job. Essentially it became his life.

Fred's father, a dock worker, had died several years ago at the age of eighty, a year after his mother died. Fred's grandfather had emigrated from Russia during the Jewish pogroms even though he had converted to Christianity. His mother was a hard working homemaker of German immigrant stock, who had made their modest apartment a comfortable and welcoming home. Her death had laid his father low, and his father never recovered his jovial air. His father had seemed healthy and took his dog, Slippery, for daily walks, but it was obvious he had lost his will to live. He died in his sleep.

Fred had admired his father, who had instilled in his son the importance of hard work and giving back to the country, emphasizing education, the importance of humility, and the right of all people to live a productive and fulfilling life.

After the divorce, Fred occasionally went on dates over the years, but didn't find anyone that seemed to engage well with his taciturn personality until he met

Maggie. She was divorced and had her own life. She was talkative, but not garrulous and shared his love of movies, music, and theater. She had two grown daughters. One was happily married, living in Saugerties, an upstate New York small community, who had a daughter that Maggie saw regularly. Maggie loved being a grandmother. Fred enjoyed being around Maggie's granddaughter, and relished playing with the rambunctious child. Her other daughter lived in Marin County, California and was unmarried.

Although Maggie often expressed her worries about the dangers Fred faced daily, she tolerated the broken dates and days when he wasn't available. They suited each other well. He heard secondhand his team was grateful that he had found someone, since it made him much easier to deal with, tempering his abruptness and dictatorial nature.

He knew he was a hard task master. Many agents had not lasted long on his team. The oldest team member, Jeff, was an easy-going agent, who didn't seem to mind Fred's sarcasm and demanding nature. Jeff was a tall, extremely handsome blue-eyed man, who had quite the way with the ladies. His good looks came in handy in interrogations, but made him stand out in a crowd. Fred was grateful that Jeff had stuck with him and expected that Jeff would become team leader when Fred retired—something he thought about from time to time.

Fred enjoyed the diversity of thought that Mary Garcia brought to the team and believed she was turning into a top notch agent. She took no gruff from the often joking somewhat purposely sexist Jeff. She was a martial arts expert, who, although slight, could bring down a man twice her size. The good natured banter between Jeff and Mary often gave Fred a chuckle. The newest addition to his team was John, a tall and spindly young man, who was a whiz with computers. He and Mary got along well and joined together in sarcasm directed at Jeff. Fred believed he had one of the best teams in the FBI.

When the surveillance of Rasheed revealed increased visits to his associates, Fred began to think the group of Arabs was getting close to something imminent, but had no inkling what the something would be. He had obtained a warrant, and Jeff was monitoring Rasheed's cell phone calls, but Rasheed was very careful on the phone and often spoke in a kind of code that John was trying to decipher by running the conversations through numerous computer programs he had devised.

Fred hoped that whatever Rasheed was planning their surveillance and phone monitoring, and John's deciphering computer programs would eventually give them the evidence they needed to arrest Rasheed and his associates before they could launch an attack.

CHAPTER 9

Abdul tried to center his mind as he stood in the passport control line at the Berlin airport July 14, 2018. He was sweating under his sports jacket despite the air conditioning. His fake passport had passed muster at all the other borders. Nevertheless, he worried he could be randomly selected for further review. His family came to mind and he tried to neutralize his anger and sorrow by thinking of his joy of swimming. He had enjoyed swimming in the warm Red Sea and often went swimming at the college pool when his studies were getting him down.

When he had volunteered in Sana'a to train as a clandestine operator, he had no idea that they would want him to go to the US. He thought he would remain in Yemen and be used in the south for gathering intelligence or secret attacks. He wasn't sure if he wanted to return to the US, but realized his knowledge of the US would be an asset. His assignment to travel to the US to join a Yemen led Islamic cell in New York City and help execute a terrorist act sounded dangerous. He wasn't sure he liked or wanted the assignment. He worried over the assignment and thought about abandoning the rebel group even though he was prepared to die if it would help end the war. After agonizing about what course he should take for days, he decided he would accept the assignment.

The Saudis had the support and backing of the US Government and striking against the Americans would hopefully make a big impact in highlighting to the American public the criminality of the Saudi bombing campaign. The Saudis not only were using their bombing to drive the Houthi from power in Yemen, but also to be able to control Yemen and Yemeni oil.

In his month of extensive training, he had learned about a multitude of weapons, explosives, martial arts, and use of disguises, but felt he was not really adequately prepared for his assignment. He had presumed he would need to learn other skills needed to be successful as he went.

When his turn came, he stepped to the immigration officer and presented his passport. The scrutiny and prolonged stare of the officer worried him. Abdul kept his face neutral. Smiling, he knew from his training in Sana'a, could be construed as nervousness at border control. When he heard the sound of the stamp, his heart beat calmed, and he felt like smiling, but instead nodded and thanked the man in German before strolling toward baggage claim.

In the morning, after his stay in the nondescript hotel, Abdul filled out his ESTA, electronic system for travel authorization, online. An operative in Berlin had already gotten Hans a Visa credit card, used the card to establish a credit history, set up a social media account with photos of Abdul as Hans and supposed friends, and had written uncontroversial posts.

While he waited for his ESTA to be approved, he roamed around Berlin visiting the Brandenburg Gate, the Wall, the Postdamer Platz, and Alte Nationalgalerie. He was impressed by Berlin's celebration of its unification, and its cosmopolitan ambience and commerce. Unfortunately, the tourists and Germans were going about their lives with little thought for what was happening in Yemen, the same way as the

Americans. The German press denounced the bombing of Yemen, but like the Americans the Germans had other things to worry about.

Abdul thought the unification of Germany had proceeded well in contrast to the unification of Yemen. Of course the Germans had been at it since 1971 and had experienced peace while Yemen, unified in 1990, had an unending history of strife and war. What would his life be like if he had gone to college in Germany? He wouldn't have met Cindy and learned about the rampant militarism of the US or witnessed the disregard most Americans paid politics. What did it matter? He was on a mission and should not let idle thoughts distract him.

After three days his ESTA came back approved. He booked his flight to New York JFK Airport, and the prearranged hotel in Brooklyn. The next morning he took a taxi to the airport. He was extremely nervous as he waited in the immense Berlin Airport for his flight and hoped that his bag would not be searched. He had been assured it would pass X-ray scrutiny and so far it had not been a problem, but a thorough search might be devastating. The money hidden in the lining would take a lot of explaining.

He was relieved when his group was called to board the plane that would take him to the US. Upon deplaning in New York, he followed the crush of passengers to passport control. He recognized his clamped jaw and rigid stance as he waited and told himself to relax. This would be the big test. If he passed scrutiny here, he would be out of the woods and could move around America with ease.

He was glad when he was directed to stand at the line for the tall black officer, thinking he would be less likely to notice his darker skin than the next officer, who was a red-faced, overweight white man. When he moved to the tall black officer, he presented his passport, copy of his ESTA, and returned the man's 'good morning' with his practiced German accent. The man only looked at him briefly, asked him his reason for visiting the United States, and his planned destination.

"I'm just a tourist visiting your fine country," Abdul said with a German accent and slight smile. "I am staying first in the city at the Brooklyn Days Inn and plan on traveling to other destinations." He showed the officer his return ticket in three weeks, which he had no intention of using.

The officer stamped his passport, "Welcome to the United States."

Abdul collected his small bag and walked to the custom agent with his form. He tried to keep his breathing relaxed. The custom agent asked Abdul to place his bag on the metal platform and open it. The US currency stashed in the lining of the suitcase in $100 bills was $9,000, which did not exceed the import limit, but if he declared the amount, he would be subject to intense scrutiny. When he was given the money in Sana'a, he had thought it might be counterfeit, but was assured it was genuine. He was to give half to his contact in New York. If the money was discovered, it would probably end his quest. The custom agent lifted a few clothes and stared staidly at Abdul. Abdul kept his face neutral, his heart galloping.

"Thank you," The agent said. "Next."

Abdul took his time closing his suitcase, willing himself to keep his hands from shaking, hoisted the case, and slowly walked out into the lobby. He felt like shouting his success, but instead strolled outside and got in the line for taxis. The warm air and vehicle exhaust stung his nose. Such a different smell than the fresh air in his mountain village. He gave the taxi driver the address in Brooklyn of the hotel he had reserved and settled into the back seat. He felt a twitch of sorrow that he was embarking on something that would have appalled his parents. There was still time to abandon his quest and return to Berkeley to complete his degree despite the Supreme Court upholding the ban on people coming to the US from Yemen. No he was done with school in the US. He could alternatively return to Germany and enroll in college there. After obtaining another Yemen passport in Germany, he could get his credits from Berkeley transferred and complete his engineering degree. No... he had made an oath. He would fulfill his revenge and strike against the Americans.

After checking into the modest Days Inn Hotel using his Hans Zimmer credit card, he slumped down on the big bed and listened to his thumping heart. He felt as if he'd run a marathon. He had quite a few days of idle time before he was to meet his contact in which he was supposed to familiarize himself to New York City. He did not know what his assignment would be, but was anxious to get on with it. He spent the days before his prearranged meeting, traveling on the subway all over, becoming familiar with the various stations and boroughs of the City. The City was immense, seven times the size of Sana'a. He went to Central Park repeatedly and visited the Metropolitan Museum of Art, and the Natural History Museum. He kept up with the news of Yemen online and on TV.

The news of the crisis in Yemen served to solidify his resolve. He watched movies on TV and read used novels he bought near the Park. He felt as if he was suspended in time and was anxious to meet his contact. The waiting was interminable. As the day approached when he would meet with his contact, his doubts if he was doing the right thing continued to plague him.

Abdul recognized the blue LA Dodger hat and red tennis shoes of his contact, Rasheed, outside the Empire State building at the prearranged date and time, but did not talk to him or acknowledge him in any way. He followed him at a distance to the elevators and took a separate elevator to the top viewing platform. The view of the city from the platform was spectacular and brought to light the extent of towering multi-story buildings abounding in the city. He had never been up in a skyscraper and was amazed at the engineering feats that had been developed to make such tall buildings. As his contact stood looking out at the city, Abdul moved near him. When Rasheed dropped his paper, Abdul picked up the paper and handed it toward Rasheed.

"I've finished with it," Rasheed said. "Would you like it?"

"Yes, thank you," Abdul replied and walked away while Rasheed continued to gaze at the city.

Abdul rode the elevator back down, walked across the street to an alcove and waited. When Rasheed left the building, Abdul followed Rasheed at a distance. He thought it prudent that he know where Rasheed lived, but had no reason to doubt Rasheed's trustworthiness.

As they neared a residential area, he thought that another man was possibly following Rasheed as well, causing Abdul to lengthen his distance from Rasheed. When the possible follower went into a coffee shop across from the building Rasheed entered, Abdul told himself he was seeing things. He had accomplished his surveillance and now knew where Rasheed lived in case he needed to contact or find him.

Back in his hotel Abdul studied the plan he was given, hidden in the newspaper. He was to rent a car, obtain explosives from an address in Queens, drive the car near Times Square, and then detonate the car remotely. He didn't like the plan, but said nothing against it at his next meeting with Rasheed at a coffee bar at Times Square to which he had worn a false mustache, wig, and stocking cap.

Rasheed had laughed when he saw him. "What's with the disguise?" Rasheed said.

"There are lots of cameras in this City," Abdul replied. "Precautions are always a good idea."

When Rasheed smirked, Abdul wanted to smash his haughty face. Rasheed was a little shorter than Abdul and had much darker skin and a prominent hooked nose. His matted black hair was in need of a shampoo. He was wearing a black tee shirt and jeans. As Abdul talked to Rasheed, he grew increasing wary of Rasheed's haughty manner. Rasheed spoke loudly against Americans and paid no attention to those around him. Abdul wondered how such a stupid man could be a cell leader.

He had his doubts about the plan. A Times Square bombing had already been tried and intercepted in the past. The police presence around Times Square was large. Still it would create havoc and sensation if successful. He and Rasheed walked around Times Square, and Rasheed pointed out various areas he thought a car bomb could be parked long enough for Abdul to escape far enough to safely detonate. Abdul saw plenty of cameras and was glad he had worn his disguise.

After they parted, Abdul went the opposite direction but doubled back to follow Rasheed at a distance. When he saw a man, who might be the same man he had seen possibly following Rasheed from the Empire State building, standing a block from Rasheed's apartment talking to a young woman, he stopped and turned back, abandoning his pursuit. He wasn't sure if the man was same man, but didn't want the man to see him.

When he returned to his hotel, he was leery of the plan for bombing Times Square. Getting a car close enough to create maximum damage was difficult. Detonating a bomb near Times Square would generate extensive press for sure, but didn't seem like an event that would benefit Yemen that much. He would need to be caught in order to bring Yemen into the picture, otherwise it would be reported as another radical Islamic act.

He hadn't made up his mind about the planned bombing and had given Rasheed only a small amount of money. He didn't like or trust Rasheed. If Rasheed was being followed, some entity was interested in Rasheed. He would have liked to contact his Houthi handler in Yemen and find out more about Rasheed. He suspected Rasheed was a Syrian posing as a Yemeni.

If he called his Houthi handler to find out more about Rasheed, he knew it would be extremely dangerous—overseas calls were recorded by the FBI and computer programs searched for key words. He wanted revenge, but didn't want to be a martyr for a plan that would fail. He hadn't come all this way to fail. He would try to get some semblance of sleep and decide in the morning what he should do.

CHAPTER 10

Fred Sampson, followed Rasheed as Rasheed entered the Empire State building. The day was warming up and although the sky was cloudy no rain seemed imminent. He watched Rasheed enter the elevator to the viewing platform and took the next elevator. He was pretty sure Rasheed hadn't seen him following him and did not know who Fred was.

When he stepped out onto the viewing platform at the top to the cooling wind, he saw Rasheed talking to a handsome man. He wondered if the man, he had not seen before, was another contact or just a random tourist. The handsome man looked Western and was dressed smartly in a blue sport coat and tan slacks in contrast to the slovenly appearance of Rasheed. The other cell members or associates he had seen were all obviously Arabic and dressed like Rasheed in jeans, tee shirts, and sneakers.

He surreptitiously snapped a photograph of the two with his cell phone, kicking himself for not bringing another agent with him, so they could follow both men. Mary had stayed watching Rasheed's apartment. He had no choice but to follow Rasheed when he left the platform all the way back to Rasheed's apartment in Queens. Mary watching Rasheed's building from a coffee shop across the street from the building informed him no one else had been to the apartment. He showed her the photograph on his cell phone of Rasheed and the handsome man. She had not seen the handsome man before.

In the morning Fred sent the photo of Rasheed and the handsome man to FBI Washington headquarters asking if there was any information on the handsome man. His penchant to often work alone, believing other agents might stand out more than himself and couldn't match his expertise built over the thirty years of his career with the Agency, was he knew unwise. He also had a penchant for not having his thoughts interrupted. His subsequent tailing of Rasheed that evening with Mary did not lead to any clues about what Rasheed was planning or the unknown handsome man.

Two days later, he lost sight of Rasheed in the morning, rush-hour crush of the subway, despite his accompanying agent, Mary Garcia, and didn't see him again until Rasheed came back to his apartment in the evening. He worried that Rasheed had discovered he was being followed, but the fact that they had stayed a good distance back was probably the reason they had lost him. It was better to lose him than to blow their cover.

The next night, he tailed Rasheed with the help of Mary to another apartment in Queens that Fred didn't have on his radar. After Rasheed left, Fred had Mary knock on the apartment while he hid out of sight around the corner. When the inhabitants of the apartment refused to answer the door, Mary identified herself as FBI. Luckily, Mary was standing to the side of the door as gun fire ripped through the door. Fred called for backup and joined Mary on the other side of the door. He was glad that he had trained Mary to always take the safest position. His training had paid off. If she had been hurt, he would have never forgiven himself.

Fred banged on the door with his Glock pistol. He also carried a .38 special revolver in an ankle holster. He liked a revolver as back up because they never jammed. He was often called old fashion. "FBI. You are surrounded. You have no choice, but to give up."

In response, the occupants in the room answered with additional gun fire. Mary wanted to bust in, but Fred cautioned her to wait for back up. The occupants, judging by the different sounds had more than two weapons. "You can't escape," Fred called. "You're making this much more difficult than it needs to be." His statement was met by silence.

When the city SWAT team in bullet proof vests, helmets, and carrying shields arrived, they burst open the door and went in returning fire. Fred squinted against the acrid and sour smell from all the gun fire as he entered. All four of the assailants were dead and one of the SWAT team was wounded in the leg. Inside they found a bomb making factory with enough C4 explosive to blow up the entire block and a map of the City folded to Times Square and the surrounding streets.

Fred with three other agents went to Rasheed's apartment after the raid on the bomb factory and arrested Rasheed without incident, charging him as an accomplice in the bomb making factory. Fred was congratulated by his superiors for disrupting the terrorist plot, but they found no evidence of what had been planned other than a map of the City folded to the area around Times Square. Rasheed claimed he had met the inhabitants of the bomb factory at a restaurant, and, when he visited, he saw no bomb making materials. He knew nothing about any terrorist plot.

The FBI lab would try to trace the origin of the C4 and hopefully that would lead to others involved in the plot. The following day Mary and Fred went to another apartment Rasheed had visited. After knocking on the door, the door was answered by a slim teenage girl with sad dark eyes wearing a black scarf and dark blue, floor-length dress. Fred identified himself and Mary and asked if her parents were at home. The girl invited them in. The mother, a rotund women with a black head scarf and black full length dress was sitting on a sofa with a young boy, maybe 8 or 9, and a teenage boy. They were a Syrian refugee family. They told Fred that Rasheed was from the same town in Syria and was helping them to adapt to their new country. The father was working at a nearby restaurant as a dishwasher. They did not know Rasheed had been arrested and was implicated with terrorists. They seemed innocent enough to Fred, but he would keep up the surveillance on them.

When Fred encountered two of a group of men, who Rasheed had visited repeatedly and who Fred had had under surveillance for several weeks, leaving their apartment with large suitcases, Fred called for a warrant and he and Mary followed the two. When Fred received acknowledgement of the warrant, he and May pulled the two in for questioning, and their suitcases were searched. The suitcases contained weapons for which they had no permits. Fred ordered a raid on the apartment and the other two Arab occupants were arrested. The apartment contained additional weapons and a small amount of explosives. Two of the four were from Syria and two were from Libya. Fred's fame increased. His boss was very congratulatory. Fred felt good about his success, and Mary basked in the praise she received. She was turning into an excellent agent.

Fred did not rest on his laurels. Rasheed's cell he felt was finished. If there were other members, they would have gone into hiding. He had a nagging suspicion that the handsome man at the Empire State building was involved in some way. A local FBI alert was circulated with Fred's photograph of Rasheed and the handsome man, asking agents to be on the lookout for the handsome man. Fred sent the photograph to Immigration Services asking if the man was a person, who recently entered the country.

When Fred received the news that the handsome man, Hans Zimmer, a German passport holder, had enter the US at the JFK Airport weeks earlier, he immediately requested all FBI offices to be on the lookout for Hans Zimmer. A week later a hotel address in New York City for a Hans Zimmer was sent to Fred. Fred gathered Mary and Jeff, and they went to the address. Hans Zimmer had left over a week ago, and the hotel had no idea where he was headed.

As the weeks went by, no information on Hans Zimmer was forthcoming. The man had disappeared without a trace. Fred didn't think Hans was an Arab like Rasheed and the rest of the dead bomb makers or associates. For some reason that he couldn't put his finger on, he doubted the man was German even though his features and complexion could be that of a German. The face of Hans haunted him to no end. He strongly believed he needed to find this man.

CHAPTER 11

In the morning Abdul rose early and went to the vicinity of Rasheed's apartment. He wanted to confirm his suspicions that Rasheed was being surveilled. He noticed a man and a woman, who appeared to be watching Rasheed's apartment building, from a parked car. Not wanting to get too close, he couldn't be sure. When the man got out of the car, something about the way the man carried himself made him wonder if this was the same man he thought had been following Rasheed.

What seemed abundantly clear was that the police or FBI were possibly on to Rasheed. He needed to abandon working with Rasheed and get out of town as soon as possible. He returned to his hotel, stopping periodically at subway stations and reversing direction to make sure no one was following him. After checking out of his hotel, he took the subway to the bus station and bought a bus ticket for Chicago. He choose Chicago on the spur-of-the-moment because it was a large urban city with a significant Muslim and Yemeni population and was far enough away that he felt assured no one would be looking for him there.

At the bus station, he wore a stocking cap and false mustache and kept his head down, so that any surveillance cameras wouldn't reveal his face. He was on his own and knew of no other contacts in the US, except for a woman, Zahra Basha, a professor at the University of California. He was only to contact her in San Diego as a last resort for aid to leave the US. He thought the planning by his handlers had been poor. There should have been a back-up plan besides Zahra if the original plan ran into difficulty. Although disappointed that his only assignment for revenge was over, a part of him was glad he had not participated in the bombing of Times Square.

On a stop of the bus at a terminal for the bus cleaning, he saw the newspaper account of the raid on the bomb making terrorists and arrest of Rasheed Malika. His doubts about Rasheed and cautious following had saved him. He wondered if he had been seen with Rasheed by any government agents. He thought back about his two meetings with Rasheed. He was in disguise at the coffee house and had kept his head down. He remembered Rasheed laughing at his disguise. He hadn't seen a camera, but they could be easily hidden. On their walk around Times Square, Abdul was undoubtedly captured on security cameras, but again he had kept his head down and was in disguise. Then there was the first meeting at the Empire State building. He remembered the man who had looked directly at him and his own surprised reaction. The man had a cellphone in his hand and was the same build as the man that he thought was following Rasheed. He would file the man's face in his memory.

After arriving in Chicago on July 29, 2018, Abdul rented a room at a hotel near the Chicago University under an assumed name after lifting a wallet from a student at the Student Union and replacing the picture on the student's ID with his. He was now Frank Harmon with dyed reddish brown hair and fake mustache that he had applied in a bathroom at the University. He paid cash for the room and spent days taking the elevated train, moving around the city, familiarizing himself to the City layout, and trying to come up with a viable alternate plan.

He visited several mosques in Chicago, trying to connect with a possible Yemeni terrorist cell. He met some Yemeni young men who espoused jihadist aspirations, but had no meaningful organization. He worried about the risk he was taking seeking out possible terrorist cells. The FBI were often trying to lure people into false terrorist acts to arrest them. He varied his disguise at various meetings with young Muslims. The week passed and he had not found any viable organization or other radical Yemenis. He became depressed and felt desolate, but kept up his hunt.

The second week he grew to dislike Chicago and thought about giving up and returning to Yemen. He could fight with the Houthi or become a part of a new plan in Europe. He felt a failure. He had come all this way to give up. What a wasted trip. He had a lot of money and guile. There must be something he could do to shine light on what was happening to his beloved Yemen. He wondered what he should do as he moved around Chicago becoming more frustrated by the day.

After nearly two weeks in Chicago, Abdul had not found a Yemeni jihadist group, nor had talking to young American Muslims brought to mind any viable plan of revenge— most were either extremely uninformed or filled with hate. Perhaps, he didn't need to affiliate himself with another jihadist group. He could devise his own plan to strike back at the US for what the Saudis had done to his family. His unaffiliated situation could be an asset. Where then should he go and what could he do?

CHAPTER 12

Fred continued to investigate and follow possible suspects hoping to turn up any who had been associated with Rasheed, or others contemplating violent action rather than just inflammatory postings on Facebook and Twitter. He hadn't forgotten about the handsome man that had talked briefly to Rasheed at the Empire State Building. It had been several weeks since Rasheed's arrest, and no other information on Hans Zimmer had turned up.

The team was working on a possible new terrorist cell that centered on a Mosque in Manhattan. A group of five young men of Libyan decent, who attended the Mosque and lived together in an apartment, had posted somewhat cryptic messages on Facebook about jihad and the US responsibility for the horrific assassination of Gaddafi. Jeff had been following the group with John's help for a few weeks. There were a lot of other people, who visited the apartment. The team had identified most. The number of people involved seemed large for a terrorist cell bent on violence. Fred took his turn on surveillance, but didn't think the group of Libyans had reached a point where violent actions were expected.

Fred still found himself often obsessing over Hans despite having no real evidence that Hans was involved in terrorism. Three weeks after the initial sighting of Hans, Fred received a list of bus passengers to Chicago from New York that included Hans Zimmer. He wondered why it had taken so long for his enquiries about Hans to bear fruit, but was overjoyed to have a lead to pursue. He sent an email to his friend

Richardson in the Chicago office, explaining his interest and asking Richardson to look at the security camera footage at the bus station for Hans Zimmer on the day he would have arrived in Chicago, July 30, 2018.

Two weeks later when Fred arrived at his office, feeling heavy from his late night with his Irish whiskey, there was email from Richardson. He opened the email and studied the attached photograph of a man at the Chicago Greyhound Bus Station from a surveillance camera. As Richardson explained in his email, he had obtained the camera footage of the bus station for the arrival date as requested, but had not seen an image of any man that might have been Hans. Richardson had worked with Fred briefly in New York and knew if Fred was looking for someone it had to be important. Consequently, he viewed footage of the weeks after the arrival in case Hans travelled on by bus even though there was no listed passenger buying a ticket named Hans Zimmer at the Chicago station. He had spent many hours reviewing the footage when he saw the man with his head down, mustache, and stocking cap. It had stirred his interest, and he had the photograph run through their facial recognition software. It came back with only a 40 percent match, but it was enough to email the photograph to Fred.

Fred printed the photograph, which he thought could be Hans and sat studying it. The man in the photograph was standing in line to board the bus to Albuquerque. He wore a stocking cap, had a different hair color, a mustache, and his face was not fully visible. Fred gave the photograph to John to run his enhanced program of facial recognition against the photograph of Hans.

If the photograph was indeed Hans, he wasn't a tourist. A tourist wouldn't be wearing a disguise. Was Rasheed just a stop on Hans's way to join a terrorist cell in Chicago? But why stay such a short time? Maybe Albuquerque was his original intended destination and the stops in New York and Chicago was for funding or other support. He sent an email to Richardson, thanking him for the photograph and his diligence searching the camera footage. Richardson had gone way out of his way to help.

Fred got a cup of the brewed coffee that had already thickened on the hot plate and sipped the disgusting brew as he waited for the results of the facial recognition comparison from John. John's facial recognition software came up with a fifty percent chance that they were the same person. A better result than the Chicago's office facial recognition software, but not enough, he was sure, to convince his boss to let him travel to Albuquerque. He placed the photograph in his desk drawer.

Several days later he took out the bus station photograph and sat staring at it. The more he looked at it the more he was convinced it was Hans. He thought he should show the bus station and passport photographs of Hans to Rasheed, who was in jail awaiting trial. He knew Rasheed would never admit he knew the man, but his initial reaction on seeing the photograph would be interesting and possibly revealing. Fred drove to the New Jersey State Prison where Rasheed was housed.

When Rasheed was brought to the visiting room, shuffling along in his leg irons and handcuffs, Fred stood. "Hello, Rasheed. How's prison?"

Rasheed, with dark shadows under his eyes, looked menacing at Fred and sat down. "What the fuck do you want?" Rasheed spit out as if the sight of Fred made him sick.

"Are they treating you okay?"

"Why the fuck would you care?"

Fred smiled widely before answering, "I like to know if our prisons are treating the inmates properly so they can be rehabilitated."

"A fuckin' comedian. Ha-ha. As I said, what the fuck do you want?"

Fred tossed the bus station photograph of a possible Hans on the table.

Rasheed looked at the photograph briefly before looking up at Fred. "Who's this?"

"We think it might be Hans Zimmer in Chicago."

"And who's Hans Zimmer supposed to be?"

Fred tossed on the table Hans's passport photo. "He's one of your accomplices."

"In your dreams, asshole. Never saw the man before."

Fred picked up the photographs. "Enjoy your stay, Rasheed." He nodded to the guard. "We're finished here."

Fred had noticed a slight interest in the bus station photograph when he first slipped the photograph on the table. When he tossed down the passport photo, Fred thought he saw a definite stiffening. The statement that

Rasheed never saw the person in the photo was definitely a lie. Fred was convinced Hans had been an accomplice with Rasheed, and the bus station photograph was Hans in disguise.

Even if he could get approval to visit Albuquerque, where would he look for Hans Zimmer? Albuquerque, a city of a little over half a million, was not a large city, but finding Hans would be nearly impossible without more to go on. He remembered meeting an agent from Albuquerque, who he had had a few drinks with in D.C. after a seminar. He racked his brain for the agent's name. He couldn't recall. He fired up his computer and searched the Albuquerque office names. There he was, Jerry Sunu. He telephoned Sunu and referenced their meeting at the seminar last year. Sunu remembered Fred and congratulated him on disrupting the bomb plot and arrest of Rasheed.

Fred told Sunu about Hans Zimmer, the bus station photograph, and his feeling that Hans was a person of interest from Rasheed's terrorist cell. Fred emailed the photograph from the bus station and Hans's passport photograph to Sunu and asked if he would be willing to check the cameras at the Albuquerque bus station for the disguised Hans and possible other locations in the City. Sunu told him he had heard about Fred's famous gut instinct and promised he would keep a look out.

CHAPTER 13

Abdul was happy he had come to Albuquerque and, against his better judgement, had sought out Cindy. His time with Cindy felt like a different life from the failed quest that had led him from Yemen to the US. Unburdening himself to Cindy about the bombing of his Yemen home had been freeing. He still was plagued by his recurring nightmares that kept the hatred for what the Saudis had done to his family forefront in his mind, but it did not seem as debilitating as it had in New York and Chicago.

He and Cindy went out together to dinners, movies, and theater productions over the days in Albuquerque. They were having fun together. He felt so good in her company that he strongly considered giving up any retaliation against the Americans. He could just return to Berkeley complete his degree and then possibly go to graduate school at the University of New Mexico. He could try and make a life with Cindy and forget about revenge. He could join Cindy in her pacifism and work to get enough sentiment in the US against what the Saudis were doing to Yemen to stop the destruction.

One evening after returning from a delicious meal at a Thai restaurant to Cindy's house, Cindy said, "There is a meeting of Nuclear Watch New Mexico tomorrow night. I usually go. Would you like to come with me?"

"What is Nuclear Watch New Mexico?"

"It's an organization whose goal is to inform the public about nuclear research, the dangers of this research at our National Labs like Sandia and Los Alamos, and the importance of transitioning these Labs to peaceful research that would benefit people and not more hideous ways to kill them."

The phrases 'nuclear research' and 'hideous ways to kill them' ricocheted like a bouncing ball in his brain. He remembered how his visit with Cindy to Los Alamos, last Christmas holiday had upset him. His almost ignored goal of formulating some kind of attack to bring the travesty of what was happening to Yemen sprang forth with renewed importance. It was crazy to think he could live in the US after what the US support of the Saudis had done to his family. He needed to get back on track and come up with a plan for revenge. Maybe there was something he could do at one of the Labs that would be a bold statement.

"Yes, I would like to go with you," Abdul said.

"Great. Let's go to bed. I have an early class tomorrow." Cindy took his hand and pulled him up the stairs.

He could feel the rising anticipation as he followed her lithe form. Contacting her had been rewarding and freeing. He loved her, but knew they could not settle down together and live happily ever after. They made delicious, thrusting love, and Cindy fell asleep afterwards in his arms. He watched her beautiful face as she breathed the calm breath of deep sleep. He wished he could sleep like that.

In the morning Cindy awoke after Abdul had already taken a shower and dressed. "Abdul, what's happening? You're already up and dressed. Where are you going?"

"I'm going for a walk. I didn't sleep well." He gazed down at her beautiful body as she rose to give him a good morning kiss. Her kiss felt luxurious and for a few seconds he doubted his renewed determination. Being with her had assuaged his overwhelming sorrow. He owned her so much, but he owed his family more. "I need to do some research on different graduate schools and want to clear my head before diving into my investigations. I'll come back around 5:00, and we can go out to eat and then attend your meeting."

At the Nuclear Watch New Mexico meeting, Abdul was appalled by the talk about the planned updating of nuclear triggers, expansion of new nuclear weapons, and increased nuclear weapon research activities at both Sandia and Los Alamos. The next day he spent most of the day researching both Labs on the internet. His thoughts coalesced around some kind of attack at the Los Alamos Lab. Its remoteness would allow an attack there easier than the Sandia Lab.

The meeting had given him the idea for his attack, but had exposed him, since all the attendants learned his real name and that he was from Yemen. His attendance had been an error even though it was the catalyst that renewed his determination for revenge.

He wondered if there could have been an informant at the meeting. None had seemed too inquisitive, but there was an individual who was taking pictures with his cell phone, who did not try to talk to Abdul as most of the other attendees did. Abdul made sure the individual never got a full face photograph of him.

He needed to consolidate a plan and begin action. If there was an informant, he would need to move quickly although there should be no adverse information on Abdul Salaamed. If he had been spotted with Rasheed by the police or FBI, they would likely be looking for Hans Zimmer in New York or Chicago. Since he had used the fake student ID to purchase his ticket to Albuquerque, there should be no one looking for Hans Zimmer in Albuquerque.

When Cindy awoke in his arms after a wonderful satisfying night that he understood would probably be his last, he pulled her to him and held her tightly, holding back his tears. "Unfortunately, I have to leave for a while. I have an appointment at the University of Arizona in Tucson about graduate school there. I'll be back though in a few days."

She grasped him tighter. I wish I could go with you, but I have an important class I don't feel I can miss. It has been so wonderful to have you near again." She sat up. "It will be hotter than hell in Tucson. Good reason to hurry back."

"Don't worry I'll be back as soon as I can." He wondered if his lie was visible in his face, but her hug and kiss testified that she had accepted his lies. Gazing into the depth of her deep blue eyes, he felt an immense qualm of disappointment and sadness that he would never hold this beautiful women in his arms again.

The majestic mountains of Northern New Mexico were spectacular as he drove up the highway in the bright sun. He had switched the license plate and added saddle bags to the motorcycle to make the cycle appear different and less likely to be recognized as stolen. He relaxed as he drove, the azure sky hosting isolated billowing clouds. The sunny weather felt good as he motored north. The landscape reminded him of his home in the mountains of Yemen. A home if he made his statement he would probably never see again.

When he arrived in Los Alamos, he got something to eat at the Central Grill restaurant in downtown Los Alamos. The restaurant was crowded with mostly adults taking their lunch break. Many he surmised worked at the Laboratory. Could he kill these people? Was their association with an entity that was engaged in developing weapons of mass destruction enough to make them guilty enough to die? His innocent family had been killed. They had done nothing to deserve their death sentence. He scoffed at his meekness. He was essentially at war with the US— a behind the lines combatant— and should act accordingly.

After lunch, he drove across the bridge toward the Lab. He passed the multi-station security entrance to the Lab area that all vehicles had to stop at to show their badges. It would be impossible for him to gain access through the security check without a Lab ID. At night he might be able to sneak around the security access, but suspected there were many security cameras. He noticed a few.

He stopped down the road from the security entrance and watched the cars entering. The scrutiny the guards were giving the badges and occupants of the vehicles seemed only cursory. Perhaps he could steal a Lab badge and change the photo with his. He should have paid more attention to the badges he saw at lunch in order to determine how hard it would be to alter the badge. Student IDs were easy to alter. Driver's licenses and passports required more sophisticated equipment.

His decided that doing something dramatic at the Los Alamos Laboratory would strike a resounding blow against the criminal Americans. He would need to obtain explosives, but didn't think that would be difficult. Dynamite used in construction would be easy to steal and ammonia nitrate and diesel fuel was readily available. With a badge he could gain access to the Lab and plant a bomb. He would go back to Albuquerque and research the Lab for the best place to attack.

Abdul settled in at the Albuquerque student union coffee shop. He stole an internet ID and password from a person at the student union, who he had watched log in. He didn't think it safe to use his Hans Zimmer or Abdul Salaamed IDs any more. After the student left, Abdul spent hours on his laptop, learning as much he could about the Los Alamos National Lab. He discovered that spent nuclear waste at the Lab was stored in the Tech Area 54 location adjacent to Pajarito Road and was quite near the community of White Rock. His further research confirmed that indeed nuclear waste was stored in that area. He wanted to get a look at this Tech Area 54.

Blowing up nuclear waste would create havoc, possibly eliminate the Lab from further use, and kill some of the weapon researchers. It would be a bold attack against the criminal American war making establishment.

In the morning, another glorious day of bright sun and a beautiful blue sky dotted with a few clouds, he drove the motorcycle north toward Los Alamos. Instead of taking the winding route to the town center, he turned off toward White Rock and went past the community of White Rock to the intersection of Pajarito Road. When he saw the security station on Pajarito Rd a brief distance up the road that everyone had to stop at, similar to the one he had seen just across the bridge from the Los Alamos town site, he realized there was no way he could get a good look at the Tech Area 54 from the road.

He turned around and drove back through White Rock and pulled off out of town about a half a mile from the traffic light at Rover Road where the gas stations were located. He pulled the motorcycle under the barbed wire fence and hid it near an arroyo, covering it with tree branches. He hiked through the sparse pinon forest to the hilltop north of Tech Area 54. Many of the pinon trees were dead or dying, attacked by insects, another insidious result of global warming.

The Americans had elected a stupid idiot, a climate change denier as their President. This orange-faced buffoon had sucked up to Saudi Arabia and gave the military even greater license to support the Saudi's reign of destruction on Yemen. The moneyed class supported the buffoon, who had given them the tax cuts they wanted and a Supreme Court Justice that would turn the clock back on progressive issues and ignore global warming.

He watched Tech Area 54 through his binoculars as he lay under a pinon tree. The large white tents would be easy to blow up with a rocket launcher. The resulting explosion would release untold amounts of deadly radiation since these idiots actually allowed nuclear waste to be stored so blatantly out in the open. This could be his plan of retaliation. He could shoot the rocket from where he was lying and create serious havoc, contaminating the Lab and the surroundings with a death cloud of nuclear radiation. He wouldn't need a Lab badge. This would be even better than a car bomb or a bomb in a building at the Lab. Perhaps the cloud of death would float out beyond Los Alamos.

Would he be able to escape before the radiation reached him? Maybe not since the prevailing wind was from the southwest. If not, then he was ready to die. He returned to the motorcycle, rolled it back to the highway, and drove up the truck route to the town center. He went to the Starbuck's coffee shop, settled down at a table, and took out his laptop.

As he listened to the inane conversations around him, he hated the jovial attitude of the patrons. The place was crowded and was obviously a popular meeting spot. He would have liked to blow-up the coffee shop in this town dedicated to death and destruction as well. After several hours as his anger level rose, he settled on the idea of blowing up the spent nuclear waste at Tech Area 54. How then could he obtain a rocket launcher? In Yemen, Iraq, and Syria it would easy. In the US, he could possibly obtain one from a military base by inducing or bribing someone working at the base to steal such a weapon. This could be difficult if not impossible, but it would be worth a try.

He didn't want to go to any of the bases in New Mexico. It would be better if he was able to find the weapon in another state. His internet search turned up Fort Carson in Colorado Springs with a large Army training area and munitions storage as a good prospect. The Air Force Academy was there and the right wing conservative organization, Focus On The Family. There'd probably be a militia organization there as well. It seemed militia organizations often stockpiled weapons for their expectation of a coming revolution. He had learned about militias from Cindy at college.

He'd research them further and maybe pose as a militia member so he could meet other militia devotees.

He rode back to Albuquerque and waited until it was dark to search the downtown area for a vehicle that would be good to drive to Colorado Springs. He found several SUVs that would be suitable and selected a white Honda HR-V. He had stolen a jimmy-slide from an AAA wrecker truck to easily open the door and hotwire the ignition. He drove away, stopping at a parking lot to switch plates with another SUV. He had stolen another student ID and switched the picture. He was now Sidney Wallace.

CHAPTER 14

Fred continued to obsess over Hans Zimmer. He checked his emails several times a day, hoping for some information from Sunu. He knew he needed to concentrate more on the group his team had under surveillance. He was doing a disservice to his team with his worries about Hans. He tried to put Hans out of his mind and threw himself into the surveillance. He and Mary took their turns on the stakeouts and cautious followings of the group. He often found himself daydreaming about why Hans had gone to Albuquerque and if he was still there. Hans was like an irritating splinter that he found hard to ignore. The only time he could put Hans out of his mind was when he was with Maggie. He was glad that she tolerated his obvious distress.

After several weeks, Sunu telephoned and sent Fred a photograph of a man from a surveillance camera that had come to light in an auto theft investigation of a white Honda SUV. The man in the photograph had never been found and there was no evidence linking him to the auto theft. He was recorded in the vicinity of the theft. Sunu had been working on a multi-state auto theft ring that had been active in New Mexico, Arizona and Colorado and was possibly linked to a Mexico drug cartel.

When Sunu reviewed camera footage in the area for any of the known suspects in the car theft ring, he came upon the image of the man he vaguely thought could be Hans Zimmer. It wasn't a clear enough image to positively identify the man as Hans, but it might be. The image was at night and of poor resolution, but when

Fred saw it, his hair stood up on the back of his neck. His gut told him it was Hans with no disguise. He had the image run through John's facial recognition software, and it came back sixty percent. He thanked Sunu and asked if the stolen SUV had been found. It hadn't. Fred asked Sunu to send him the particulars on the vehicle and continue to keep him in the loop on the car and any more sighting of a possible Hans. He wanted to hop on a plane and fly to Albuquerque, but knew he needed more information.

A week later Sunu sent Fred information on the recovery of the white SUV in Albuquerque. Fred asked Sunu to have the vehicle dusted for prints. Sunu was reluctant to get the FBI involved in a recovered run of the mill stolen vehicle, but Fred convinced him it was important. Sunu had the local police dust the vehicle for finger prints. He was surprised when the vehicle had no prints whatsoever. It had been expertly wiped clean.

When Fred got the information of the vehicle being clean and the license plate being ditched, he went to his boss and explained his theory on Hans Zimmer and the circumstantial evidence that he might be in Albuquerque. His boss considered Fred his best agent and knew his famous gut intuition had led to many arrests. He was reluctant to lose Fred's expertise if only for a short time, but sanctioned his trip to Albuquerque.

CHAPTER 15

Abdul drove into Colorado Springs on August 25, 2018 and found a motel in the vicinity of Fort Carson. He checked in using his Sidney Wallace identification. The next evening he visited the bars near Fort Carson, dressed in camouflage trousers, work boots, and blue cotton work shirt. He practiced the rural, almost southern way, people in the bars spoke and portrayed himself as a Montana militiaman, who had been with Bundy during the standoff with federal agents in Nevada. After two days of conversations with various bartenders and patrons, asking if there were other like-minded freedom fighters present, he was finally directed at a bar called the Amory to three men sitting around a table, drinking beer, and talking animatedly. He told himself he needed to drop his natural reticence and try to talk to the three. This could be the opportunity he was looking for.

He purchased a pitcher of beer and walked to their table. The bar was small and many of the tables were vacant. The walls had knotty pine paneling and the floor was oak that displayed the many years of spilled beer and heavy boots. Most of the wall decorations were old promotional beer or whiskey advertisements. Only one patron was a woman, sitting at the bar with a man, who was many years her senior.

"Hey guys, mind if I join you... my name's Sidney," Abdul said before slinging his head toward the bar. "The bartender said you men were patriots like myself." He set the pitcher down on the table. "Peace offering, help yourself." Two of the men eyed Abdul with a frown, but the third smiled. Abdul smiled back, pulled out a chair, his heart racing, and sat down. He hoped his anxiety wasn't apparent in his face. "I'm from Montana. Just got into town. Heard this was a patriotic town. Focus on the Family and all." He leaned forward and lowered his voice. "Had to escape my old lady. She wanted to have me arrested." He waited for their reaction, his heart thumping so loudly that he wondered if the men could hear it.

"Thanks for the beer," the third man said. He was tall and thick in the shoulders, but had a noticeable stomach paunch. He wore a 'Make America Great Hat' and sleeveless black tee shirt, emblazoned with a white skull, his multicolored tattoos proudly displayed across his once toned arms. His black, heavy work boots were outstretched as he slouched back in his chair and studied Abdul with his pale blue eyes. "So what did ya do to your wife?"

"She's not my wife, but we've been living together a few years," Abdul replied. "Oh, you know how women can get. I just set her straight. Hell, I hardly slapped her. She called the police, and I hightailed it out of there. I don't need any trouble with the law."

"Why's that?" the third man asked as he pulled in his feet and sat upright.

"I had a possession charge when I was younger," Abdul replied. He was having a hard time getting a read on the big guy. "If you've got a prior, the Sheriff in Hammond can be pretty intimidatin'. I didn't want the agro." Abdul took a deep gulp of beer and forced a smile. He consciously fought his apprehension and jollied his voice. "Here let me top you guys up." He picked up the pitcher and filled up all of the three's glasses with beer. "What are you guys into?"

"Why do you ask?" the third man said, placing his hands on the table.

"No reason," Abdul answered and settled back in his chair. "Just tryin' to make conversation. I'm new to town and want to meet like-minded people. I don't mean no offense." He took a drink of beer. "I was in the Militia of Montana and was lookin' to find a similar group here. I like it here. The mountains are spectacular. I was hopin' to get a construction job. You know of any projects here about that are hirin'?"

The third man tilted back and smiled. "I'm Ray," he said. "This here is Frank." Ray pointed to the man on his left and then to the man on his right. "And this is Jess." Ray studied Abdul in silence.

Abdul wasn't sure whether Ray was playing with him or had genuinely dropped his aggressive stance. "Pleased to meet you all," he said and extended his hand to Ray, who grasped it and squeezed, making Abdul wince. Frank and Jess shook hands with him normally. He waited in silence a few moments, his hand smarting, as the three just stared at him, then said, "Well, if I'm interruptin' somethin', I'll mosey back to the bar." He stood and tried to stifle any disappointment in his expression.

Ray laughed. "Nah, you're cool." He pointed to Abdul's chair as if the previous conversation had been a game. "So who started the Militia of Montana?"

Abdul sat back down. "John Trochmann in 1994." He had studied the Montana Militia and was glad he was prepared for their interrogation. He felt a glimmer of hope he could string this group along.

"What did ya say your name was?" Ray asked.

"Sidney... Sidney Wallace."

"Is that your real name or did you change it to Wallace?" Ray asked as he extended his long legs again to the side of the table.

"No, it's my real name. I know you might think I changed my last name to Wallace because of Governor Wallace, but, no, that's my real name."

"You got ID."

Abdul wasn't expecting this. Shit... there was nothing else to do but show them the student ID and hope they didn't scrutinize the altered identification closely. "I've got an old ID when I was a student in Albuquerque." Abdul laid his stolen altered ID on the table and prepared himself for an altercation.

Ray picked up the ID, glanced briefly at it, and tossed it back on the table. "You ain't got a Montana driver's license?"

Abdul scooped up the ID and placed it back in his wallet. "Nah, my license was revoked." He was relieved that Ray's hadn't given the ID more scrutiny.

"You drove down here without a license?" Frank laughed. His slack thin face and drooping, bloodshot brown eyes testified that he'd already consumed a good deal of beer. His ears stuck out and gave his face a comic appearance. "You'll never get a job here without a license."

Abdul resisted the urge to laugh at Frank and nodded, raising his eyebrows. "Probably so" Abdul leaned into the table and lowered his voice. "You guys don't know where I could get a set of documents— if you know what I mean?" He scrutinized the three to see their reaction, wondering if his question was too provocative. Frank and Jess were obviously surprised by his question.

Ray's face betrayed no emotion as if he hadn't heard the question, looking off toward the bar. Slowly he pulled in his legs and tilted forward, facing Abdul with a menacing expression of puffed lips and scrunched face. "Do we look like crooks?" he said in a low guttural tone.

Uh-oh, Abdul worried he had overstepped his bounds. "No... no, of course not." He wanted to leave, but knew leaving abruptly after what went down could be dangerous. A fight would be disastrous, and the police could be called. He thought he could easily handle Frank and Jess, but Ray could be difficult. "How about another round on me."

"If you ain't got no job, how come you're throwin' money around?" Frank asked.

"Easy, Frank," Ray said. "Don't be rude." He eyed Abdul with half-closed eyes. "Fake papers can cost a lot of money."

"Yeah, I suppose so. Forget it." Abdul raised his hand. "Bartender, when you have a chance would you please fill us another pitcher." He would need to string these men along for a time in order to leave safely. When the bartender placed the beer pitcher on the bar, Abdul retrieved it and topped up each of their glasses. "I'm sure glad to hear Trump is goin' after all the illegals. We need to enforce our damn laws. Shit, these illegals come in here and steal our fuckin' jobs. Findin' a construction job with good wages is almost impossible anymore. Hell, in Hammond almost all the construction jobs have gone to wetbacks. It's a damn crime. Shit, whenever, I apply for a new construction job, the first thing they want to know is if I speak Spanish."

"Yeah, if you go to construction sites here, all you hear is fuckin' Spanish," Ray said. "Not to mention all the damn restaurant kitchens."

"Fuckin' right, man," Frank said. "This is America. They shouldn't let anyone in who don't speak English."

"You're right there," Abdul said.

"At least here, Ole Max's got a white guy in the kitchen," Jess piped up, his first words since Abdul sat down. He scanned the group nervously as if to gauge how his statement was received. He had a short, stocky build. His beige work shirt had stains down the front and his shaved head, looked like multicolored tapestry as it reflected the light from the liquor signs. His teeth were yellow and he was missing a canine tooth.

"Yeah, Max don't hire no illegals," Frank said. "He was in Nam, I hear. Got a purple heart. He's a true patriot. If he wasn't so old, he'd ah made a good Militia recruit."

"I heard Max's got cancer and that's why he don't come round much," Jess said. "Jack, the bartender, said Max was thinkin' of sellin' the place."

"Yeah, I heard," Ray said. "Maybe we should chip in and buy the place."

"Shit, that would be cool," Frank said.

"Don't hold your breath," Ray added, laughing. "Nah, I hope Max recovers and keeps the bar." He watched Abdul as if he expected Abdul to speak, then took a long drink of beer. "We'd be hard pressed to come up with the money."

Ray, Frank, and Jess discussed the things they would do if they bought the bar to improve the place. Abdul praised their ideas. Ray bought the next pitcher and Abdul's danger scale slipped down a notch. He was confident he could now leave without being attacked. "Well, I guess I'll hit the road. Get up in the mornin' and make the round of construction sites. I enjoyed talkin' with you guys. Maybe I'll catch you here again. I like this bar."

"Where you stayin'?" Ray asked as he extended his legs and settled back.

Abdul studied Ray's face and posture. He decided it was a simple enough question with no alternative motive. "I was plannin' on sleepin' in my car tonight." He didn't want to reveal the motel he was staying at.

"No need, Sidney," Ray said. "I've got an extra bed in my trailer. You can bed down there tonight."

"Oh, that's kind of ya. I don't want to put you out." Abdul wasn't sure if accepting Ray's invitation was wise. "I've got a comfortable mattress in my SUV. I'll be alright."

"No I insist," Ray said. Ray's voice and demeanor had changed dramatically to a more friendly tilt. "I like what you've been sayin'. I'd like to get to know you a little better. We're members of the Colorado Freedom Militia and we're always lookin' for new qualified members."

Abdul didn't know how to respond. The change in Ray gave him qualms. The three could be thinking of robbing him or some other nefarious action. He wondered if he should risk it or leave. He decided that maybe the risk was acceptable. He wanted to learn more about the Freedom Militia. He had a knife in his pocket and he had trained in Sana'a how to use it. Getting accepted by the Freedom Militia might lead him to a rocket launcher. "I'll take you up on your offer. How about some snacks to go with the next round."

"I'd go for a burger and fries," Frank said. "They do a great burger here."

"I'm not hungry," Ray said, "but go ahead. Frank's right the burgers here are good."

Abdul, Frank and Jess ordered burgers along with another pitcher of beer. Abdul sensed that the group had relaxed, following Ray's lead, and were quite talkative about their Militia as the beer flowed.

Abdul followed Ray's truck to the outskirts of the city. The narrow trailer was on a lone property surrounded by empty fields of sage brush. Ray ushered him inside. The trailer interior was tidy. The green carpeting was a little worn and the beige fake wood paneling on the walls added a cheap spacious atmosphere to the small trailer. The living area contained a black, vinyl sofa, black, vinyl, recliner-chair, large flat screen TV, and a large gun cabinet with an assortment of rifles.

Abdul walked to the gun cabinet. "Nice collection."

"These are my babies." Ray unlocked the cabinet and pulled out a rifle that had obviously been used extensively. "AK-47, Russian made. The real deal. Here feel the weight of this baby." He handed the rifle to Abdul.

Abdul jostled the rifle up and down, then put it to his shoulder and sighted down the length of the trailer. "Excellent weapon."

"You been in the military?"

"Yeah, I was in the Rangers. Two tours in Afghanistan. How about yourself?"

"No... I'm not much for gettin' blown up. I respect those that served. Don't get me wrong. Service to your country is a high form of patriotism."

"I understand. I saw a lot of my buddies get blown up. After my service was complete, I was glad to get out. Seventeen years in Afghanistan and what have we achieved?"

"You're damn right there. Waste of our boys if you ask me. Them damn rag heads.... Let them damn Arabs kill each other."

Abdul smiled. He wanted to slit Ray's throat. It would be so easy. Instead he handed the rifle back "Yeah, we need to keep them out of this country." He was amazed at the change in Ray from his belligerent alpha male posturing at the bar to his bosom buddy persona. He'd need to be very careful how he handled the mercurial Ray.

When Abdul woke early in the morning, he stepped out of the trailer and breathed in the cool mountain air. The sun was beginning to emerge over the mountains. The sagebrush was changing from dark green to a silvery green with the brightening sunlight as the scent of the sagebrush intensified. He had the urge to pray as he had been taught and done so many times over the years, but that was behind him now. He wondered if Ray knew anyone who could obtain a rocket launcher, a SMAW, shoulder-launched, multipurpose, assault weapon, as they were known in the military. He had trained on the Russian made SMAW in Yemen and knew that with a range of 500 yards, he could blow up the tents and buildings at Tech Area 54 with such a weapon. He would stay a few days, act like he was looking for work, and see what he could learn about the Colorado Freedom Militia and Ray.

Ray opened the trailer door. "Whatcha doin'?"

"Just breathin' in the fresh air. You've got a good spot here."

"Yeah, five acres. Just over the hill is my shootin' range. The boys come out here on the weekend. We have a grand old time. Some old coot owns the rest of the property around here, so we're well isolated."

"Sounds like fun."

"You want some breakfast?"

"Nah, I'll take off and make the rounds of construction sites before they get busy. I'll catch a coffee and something to eat on the way at a fast food joint."

"It's no trouble for me to fix some eggs and sausage. I need to head out to work too."

"Thanks, but I should be on my way." Abdul walked back toward the trailer "The early bird gets the worm as they say."

"Yeah, I understand. Say, why don't you come back to the Armory Bar tonight? You can meet some of the other Militia. You can stay here in the trailer as long as you need. I bet that bed felt better than that mattress in the back of your car."

"Yeah, it did." Abdul stepped up into the trailer and shook Ray's hand. "I don't know how to thank you. You've been so kind." He fetched his bag and slapped Ray on his back. "I'll see you tonight at the Amory. You have a good day." He stopped at the trailer door and smiled back. "I'm glad I met you and your friends." He nodded and left, thankful and surprised that Ray had asked him to stay as long as he needed. He relished the idea that he made a good impression as he got into his stolen SUV, but wondered if Ray could have an alternative motive as he drove off.

In town he settled at a diner and ordered a full breakfast. He was feeling quite good. He had made good contacts and needed to lead the group on. He was a little worried about the stolen SUV. He could steal another here and abandon the Honda, but that could lead to a search for him in Colorado Springs if somehow he had been linked to the stolen car— a remote possibility. He'd hang around a few days get the feel of these Militia men, go back to Albuquerque, dump the vehicle and take the bus back to Colorado Springs where he could steal a motorcycle. If he was able to obtain a SMAW, he could steal another vehicle to take it back to New Mexico.

CHAPTER 16

Fred landed at the Albuquerque Airport and was greeted by Sunu when Fred came out from the secure area. Sunu had developed quite a paunch since Fred last saw him in DC, but Fred recognized his bushy hair and stellar smile like a kid that had been offered an ice cream cone.

"Welcome to Albuquerque," Sunu said in his gravelly voice that didn't at all mesh with his smiling face. "Have you been here before?"

"Not for many years," Fred answered as he shook hands. "Came through on a family vacation."

"I didn't know you were married."

"I've been divorced for many years." Fred placed his hand on Sunu's back and ushered him forward. He liked the small size and spaciousness of the airport. Quite a change from the bustling JFK. "Any other sightings of Hans?"

"Not a one," Sunu replied as they walked along the hall toward the escalators going down to baggage claim.

"Did you review surveillance cameras near the area where the stolen SUV was found?"

"No... since the vehicle was recovered, it had no significance in our investigation of the car theft ring."

"Would it be possible to get the camera footage in the area for the days before the vehicle was found?"

"That could be difficult. You'll have to talk to my boss about that."

"Don't you think it was unusual that the stolen vehicle was wiped clean and the license plate removed?"

"It's unusual, I suppose. The police don't usually dust for finger prints on a recovered stolen vehicle. Most recovered vehicles were taken for joy rides and abandoned. I imagine that a smart joy-rider might remove the plate and wipe the vehicle down." Sunu almost tripped on the escalator as he talked. His paunch didn't help his vision. "The owners are overjoyed to get their vehicles back and that's usually as far as it goes."

Fred got permission from Sunu's boss to go around the area where the stolen SUV was abandoned. He asked to see the camera footage at the stores and banks in the area, viewing the few days of film before the stolen vehicle was found at each location. He was down to his last camera and was disappointed that he hadn't found an image of someone, who could have been Hans, when he came across an image from the outside camera of a bank that showed a man in a stocking cap and beard, who was keeping his head purposely down as if he had something to hide. It reminded him of the film image from the Chicago bus station. He was about the same build as Hans. Although Hans did not have a beard, he could have easily worn a beard as disguise. In the Chicago image, the man had a mustache and a stocking cap of a different configuration. Fred felt in his gut the image could very well be Hans.

Fred went back to FBI office and placed the photograph of the bearded man on Sunu's desk. Sunu picked up the photograph and laughed. "Fred you're grasping at straws here. Your man, Hans, doesn't have a beard. Sure the man in the picture's about the same build, and he's definitely keeping his head down. So what?" Sunu shifted in his chair and leaned back. "Maybe the bearded guy always walks like that. The picture of the man in Chicago had a different cap." He bent forward and held the photograph toward Fred. "I suppose it could be him."

Sunu dropped the photograph on his desk and stared up at Fred. "Do you think Hans would wear a fake beard and stocking cap in the heat and ditch a car in broad daylight?" He took a deep breath and pushed his hand through his curly hair. "If Hans was the one who stole the SUV downtown and later abandoned it on the other side of town a few days later, what was his purpose with the car? If you think Hans is some kind of terrorist, what's he doing in Albuquerque?"

"I have no idea. To be honest, I have no evidence that Hans Zimmer is even a terrorist." Fred slumped down in the chair at the side of Sunu's desk. "It's damn strange that he would just disappear right after we arrested Rasheed. I saw him talking to Rasheed. There was some reason why they were talking."

"I'm sure there was. Could it have been just a friendly comment about the view up there?"

"I doubt it. He seemed embarrassed that I had saw him talking to Rasheed."

"I'd like to help you. I know you've foiled more terrorist plots than anyone else in the Bureau. You're a walking legend."

"Don't get maudlin on me, Sunu." Fred squished his lips together. "Shit, I guess I've hit a dead end. I'll go back to New York and get out of your hair." Fred rubbed the back of his neck as he twisted it back and forth. "Thanks for your help." He tapped the desk with a frown. "I'll call and make reservations and hopefully take off in the morning. Can I take you and your wife out for a farewell dinner?"

"Now you're talking my language," Sunu said, rubbing his ample belly. "That would be nice. How about we meet you in the lobby of your hotel, say 7:00?"

When Fred returned from Albuquerque, he was distraught and even more taciturn than usual. His team sensed his mood, and, once Fred answered their initial questions on how his trip had turned out, they didn't broach the subject again. They brought Fred up to speed on what they had been working on while he was gone. He joined them in the continued surveillance of Libyans and a far right white nationalist group that had recently been involved in vehement and bloody bar fight.

He still wondered about Hans and the stolen vehicle. He felt in his gut that it was Hans who had stolen the white Honda, but nothing made sense. Why steal a vehicle, keep it for a few days, then leave it in a different part of town. Maybe Hans needed to go on an excursion somewhere for a few days and was worried the stolen vehicle could be traced to him. If the picture in the vicinity of the theft was Hans, maybe Hans thought someone saw him, who could identify him near the vehicle. For safety he ditched it. Or maybe it was his routine to steal vehicles for only a short time to be on the safe side. He needed to call Sunu.

"Sunu," Fred said when Sunu answered.

"Yeah, Fred, what's up?"

"Were there any vehicles stolen in the area where the Honda was ditched in the days or nights after that photograph of the man in the beard?"

"Jesus, Fred, I see you're still obsessing over Hans Zimmer. Do you know that Albuquerque is the number one city for auto thefts? We had over 9,000 last year. I don't know, but I'll check for you. Don't you have other terrorism suspects in New York you're looking at?"

"You know we have. Thanks for your help. Call me."

Sunu called after a few days and gave Fred the particulars on two vehicles stolen in the broad area around the University near the day the Honda was left. Fred asked Sunu to keep him informed if any turned up abandoned or apprehended, hoping one of the vehicles could lead to the whereabouts of Hans— a long shot at best.

Fred tried to put Hans out of his mind and focus on the suspects his team were following. He hadn't called Maggie since his return and had ignored her telephone message to call her. He felt he was unfit company and didn't want to drag Maggie into his obsession over Hans. Deep down, he knew he was being stupid. Often upon return to his apartment after work, he would take out the Irish whiskey to calm his mind and end up in front of the television asleep.

The Libyans, the team was following, were definitely radicalized, but didn't seem to be working on a specific plan. When the Libyan group's jihadist rhetoric increased dramatically on Facebook and then strangely ceased, Fred had the team step up surveillance, worrying something was imminent. Jeff, John, Fred and Mary took turns with the increased 24 hour surveillance. Jeff alerted Fred when another unknown person moved into the apartment with a big suitcase, thinking they needed to get a warrant to search the apartment. Fred was reluctant to ask a judge for a warrant, believing they needed more probable cause. The social media rhetoric and another tenant with a big suitcase wasn't enough evidence to convince a judge.

CHAPTER 17

Abdul went to the Amory Bar in the late afternoon. He wanted to be already settled there when Ray and his friends showed up. When Frank was the first to arrive, he raised his hand. "Hey, Frank, over here."

Frank shuffled to the table and took a seat. He lurched to one side when he walked. Abdul wondered if he had a handicap. "You have any luck finding a job?" Frank asked.

"Nah, I might have if I'd had my tools. I was stupid for leavin' them in Montana. I bought a hammer, hand tools, and a tool belt here, but they wanted someone with their own power tools." He poured a glass from the pitcher for Frank. "Here, wet your whistle."

Frank grabbed the glass and took a long swallow. "So... you stayed at Ray's last night?"

"Yes, he's got a nice spot— quiet and private."

"You should've asked Ray for some power tools. He's got about everything."

"Well, I don't like to use other people's tools. You know a man's tools are sacrosanct."

"Sancro what?"

"Sacrosanct... it means very important almost like religious. I should've gathered up my tools when I left, but thought I needed to hightail it quick out of Montana 'fore the Sheriff found me. I'm thinkin' of goin' back tomorrow, pickin' up my tools, and findin' out if they're still lookin' for me."

"I bet Ray showed you his rifle collection, didn't he?"

"You couldn't miss his display case." Abdul poured Frank another glass of beer. "It's a fine collection."

Ray and another man in an Army fatigue uniform with a specialist insignia entered the bar and made directly for Abdul and Frank. "Sidney, I'd like you to meet another good friend of mine, Steve Moore."

Abdul stood and shook hands. "Pleased to meet you." He sat back down with Ray and Steve and poured Ray and Steve each a glass of beer, and topped up his own. He didn't mind drinking beer and liked the taste, but made sure he didn't consume too much that would significantly impair his abilities. He needed to stay sharp and alert, ready to adapt to any scenario.

Steve was short and had a chubby face with ruddy cheeks, reddish hair, and small nervous lips. His eyes seemed to often roam around the room as if he was looking for an assailant.

"Sidney was in the Rangers," Ray announced. "Did two tours in Afghanistan."

"I was in Iraq," Steve said. "I was glad when we got the hell out of there."

"What's your MO?" Abdul asked.

"I'm in supply now," Steve said. "Fort Carson has one of the largest stockpile of munitions in the US."

Abdul felt his heart beat take a leap and took a slow deep breath. "Wow, I bet you've got all kinds of weapons."

"You name it and I bet we've got it."

Abdul would have loved to ask if he had access to a SMAW, but knew it would be stupid and premature. "How long you been in?"

"Ten years. Joined when I was eighteen. Don't know if I've got the stomach to last another ten and retire. The way this country is goin', I'm thinkin' of leavin'." Steve squished his lips to the side and shook his head.

"Yeah, I know what ya mean," Abdul replied. "When I left, the number of Mexicans and blacks was growin'. What's it like now?"

"You wouldn't believe it. Women in combat units. The Army is goin' down the tubes big time. There's even damn Muslims now."

After several more pitchers of beer and the arrival of Jess, Ray suggested going to Hooters to get something to eat. They were all in agreement. Abdul thought that Hooters was a demeaning place with its assortment of big-breasted waitresses flaunting their sexuality for tips. He recognized the beauty of the female form, and didn't believe women should hide their form in burkas or should be forced to wear head scarfs, but thought the flaunting of sexuality was an affront to women.

His mother always wore a scarf in public or when his father was home, but often went bare-headed in the home when it was her and the kids and did not hide her beautiful body from the children, but always told them to never tell their father. He thought the Moslem restriction requiring women to keep their hair covered in public misogynistic and medieval. He realized how much his schooling at Berkeley and his relationship with Cindy had changed him. He now thought most religions were stupid means to control people—something before he left Yemen he would have never espoused.

He remembered Cindy's beautiful body the first time he saw her naked. She had taught him so much. Oh how, she would be against and hate what he was planning to do. Cindy was a Buddhist, which among religions seemed the least restrictive to Abdul. He didn't know if he believed in reincarnation or heaven. What did it matter? If he died in his quest, he had no illusion that he would be martyred and go to paradise for the lives he would take.

The food at Hooters was tolerable, and he had to admit many of the women were beautiful. He thought about Cindy, and a part of him wished he had never embarked on this endeavor to strike back at the Americans for killing his family. Could he give up his retaliation and settle down in America with Cindy? No it would never work. They were from different worlds.

After dinner, the five returned to the Amory bar where some additional men Ray knew were at a table. They pulled two tables together and sat down with the other men, who Abdul learned were all Colorado Freedom Militia members.

Abdul joined in the conversation about how immigrants, blacks, homosexuals, and Jews were taking over, and the salacious comments about the waitresses at Hooters. They professed how happy they were that Trump was finally kicking all the illegals out and would build a wall to keep others from coming. He was amazed how Trump had fooled these racist nuts. Fox news and the other right wing media had done an excellent job of keeping these fools in the fold. He felt his trip to Colorado Spring was developing nicely. Maybe Steve or another militia nut could get their hands on a SMAW or another weapon that would be suitable for his plan.

At about eleven Ray said he needed to be going. He rose and rubbed Abdul on the shoulder. "Come on let's head back to my place. You're comin', aren't ya?"

"Sure," Abdul said. He shook hands with all the men. "Sure glad to meet so many like-minded individuals. It was fun. Hope to see ya all soon."

When they were outside in the parking lot. Ray stopped and turned to Abdul. "Jesus, Sidney. You'd think you were runnin' for office."

"Ray, my Mama taught me to always be polite to people except of course for Blacks and Mexicans."

Ray laughed uproariously. "Your mama knew what she was talkin' about." He slapped Abdul on the back rather hard. Abdul bristled, but kept smiling. "Do you need to follow me or can you make your way to my place on your own?"

"I can find it. You sure you're all right to drive?"

"Fuck yes." Ray punched Abdul's arm. "I'll meet you at my place. I left the gate unlocked before I came. So open it and drive right up. I'll be along. I need to stop at my post office box to get my mail."

Abdul was watching Fox news with Ray and sipping bourbon when Ray got up, unlocked the rifle cabinet. He tossed Abdul an M-16 rifle. "Here make yourself useful and clean this baby. Frank used it last, and he's a fuck up when it comes to cleanin' weapons." He handed Abdul the metal tin with barrel brush, cloth swabs and rifle oil. Abdul wondered if this was a test. He quickly broke down the weapon and began cleaning the barrel.

"I'm off work tomorrow," Ray said. "Would you like to do some target practice late mornin' or do you need to hit the construction sites?"

"I can take the day off from job huntin'. I was thinkin' of headin' later in the day to Montana to pick up my power tools, clothes and shit, and check to see if the Sheriff is still lookin' for me."

"You think that's wise. I've got all kinds of power tools you can use. I used to work in construction, but I've got an easy job now as UPS dock supervisor. The hours can be hard. I sometimes have to work on the weekend, but it's a hell of a lot easier than swingin' a hammer."

"I know what ya mean. Don't worry. I should be able to sneak into Hammond with no problem. My old lady will have calmed down and will probably try to get back in my good graces, but I've had it with her. She let herself go. She was a real looker when I met her."

"Damn, you're a helluva shot," Ray said when he pulled Abdul's target at the rifle range after a round of target practice late morning. "You must have been a damn-fine Ranger."

"I don't know about that. My Dad taught me to shoot when I was just a kid. He loved to go huntin'."

"Yeah, my Dad was big on huntin' too. This fall we should go elk huntin'. I know this private ranch where we can go. The owner's a Militia member."

"I'd like that. Your Militia group seems to be a bunch of interestin' guys. That Steve character was a nervous, shy one. How long have you known him?"

"Couple of years."

"It's unusual for active duty military personnel to be in the Militia. We had some in Montana, but they were discouraged. If Steve's commandin' officer found out Steve was in a local militia, he'd be in trouble and the Militia could be investigated."

"Yeah, but Steve wouldn't squeal. He's the only active duty member we got. Most members are ex-military or just concerned about the country. No way Steve could be an informant."

"He seemed like a nice guy. I wasn't implyin' anything."

"He'd do anything for one of us."

"So what do I need to do to become a member of the Militia?"

"I knew you'd want to join. I got an application back at the trailer. Let's go back and fill it out." Ray picked up his AK-47 and started back toward the trailer. Abdul shouldered the M-16 and caught up with Ray. Ray turned to Abdul and smiled as if he was thinking of a joke. "You know, I've also been thinkin' about your lack of driver's license. It'll be hard to get a job without one. I know a friend at the DMV. I think I can get you a Colorado Driver's license, but it'll cost ya."

"Really. That would be awesome, man."

"It's the real deal, so unless you get arrested it will work even for a traffic stop. You'll be in the computer. If you have your birth certificate and social security card it will be a lot cheaper and easier."

"No such luck, I'm afraid. They burned up in a fire we had at my trailer. My old lady was smokin' in bed."

"That's unfortunate. The fee jumps to $2,000 without any documents."

"I think I'll be able to handle that. I'll have it for you when I come back from Montana tomorrow if all goes well."

CHAPTER 18

Fred told himself he should forget about Hans Zimmer, but knew he wouldn't. His intuition or his gut, as he liked to call it, was usually spot on, but he had nothing concrete to go on. There were plenty of government facilities in New Mexico that would be suitable entities for a terrorist attack. There was Sandia National Lab, Kirkland Air Force Base, and of course the famous Los Alamos National Lab. All of which had nuclear weapon material and would be good targets for terrorists. He contemplated what target he would choose if he was a terrorist. If Hans was checking out sites for terrorism maybe he was picked up on a camera near one of the sites. For that matter, the Airport itself would be a good target.

He knew sending a picture of Hans to the various sites and asking them to review their camera footage would be futile. His boss would not approve his return to Albuquerque without some further evidence.

In the days after his return, Fred got back into the swing of things, but couldn't shake the maddening feeling that Hans was out there in New Mexico planning something horrendous. His drinking of Irish whiskey became a nightly experience. He realized his boss noticed Fred's ill humor and seemed to be keeping an eye on him. He knew he should show more interest in what was going on with his team and get more involved in the teams surveillance of the Libyans. Nights, he had dreams about Abdul and often felt unrested in the morning. What was it about Hans that infected his mind so?

One morning a week after Fred returned, Fred's boss, looking like his shoes were to tight, approached Fred's desk. "Fred, would you come into my office."

"Sure, Boss," Fred replied, suspecting he was going to get a dressing down.

"You don't seem yourself," his boss said as he indicated the chair in front of his large mahogany desk with the photograph of the Director on the wall behind. He was a big man with a fringe of gray hair around his head and a shiny bald spot. He had been a college football linebacker and was an imposing presence. "You've come dragging in most mornings with bloodshot eyes." He paused to stare sternly at Fred. "I'm not going to ask what's going on. We've already gone over what you have on Hans Zimmer. There doesn't seem to be much of anything there."

"You're right, Sir. I don't know what it is, but I can't get Hans out of my mind. I've got this nagging feeling...."

"Stop right there," the boss interrupted angrily and placed his hands on his desk straightening in his chair. "We've got fish to fry here. You're no good to your team in this condition. You've alerted the Albuquerque office. Let them handle it." He dropped his arms and leaned back in his chair. "Maybe you should take a vacation. Take Maggie someplace exotic. Get away from it for a time. Take her to the Bahamas or the Caymans. Relax on the beach and get your head straight." He raised his hand to stop Fred from replying. "You've got plenty of accrued vacation."

"Yeah, Boss, maybe that's a good idea." Fred hadn't been on vacation in he couldn't remember how long.

In the evening, Fred dropped his consternation and phoned Maggie, knowing full well she would be angry for his brief shunning. "Hey, Maggie, how's it going? Sorry for not returning your call. I've been swamped at work. Would you like to go to dinner tomorrow night?"

"Jesus, Fred, what the hell is going on? I know you've been back for over a week."

"I've been in a funk. I don't know what's happening to me. I am profoundly sorry for my behavior and want to make amends. Please...."

"Enough already," she clipped, then laughed nervously. "Yes, dinner tomorrow night sounds lovely."

Fed and Maggie went to the Gotham Bar and Grill in the Village and each had the lobster. Maggie looked smashing in her black sleeveless dress. She, like many middle-aged women, was sporting some excess pounds, but still had an alluring countenance and figure. She dyed her long black hair very tastefully leaving some gray highlights and her hazel gold flecked eyes were haunting.

As they were sipping their coffee after a delicious dinner, Maggie reached across the table and grabbed Fred's wrist. "What's bothering you Fred? You're a million miles away. What happened to you in Albuquerque?"

"I'm sorry Maggie. I'm poor company. The problem is nothing happened in Albuquerque. I believe Hans Zimmer was in Albuquerque, and I feel in my gut he's planning some terrorist plot."

"Who's Hans Zimmer, and why do you suspect him?" Maggie asked.

Fred was crazy about Maggie, but doubted he would remarry. She had been divorced for five years herself and probably wasn't interested in jumping into marriage either. He enjoyed her company and knew she worried about him. She had told him she thought he took unnecessary risks. They had been dating for a little over a year. He was apprehensive of saddling her with the same fears that had driven his wife away.

"I saw Hans talking to Rasheed atop the Empire State building viewing platform," Fred said. "When Hans saw me, he looked embarrassed and left the platform. I think he was involved with Rasheed in some way." He grit his teeth at the image his words brought to mind. "He's German, and he disappeared after we arrested Rasheed. I think a surveillance camera footage of him turned up in Albuquerque by chance because of a local investigation there, but there's no trace of a Hans Zimmer in Albuquerque or anywhere else. It was a dead-end. I should have looked at possible terrorist targets in the area more closely. I don't think I did due diligence. Maybe I'm getting too old for this game."

"Oh, Fred." She squeezed his wrist. "Don't be silly. From what I know you're one of the best FBI agents in the country. Foiling Rasheed's bomb factory undoubtedly saved enumerable lives. Don't be so down on yourself."

"Thanks Maggie. I'm sorry for not contacting you as soon as I got back." He reached across the table and took her other hand. "Thanks for forgiving me and coming out tonight."

After an enjoyable sleep over with Maggie, Fred felt renewed. He was lucky that a considerate woman like

Maggie wanted to be around him. He returned to his apartment early in the morning and after a quick shower went to the office. As he sat at his desk, he considered the possibility of a vacation. Maggie worked for herself doing fund raising for various non-profit organizations and would probably be free to take a vacation with him. He went online and checked various destinations on Travelocity. Many of the Caribbean destinations certainly looked inviting, but he was fooling himself. He couldn't leave the US while Hans was still out there. If something happened while he was gone, he'd be devastated. Besides, he knew he wouldn't be able to relax on the beach as long as Hans infected his brain. He did accept though that getting away from the office for a while would probably be beneficial.

The thought of a vacation in New Mexico hit his consciousness like a bolt of lightning. He knew Maggie had never been. They could stay in Santa Fe. Maggie would love it there—the Land of Enchantment. It really was enchanting, and he could check out the various targets and maybe get a feel for what Hans was planning. He called Maggie and invited her over for spaghetti, one of the few dishes he could make well. He owed Maggie, since he had been to her place enumerable times for delicious meals and sensuous romps in her queen size bed that smelled heavenly.

After dinner as they lay entwined in his bed in clean sheets he had changed especially, he asked her if she would fancy taking a vacation with him to New Mexico. She asked if it would be a real vacation or was he wanting to go to look for Hans. He admitted it would be both. He had gotten some material on New Mexico and

Santa Fe from a travel agent and showed her the brochures.

"It looks wonderful. I would love to go, but if you're going to be gone most of the time off on your own hunting for Hans, then you better go alone."

"I won't lie. I will be hunting for Hans, but we'll do it together. I won't abandon you. You'll have a good time. I guarantee it."

"Oh, a guarantee from the famed Fred Samson. How could I resist?"

Fred took her into his arms and kissed her rose colored lips. "Shall we leave next week?"

"I'm ready and willing," she said as she slipped her hand down his stomach.

CHAPTER 19

Abdul reached Albuquerque late in the night and went straight to his rented room. He was tired after the drive and needed sleep to think straight. In the morning, he awoke, remembering the dream that would not let him be. He had become inured to the dream somewhat, but its memory on waking was always debilitating.

After taking a long shower, he applied a fake beard and wig. For a brief second, he considered seeing Cindy one more time, but knew it would be stupid and wouldn't be fair to Cindy. He drove the SUV to the area west of the University, parked on a quiet street, removed the license plate, and tossed it into a nearby dumpster before walking several miles in the back streets to his rented room. After packing up, he hopped on the stolen motorcycle, stored under a tarp in the backyard, drove the motorcycle to the vicinity of the bus station, and abandoned it on a side street. The blue skies of the warming day were a welcome sight as he walked to the bus station. After purchasing his ticket to Colorado Springs, he went to a nearby restaurant and had a late lunch.

Upon arrival in Colorado Springs in the early evening, he walked to a restaurant. He didn't want to arrive at Ray's until later in the evening, thinking Ray was probably at the Amory Bar, and he wasn't ready, just yet, to adopt his racist persona. After a leisurely dinner, he walked a mile from the bus station and looked for a suitable motorcycle to steal. He found a large Harley that would be a comfortable ride, switched the license plate with another motor cycle, hotwired the motorcycle, donned the helmet he had brought with him, and drove off. He arrived at Ray's late in the evening. The gate was unlocked and Ray's truck was parked outside the trailer. When he roared up on the motorcycle, Ray came out with his AK-47.

After Abdul removed his helmet, Ray lowered his rifle. "Jesus, you had me goin'. I wondered, who was stupid enough to ride up here at this hour." He thrust his arm out palm up. "What's with the motorcycle?"

Abdul smiled and walked up to Ray and handed him an envelope. "Two thousand, my man." He ignored Ray's surprised expression and shepherded him inside the trailer. "I sold my car to a friend in Hammond and bought me a motorcycle."

"Looks like a doozy. Can I take it for a spin?"

"Sure, as soon as I register it here after I get my license. I'm not sure, but I think the guy who sold it to me wasn't technically the owner, although probably in reality it was his. It was registered to his wife."

"Shit. I don't want no trouble with the law."

"Not to worry. I'll leave it here under a tarp until I get a driver's license. I doubt that his wife reported it as stolen, but I thought it would be better to leave it under wraps until I can register it here." Abdul laughed. "The guy and his wife weren't on speaking terms." Abdul settled on the couch.

"You want a beer or are you hankerin' for a little whiskey," Ray said, raising his eyebrows before strolling to the kitchen.

"Well, now that you mention it, a little whiskey would go down well. It was a long drive down on the motorcycle."

"I figured you'd go for some whiskey. I picked up some Maker's Mark especially. It should go down real smooth." Ray filled two glasses half full of whiskey, sauntered over to Abdul, handed a glass to him, clinked his glass with Abdul's, then sat in the recliner, and took a long sip. "Woo, that goes down nicely."

"Thanks, this is just what I needed." Abdul held up his glass and nodded with a wink. "Hey, I sold all my tools and some other sundries as well, so I'm all right for money for a while. Don't need to look for a job until I get that driver's license. I can hang out here if it's cool or rent a place in town."

"How you gonna get around?"

"Well, if it's convenient, I thought you could drop me in town when you leave for work, and I can meet you after work at the Amory Bar. If you're tired of me or I've transgressed your hospitality, I'll leave."

"You know you sure talk funny sometimes. Transgressed... nobody I know uses a word like that." Ray walked to the refrigerator and tossed Abdul a beer. "Catch."

Abdul, caught unawares, was just barely able to hang on to the beer with his left hand without spilling the rest of his whiskey in his right. "Those years of college in Albuquerque must've tainted my vocabulary. Good thinkin' on the beer. A beer chaser is just what the doctor ordered."

Ray joined Abdul in laughter. "You are trip." He put his arm around Abdul's shoulder as he sat next to him on the couch. "Of course you can stay." He got up and moved to the recliner. "I was worried when you didn't show earlier today."

Abdul thought Ray might be a latent homosexual. He noticed that Ray liked to touch him, something he hadn't noticed Ray doing with his other friends. When the discussion turned to gays, Ray was the most vehement in denouncing them. In Yemen homosexuality was against the law and could be punishable by death. Of course it existed, but was kept extremely secret. Cindy had opened his eyes to the realities of homosexuality, and he did not begrudge those so inclined. When he first arrived at Berkeley, he had been angered by male students, who seemed to be unduly interested in him, or those, who openly professed their homosexuality. He had learned so much from Cindy.

"I'll talk to my friend tomorrow," Ray said. "Glad you made it back. I think I'll hit the sack. You comin' with me into town tomorrow or you want to hang out here?"

"I'll hang out here if you'll pick me up after work before you go to the Amory Bar."

"Okay." Ray got up and rubbed Abdul's back as he passed, proceeding toward his bedroom. "I'll try and leave work a little early. He turned back and smiled at Abdul. "Good night."

In the morning Abdul fixed Ray some eggs and sausage and walked with him out to Ray's truck.

"See you then around 5:30," Ray said as he tapped Abdul on the shoulder. "Thanks for fixin' me breakfast. I'm glad you're stayin' with me. I like your company. It can get lonely out here on my own." Ray opened his truck door. "If you want to use the rifle range, feel free except no shootin' early in the mornin' or near sunset. I left the display case unlocked."

After Ray left, Abdul searched the trailer thoroughly, making sure he put everything back as he found it. There was a loaded pistol in a drawer in a night stand next to Ray's bed. Ray's collection of books was small, a few self-help books, books on fire arms, and right wing discourses. He discovered some muscle magazines under Ray's mattress.

To make sure Ray would not find anything incriminating if he searched Abdul's bag, Abdul removed a section of the trailer skirting and buried the rest of his money in a metal container in a hole under the trailer along with his passport, credit card and other student IDs. He wondered if the Militia organization, which was apparently statewide, would do a background check on Sidney Wallace. He decided he better see what he could find out about Sidney Wallace. He connected his lap top and did a search. He learned that Sidney was from Las Cruces, New Mexico and had gone to undergraduate at New Mexico State in Las Cruces before being accepted in graduate study in Business at the University of New Mexico. Sidney Wallace in Albuquerque didn't have a Facebook page and consequently there was no photograph. His luck was holding. He thought if they did a background check he could explain away his undergraduate degree as not wanting to appear arrogant.

When Ray and Abdul arrived at the Amory Bar, Frank, Jess, and Steve were already there. They joined the group and Abdul sat next to Steve. After a few glasses of beer, Steve excused himself to go outside for a smoke. Abdul said he'd come along if Steve loaned him a cigarette. Steve readily agreed and appeared to like the prospect of company.

"Sure is a nice night," Abdul said after Steve lit his cigarette. Only a few stars were visible through the light pollution of the city. The mountain air was cool, but not unduly cold. The shining sliver of a moon looked like a silver scimitar. "I gave up smoking a few years ago but often like the occasional smoke."

"Good that you gave it up," Steve replied. "I've tried to stop many times. As soon as I have beer, I get the cravings."

"Are you married, Steve?"

"Used to be, but, when I was in Iraq, she cheated on me with an old friend. After I got back and learned about the affair, I confronted her. She cussed me out and told me she wanted a divorce— she was in love with Hal." Steve lowered his head and composed himself before looking again at Abdul with wet eyes. "She had tried to make a go of it. She said I was a changed man, and she couldn't take livin' with me anymore."

"I'm sorry."

"She was right about being a changed man." Steve shook his head and puffed out his lips. "Fuckin' war will mess with your head something awful. I'm just now startin' to feel whole again. I had PTSD big time. We hit an IED in Iraq that blew the shit out of the front of the Humvee, shredded my buddies in the front, sent a piece of shrapnel through the head of the guy next to me in the back, and sliced my shoulder nearly off." He took a quick drag on his cigarette, his hands shaking. "I was the only survivor. When I got back, the Army doctors tried to help me out, but talkin' to them wasn't helpin' much. The Freedom Militia has been a god-send for me.”

Steve took a deep draw on his cigarette and squinted against the smoke as he exhaled. “This country is goin' to hell in a hand basket. There's gonna be a civil war, I bet. The damn blacks, Mexicans, Jews, gays, lesbians, and other deviants are gettin' so uppity, thinkin' they're as good as us. Not to mention the damn Muslims.” He got up on his toes. “Fuckin' creeps.” He spit. “I'm so happy we have Trump in the Whitehouse. I recently started goin' to church again and that has helped too. This should be a Christian Nation. We need to change the constitution.”

“No shit, brother.”

“You go to church?”

“Haven't been in I don't know how long.”

“I been goin' to the Evangelical Covenant Church that some of the guys go to. If you want, I'll take ya some Sunday.”

“Yeah, that might be nice. Does Ray go?”

“Nah. Ray's not much of a Christian. Don't get me wrong he's a good guy and solid militia member. I think his parents put him off church for life. Damn Catholics.” Steve took a long drag on his cigarette and blew the smoke out through his nose as he tilted his face skyward. “There are some fine single and divorced ladies that attend the church if you're lookin' for a girlfriend. Frank told me about your wife in Montana callin' the cops on ya.”

“She wasn't my wife. We was just livin' together. Have you got a girl friend?”

"I been out on a few dates with a girl I work with at the Base." Steve blew air out between his pursed lips. "Pretty young thing. Boy, does she get the abuse from the non-coms and officers." He frowned and clamped his jaw. "The damn Supply Captain touched her up." He made a slice with his finger across his hand. "I feel like cuttin' his balls off." He took another drag on his cigarette and blew the smoke skyward. "We haven't gotten serious yet. I don't want any premarital sex from her. I'm not sure if I like her enough to want to marry her. I'm takin' everything slow. She came to church last Sunday, but I'm not sure she liked it much."

Abdul thought that now would be an opportune time to find out about Steve's supply job. "You like workin' in supply?"

"Yeah, it's quiet work and hardly anybody gives me any shit except that damn Supply Captain, but he don't come round much. The fuckin' sergeant is gone, God knows where, most of the time." Steve took a short drag on his cigarette. "I've been tryin' to straighten out the records. You wouldn't believe how fucked up they are. Shit we got all kinds of arms that aren't on the books."

"I know what you mean. Sometimes the Army's so fucked up it's a wonder if they know their head from their ass."

Steve laughed and choked on his cigarette. "You're right there."

Abdul thought he needed to broach the subject of weapons if he was ever going to find out if Steve was someone he could manipulate. He didn't think Steve would be susceptible to bribery, but subtle inducement might work. "So what kind of arms do you stock?"

"If the Army uses it, we've got it."

"That's a lot to keep track of."

"Yeah, sure is. I think I do a pretty good job of it. The rest of the guys I work with are lazy fuckers that don't seem to give a shit. I'm correctin' their work all the time."

Abdul had to bite his tongue so he didn't ask about SMAWs. The fact that Steve took some pride in his work might work against Abdul convincing him to steal a SMAW. Abdul would need to be very careful how he handled Steve. He needed to go slow and convince Steve he was his loyal buddy. He put his cigarette out and field-stripped it. "Shall we go back in? I think a beer is callin' my name."

CHAPTER 20

Maggie rolled over to watch Fred with his half-closed eyes. He had always been a rover in his sleep, but last night he had almost pushed her over the edge. He remembered his dream of chasing Hans and opened his eyes wide. "Christ, I was dreaming of that damn Hans last night," Fred said and sat up.

"You definitely have Hans on the brain," Maggie replied. "This is a beautiful old hotel. Santa Fe is such a lovely city. I'm so glad I came with you." She moved to Fred and gave him a quick kiss. "What's on the agenda today?'

"I thought we could have breakfast in the hotel's covered atrium and go for a stroll around the Plaza after."

"What about your monomania with Hans."

Fred laughed. "I haven't forgotten." He grabbed Maggie and pulled her back down in the bed. "I thought we could drive up to Los Alamos this afternoon, have a look around, and get a feel for the town. There's a museum there. I've never been. But first we need to properly christen this bed.

"Ahh, how nice."

The road from Santa Fe outside of Santa Fe was four lane and in no time they were in Pojoaque. "That's a big hotel for out here," Maggie said as she pointed to Buffalo Thunder Hotel. "It's apparently a casino too. I'm up for having a look on the way back."

"Okay, we'll do that." Fred took the exit to Los Alamos and zipped through the rest of Pojoaque past the high school and the old Otowi Bridge before the road started its winding trek up to the mesa where Oppenheimer had led the secret enclave to the development of the first atomic bomb.

As they topped the mesa, Fred pointed to the tower on the side of the road. "That's the old guard tower where the gate to the secluded Lab stood." Fred continued past the airport and into town. He drove to Ashley Pond next to the old County offices and parked.

They walked back toward the center of the small town to the Starbucks coffee house. Maggie needed a pick-me-up. The winding drive had made her sleepy. The coffee shop was full of people and seemed to be a popular meeting spot.

"You think Los Alamos would be a good terrorist target for this Hans you're looking for?" Maggie asked as they sat at a small table near the window.

Fred leaned across the table. "Let's not discuss that here," he said softly with raised eyebrows. "Too many ears."

"Sorry," she replied, slipping back and taking a drink of her coffee. "Thanks for stopping for coffee. I feel better already. I was getting a little dizzy on the winding drive, and the drop off from the steep road was a little scary. Do they get snow here? I'd hate to drive that road in the snow."

"Apparently, they can get a lot of snow, but I read the last couple of years the snow has been sparse. Global warming, I would say."

"What do you think the future holds with this climate change, the Anthropocene as they're calling it, and the threat of the sixth mass extinction?"

"Without a quick transition from fossil fuels, I think the world is doomed. You and I will die before the catastrophic conditions put humanity at risk, but today's children will face a terrifying future unless people wake up and take drastic action." He expelled a hurried breath before drinking the last of his coffee.

"Fred, I'm surprised. You've never before confided to me your dystopian vision."

"I'm sorry for my diatribe. In reality I am hopeful that the people will force governments to be more proactive against global warming, but I guess this hunt for Hans has distressed me more than I realized and has brought to the surface my worries for the world."

"I agree with you that the world's politicians need to take drastic actions to mitigate global warming, and I worry that we are running out of time to take the required actions, but I'm hopeful. I have to be for my children and especially for my grandchild's sake."

"I wholeheartedly agree. Don't pay attention to my glum ramblings." He grabbed her hand. "I apologize. I'm not myself." He lowered his head and gave it a few shakes before looking up with a smile. "Shall we go?"

"Are we going to visit the Lab?"

"Not today. I would need to get clearance. I'm supposed to be on vacation. Let's go to the museum."

They strolled down the sidewalk to the crosswalk. The blue sky was dotted with puffy clouds, and the busy street had a stream of cars. They joined the group crossing the street at the crosswalk, slowing the progress of the cars. They continued down the sidewalk, reaching the Bradbury Science Museum after a block and a half.

When they entered the museum, its cool interior was a sharp contrast to the warm day. The museum was free and the exhibits depicting the history of the Lab were well done. Replicas of the first atomic bombs dropped on Hiroshima and Nagasaki were on display. Fred was surprised how the disparate bombs had created such destruction, killing nearly 160,000 people in Hiroshima and 80,000 in Nagasaki. He knew some modern thermonuclear bombs have over three thousand times the power of these first fission bombs. The destructive power of the modern thermonuclear bombs was hard to put into perspective. One thermonuclear bomb could kill millions upon millions of people.

Fred had read about the many accidental close calls with nuclear weapons. The Cuban missile crisis had been averted by the wisdom of the Kennedys. If the military had had their way back then, it would have been disastrous. He was an advocate for removing nuclear weapons worldwide before an accident or provocation would lead to total planet destruction, but knew there was little possibility of total denuclearization. If anything the world was going the other way— inventing and deploying new nuclear weapons. They completed their tour and walked out into the sunshine.

"That was interesting but rather depressing," Maggie said as she took his arm. "I thought the display promoting the notion that the US had to drop the atomic bombs on Japan or many more US soldiers would have died because the Japanese would rather die than surrender was rather one sided. I remember reading that there was a debate among the developers of the bomb. Some said that dropping the bomb on

Japan was barbaric and instead wanted to stage a demonstration to show Japan the overwhelming power and deadliness of these bombs, hoping Japan, after seeing the incredible destruction of an atomic bomb, would then agree to surrender. The prevailing argument, as I understand it, was as the presentation in the museum purported that the US needed to drop the bombs on actual cities or Japan would not surrender and would continue to wage war. What do you think?"

"I don't know if I'm qualified to make a judgement. I know Eisenhower said that Japan was already defeated and dropping the atomic bombs was completely unnecessary. I'd align myself with his judgement. From what I've read, the US military wanted to drop the bombs to demonstrate to Russia the devastating weapon they had in order to stop Russia from entering the war against Japan and seeking additional territories in Asia."

"Oh, I didn't know that. My God, those poor Japanese." She exhaled slowly. "Imagine what a nuclear war would cause today. It's crazy. We should eliminate all nuclear weapons."

"Wouldn't that be a wonderful idea," Fred replied and placed his arm around Maggie's back. "I'm so glad you agreed to come on vacation with me."

"Yes, I have enjoyed Santa Fe, but I don't know how to feel about Los Alamos."

They walked back to the car stopping to watch the ducks skimming around Ashley Pond in the warm sun. The smell of recently mown grass hung in the air. They drove the car across the bridge and turned down the truck route. The entrance to the Lab area was a multi-station, security entrance, but only a couple of the stations were manned at this hour of the day.

Fred drove down the truck route and turned back toward Santa Fe. "Buffalo Thunder here we come." He laughed. "Are you planning to do some gambling?"

"I might try my hand at a few slot machines." Maggie replied and smiled mischievously. "That was a quick trip. What do you think? The Lab security looked pretty tight. Hans would need a fake Lab ID to get into the Lab Area to plant a bomb. Didn't look like an easy task to me. How good do you think the Lab IDs and security are?"

"No idea."

Their visit hadn't given Fred any dramatic thoughts of where Hans would attack the Lab. He thought the Lab was an excellent target, but Hans could have another target in mind. He wasn't sure what his next move should be. Alerting the Lab prematurely could be a mistake. If only he had more information. They pulled into the parking lot of Buffalo Thunder and went inside.

"It's rather smoky in here," Maggie said with a scrunched face. "Nothing like Las Vegas."

Fred followed Maggie as she perused the casino, the sounds of the ringing machines filling the air, before stopping at a slot machine where aligning four cherries was the jackpot. Maggie slipped a five dollar bill in the bill reader, and began pressing the buttons to spin the counters. She won a few rounds, but was soon out of money. "I read they had some Indian art work on the second floor. You want to have a look?"

"Sure."

It was a relief to step off the escalator on the second floor where the air was more breathable. "Between the smoke and the altitude, I was getting a little dizzy down there," Maggie said. "Wow, look at that display case of Indian pots. They're huge. Much bigger than the pots they were selling under the portal at the Plaza."

Fred moved to the front of the display case. "Impressive. I imagine it would take quite a few months of salary to buy a pot like these."

"No doubt," Maggie said with a big yawn. "I'm ready to go back to the hotel. I could do with a nap. Can we go to dinner at that restaurant Geronimo on Canyon Road tonight? My treat."

Fred laid in deep thought as Maggie slept. If Hans was here in New Mexico, would the Los Alamos National Lab be his target choice? It would be much easier to plant a bomb at the Albuquerque Airport. He wouldn't need a badge, and he could plant the bomb in a restroom easily enough and make his escape. If he wanted to blow up an Airport, he didn't need to come to New Mexico, although perhaps security at the smaller Albuquerque Airport might be less stringent.

Fred was convinced Hans was in New Mexico for a reason. He had a twitch in his gut in Los Alamos, but not enough of a feel to take restrictive actions. Blowing something up at the Lab would undoubtedly create havoc. What bigger statement could there be than blowing up a portion of the most famous National Lab in the US, the birthplace of nuclear weapons? Then again, he had no proof that Hans was still in New Mexico. He'd go with his gut. He'd call Sunu and see if he wanted to come up to Santa Fe for lunch tomorrow and meet Maggie. If Sunu came, he'd discuss the procedure for visiting the Lab. He thought Sunu would come. Sunu wouldn't miss the opportunity of lunch in Santa Fe.

CHAPTER 21

Abdul spent most days at the trailer surfing the internet and watching TV. He left the trailer door open so he could smell the fresh air. The air in the trailer was a little stuffy. Ray's collection of dirty clothes, piled in his room didn't help the smell. Some days he went into town in the morning with Ray and walked around the town or took a bus out into the countryside. He was tempted to take off on his motorcycle, but worried that someone would see him, and it would get back to Ray.

Finally after a week, Ray came back to the trailer and handed Abdul his Colorado driver's license. Abdul as Sidney Wallace was now free to ride his motorcycle. He arranged a visit to Steve's. The small two bedroom apartment near Fort Carson had a tiny ceramic tiled kitchen with a breakfast bar and relatively new grey carpeting in the dining-combination living room, which was dominated by the large screen TV on the wall and elaborate stereo system.

Steve was overjoyed at the visit and immediately opened a beer for Abdul. "What do you think of the place?"

"It's nice and cozy." Abdul took a swig of the beer. "Thanks for the beer."

Steve beamed with a big smile at the compliment. "I like it 'cause it's close to the Base. It's pretty quiet round here. Course nothin' like Ray's." He motioned Abdul to the grey and brown-flecked, cloth couch. "Take the load off." He went to his stereo. "What kind of music do you like?"

Abdul thought of the folk music he listened to with Cindy, and had to steel himself from frowning. He was glad Steve was searching the CDs and didn't see his saddened demeanor. "All kinds."

Steve placed a CD in the player and turned to Abdul. "This is my favorite song."

"I am a man of constant sorrow," the man on the CD sang.

"Oh yeah, I love this song," Abdul said. "He's got an unusual voice and sure can play the guitar."

"Yeah, for sure." Steve sat down on the couch with a big grin and took a long swallow of beer. "It's Dan Tyminski singin' the old folk song written by Dick Burnett in 1913."

"Yeah, I remember it from that movie, *Oh Brother, Where Art Thou.*"

"Yeah, I liked that movie. It was funnier than hell. Speakin' of hell. You gonna come to church with me Sunday?"

"I would like to."

Abdul went with Steve to church on Sunday and made it a regular occasion. He thought the sermons were often cloaked in racism, but tried to listen in case Steve wanted to discuss the service. After church, Abdul and Steve would meet Ray, Frank, and Jess at Ray's for target practice, and, every other Sunday they went to the Freedom Militia evening meetings, Abdul having been accepted as a member with no fuss.

Abdul still spent a good deal of time with Ray and continued to stay at his trailer. Ray seemed to be jealous of the time Abdul spent with Steve and started to deride

Steve occasionally. Abdul knew he needed to keep them both thinking he as Sidney was their friend.

A few weeks after he received his driver's license Abdul felt that he had ingratiated himself with Steve enough that he could question if Fort Carson stocked SMAWs. While they were at Steve's apartment after church, Abdul asked, "Steve, do you stock SMAWs at your supply depot?"

"Yeah, we got the old MK-153 and the new MK-153 Mod 2 with electronic sight. Why do you ask?"

"I don't know." Abdul replied. He knew he needed to be very careful how he proceeded. "Guess I was thinkin' of the times I fired them in Afghanistan. I've enjoyed shootin' weapons out at Ray's. The fun shooting brought to mind the SMAW." Abdul wanted to ask if Steve could sneak one out, but thought he'd wait and make sure Steve wouldn't balk at the idea of smuggling out a SMAW. "They're a hell of a weapon. I took out a shit load of Taliban Toyota trucks with them."

"Yeah, I've seen 'em used. They can take out a truck like nothin'. They'd come in handy when the revolution comes."

"You're right there." Abdul thought it was absurd when Steve talked about the coming revolution. How white nationalists came to such a spurious conclusion was beyond him. He'd save more talk about the SMAWs until another day. He imagined that Steve would be very reluctant to steal one. Offering money would probably not work and might insult Steve.

One Sunday morning as they were driving back from church, where the preacher had rallied against the evil of abortion and diminishing morals of the country, Steve turned to Abdul. "I've been thinkin' about them SMAWs you talked about. I'd sure like to fire one of them." He laughed. "I bet the boys would get a kick out of havin' one. Shootin' one sounds like it'd be cooler than shit."

At first, Steve's comment about SMAWs didn't grab Abdul's attention since he was day dreaming about Cindy. Suddenly he realized the import of Steve's statement and racked his brain for a suitable response. "Those SMAWs are definitely a kick to fire. They're an amazin' weapon."

"Yeah, I bet," Steve replied. "You know the Militia's got a recoilless rifle. Ray said it could take out a plane or helicopter. He said it was a lot of fun to shoot. I'd sure like to fire it, but they don't bring it out no more."

"Wow, where'd they get that?"

"It's an old type, M18. I don't know how they got hold of it. They already had it when I joined. It's one of them tripod types. They ain't got many shells for it, so that's why they don't bring it out."

Abdul considered the best way to phrase his question to Steve about getting his hands on a SMAW without spooking him. He decided the direct approach would be best. "Could you sneak a SMAW from work without anyone knowin'?" He held his breath as he waited for Steve's answer.

Steve slowed the car and glanced at Abdul. Abdul couldn't discern what the look meant. When Steve turned back to his driving and fell silent for a time, Abdul worried that he had spooked him. He waited and wondered if Steve was just going to ignore his question. Steve didn't look angry, but appeared deep in thought.

"You're damn right I could," Steve finally said and increased the speed of the car.

"Really?" Abdul didn't know what else to say. He didn't want to appear too eager.

"Hell, I could sneak anything out of supply," Steve said as he expanded his chest.

Abdul felt a surge of adrenalin. "Do the Freedom Militia go out on maneuvers for days at a time?" he asked to purposely change the subject. "You know kind of simulate what it would be like if there was a civil war." His mind was racing with ideas on how the theft of the SMAW would best be achieved.

"We haven't recently. We've got a new leader. You met him. David, the tall blond guy. He don't socialize with us much. Never comes to the Amory Bar. He's got a big ranch and thinks he's hot shit."

"If he's not very friendly, how'd he get elected?"

"Some people are so dewy-eyed about money. I think Ray would be a much better Commander than David."

"You may be right there."

Steve pulled the car in front of his apartment. Abdul got out and waited until Steve came around the car. "Thanks for taking me to church. I enjoyed it. I certainly enjoyed seein' Miss Foster." He shook hands with Steve. "I'll take off. You comin' by Ray's before the meeting to do some target practice with Frank, Jess, and I?"

"No. I got some things to do. I'll see ya at the Militia meeting. I think Miss Foster was glad to see you too. You should invite her out to coffee or lunch. She's mighty pretty."

After the Militia meeting ended, Abdul approached Harold, one of the Militia members that usually didn't hang out at the Amory Bar as they were milling around the refreshment table. He thought Harold was a stuck up member, but knew he had been in the Militia longer than most. "You ever shoot the recoilless rifle I heard the Militia has?"

Harold stared at Abdul while he finished chewing his cookie. "Yeah, I have. It's pretty old and shells for the thing are hard to come by. I don't think it's been used in a few years. It has been pretty much mothballed. The Commander has it out at his ranch in the stables under lock and key."

"I see. Sounds like an interesting weapon. I find old weapons fascinatin'."

"I suppose," Harold replied before selecting another cookie.

Abdul, intrigued by the Militia's possession of a recoilless rifle, wondered if it would work for his planned revenge. He moved through the group to Ray, who was talking to Frank. He nodded at Frank and placed his hand on Ray's shoulder. Ray turned to Abdul and immediately perked up and smiled. "Say, does the group ever meet out at the Commander's ranch?" Abdul asked. "Sounds like quite the spread." He removed his hand and reached for a cookie.

"He hosts an annual picnic there," Ray replied and looked around to see who was near before moving closer to Abdul. He leaned to Abdul's ear and whispered. "Dave worries we might steal somethin'." He laughed before taking a bite of his cookie.

Abdul judged that stealing the recoilless rifle would be much easier that convincing Steve to obtain a

SMAW. Breaking into the Commander's stables would be relatively easy.

Abdul rested his hand on Ray's shoulder again. "Steve told me the Chapter owned a recoilless rifle. You ever fire it?"

"Once a few years ago," Ray said. "It's hard to get them 57 mm shells for it. It hasn't been brought out since then."

Abdul liked the idea of stealing the recoilless rifle as a backup plan. Associating with the twenty idiots in the Colorado Springs Chapter of the Freedom Militia was taking a toll on him. He found the meetings insidious and looked forward to the time when he wouldn't have to endure these right-wing nuts anymore. The whole lot were racist assholes. The Chapter Commander was an especially infuriating, stuck-up idiot.

It was surprising how easily he had been accepted into the group. He had initially worried there might be a FBI informant in the group, but nobody came to mind. They all seemed true believers and too stupid to be putting on an act. The Commander made a point of announcing at every meeting that the group was non-violent and their primary purpose was working to influence laws, but they would be ready if insurrection began.

Abdul found the location of the Militia Commander's ranch on the internet as he lounged in Ray's trailer awaiting Ray's return from work. The ranch was a ways out of town, but would be easy to access. After researching the M18, he decided it was too old and bulky and undoubtedly wouldn't work as well as a

SMAW, but could be a fall back weapon if he couldn't induce Steve to sneak out a SMAW.

When Abdul heard Ray pull up to the trailer, he quickly left the trailer, anxious to get going and talk to Steve. Whiling away the hours at the trailer was getting old. He desperately wanted to go forward with his attack on the Los Alamos Lab.

As soon as Ray opened his truck door, Abdul said, "Hey Ray, I locked the trailer. Unless you need something from there, we can go. I'm thirsty as hell. You're out of beer. Before comin' back tonight, we need to stop at a store, so I can stock up your refrigerator."

"All right, then," Ray said and started the truck. "Hop in. Yeah, I'm dyin' for a beer too." After a few minutes of quiet as he drove off, he turned toward Abdul. "What've you been up to today?"

"I was readin' your copy of *The Turner Diaries*."

"Damn good book." Ray stretched his forehead. "You never read it before?"

"No. I heard about it, but never read it."

"That's surprising. I'd ah thought that all militia minded guys would have read it. Didn't they talk about it in Montana?"

"Oh, yeah. I know the story well enough. Just never got around to readin' it."

"We may be close to the revolution like the book talked about." Ray gripped the wheel tighter. "We've got the right leader in the Whitehouse."

"Well, if so, we'll be ready to join the fight."

"You're damn right."

Ray pulled the truck into the Amory parking lot. He got out and grabbed Abdul around the shoulder and gave him a shake. "When the revolution comes, Sidney, you and I will kick some darky butt that's for sure."

"Fuckin'-A, Ray." Abdul forced a laugh. His skin crawled from Ray's touch, and he had to consciously stop himself from hunching his shoulders.

They walked into the Armory Bar and sat down with Jess and Frank, who were already nearly finished with their pitcher of beer. Abdul ordered another pitcher and asked how their work day had been.

"Fucking awful," Frank said. "The boss was on a tear. His bitch wife must've given him a rash of shit. She's one of those half-ass liberal do-gooders. Fuck them." He raised his glass of beer. "TGIF. We need to tear one on. Jesus, I hate my job."

"Sorry to hear that, Frank," Abdul said. "Yeah, them commie liberals don't have any idea what's goin' on." He poured Frank another glass of beer. "TGIF. Say, where's Steve? He wasn't here last night either." He looked around the table.

"Who knows," Ray said. "Sometimes he gets down on himself. Give 'em a call." Ray slid his cell phone to Abdul. "When you gonna get your own phone?"

"Damn smart phones are too damn expensive. Maybe I'll get one of those cheap prepaid ones." Abdul had no intention of getting a cellphone that would allow him to be easily tracked. Not that he thought anyone would be trying to track him as Sidney Wallace. He dialed Steve's number. "Hey, Steve we're all here at the Amory. You comin'?" He waited as he listened to Steve's reply. "Okay good, see ya in a bit." He slid the phone back to Ray. "He said he'd be here soon. Had to work late."

They carried on with their denigration of blacks and immigrants and praise for Trump as they sucked down their beers. They gave no credence to the Mueller investigation, believing it was the CIA and FBI trying to tarnish Trump. It seemed to Abdul that there was plenty of evidence of collusion with the Russians already. Of course the guys only watched Fox news or listened to Rush Limbaugh, Alex Jones, or the other right wing idiots. Their stupidity amazed him. They would all drive after drinking way too much. What a bunch of careless fools.

When Steve came in, he looked haggard like he hadn't slept well and pulled a vacant chair from the next table and inserted it between Ray and Abdul. "What's up, Steve?" Ray asked. "You don't usually have to work late. Somethin' goin' on at work?"

"Inventory time," Steve said and stared momentarily at Abdul. Abdul poured him a glass of beer.

"Where shall we go eat?" Ray asked. "Hooters again. It should be jumpin' tonight. TGIF."

"Can we go someplace else," Steve said. "I'd like some seafood that's not deep fried."

"Red Lobster then," Ray said. "We can hit the Whisky Baron after. It's near there. Last time I was there, there were some fine fillies. I could do with some action tonight." Everyone agreed, and they all left.

After dinner while they were waiting for coffee, Steve nudged Abdul and asked him if he wanted to a have a smoke. Abdul agreed and walked to the door with Steve.

Outside, Steve lit Abdul's cigarette and took a long inhale of his own cigarette. "I did it."

"I see. What?"

"I got a MK-153 SMAW."

Abdul studied Steve to see if he was joking. "Really, you stole one?"

"Yep. Don't say anything to the others. I don't trust them like I do you." He nudged Abdul on the arm with his elbow. "You'll show me how to use it, won't ya?"

"Of course, Steve, no problem. Have your got rockets for it?"

"Oh yeah, plenty." Steve laughed. "I've been sneakin' out rockets all week. I've got a shit pile of 'em. The hardest thing was gettin' the launcher out. I snuck it out tonight in a pile of my fatigues from the laundry. The damn thing looks cool. I think we should lay low for a while to make sure they don't miss it. I doctored the records, so, I think we're cool, but to be on the safe side.... I could go to Leavenworth if they caught me."

Abdul's heart felt like it was going to jump out of his chest. He choked on his cigarette.

"Take it easy, Sidney." Steve slapped Abdul gently on the back. "I can tell you're as excited as me. That MK-153 is a cool lookin' mother. I was so excited when I got the thing back to my apartment I almost shit myself." Steve snickered. His chubby face with its twisted smile made him look like a small child. "I'm glad you asked me about them. That weapon would be fantastic for the civil war. We could take out a slew of blacks and Mexicans and anybody else that got in our way."

"Man, you're not kiddin'. That's fantastic." Abdul put out his cigarette and stuck the remainder in his pocket.

He didn't want to appear too over the top about the SMAW. "I'll save this for later. Let's go back in. The coffee's probably gettin' cold."

When Steve said he'd skip going to the Whiskey Baron with the rest, Abdul wanted to go with him and get a look at the SMAW, but thought better of it. Ray might get suspicious.

Abdul was deep in thought at the Whiskey Baron, the country and western music blaring, making it hard to carry on a conversation. He attempted to formulate a plan while the music had the rest of the group smiling and bobbing their heads as they watched the female dancers in their tight jeans or short skirts performing their line dance. He'd need to steal a car to transport the SMAW after somehow getting the SMAW from Steve. He had thought about taking Steve's truck, but considered it too easy to trace.

He felt sorry for Steve. He knew the best course of action would be to kill Steve before absconding with the SMAW to make sure they couldn't trace the SMAW to Sidney Wallace. The Colorado Motor Vehicles and the Freedom Militia had pictures of Abdul as Sidney Wallace that could lead the FBI to Hans Zimmer.

He remembered the man with the cell phone in his hand, who had looked at Rasheed and him briefly at the Empire State viewing platform. The look had given him chills. Could that man have been FBI? He thought he saw the same man surveilling Rasheed, but didn't get close enough to be sure. The FBI could already be looking for Hans Zimmer.

Convincing Steve to give the SMAW to him to hide at Ray's would probably be the best plan. Then again, maybe Steve would suspect him of wanting to steal the SMAW. No, he thought not. It seemed that Steve really trusted Abdul. Once Abdul had the SMAW, he'd need to come up with good story for why he had to leave for a short time without raising Steve's suspicion or just kill Steve. If he did kill Steve, he'd have to dispose of the body somewhere and have a story of where Steve went so that other militia members wouldn't get suspicious. He'd need to leave quickly after killing Steve.

Abdul drove his motorcycle to Steve's Sunday morning to join him for church. When he hit the doorbell for Steve's apartment, his heart was racing like a runaway horse. He would get his first look at the SMAW. After the buzzer rang, he opened the door and told himself to walk up the stairs slowly.

"Hey, Sidney," Steve said as he opened his apartment door. The apartment smelt of bacon and Steve was all smiles. "Come have a look." Steve led the way into his bedroom where arrayed on the bedspread was the SMAW and seven rockets.

"Man, Steve, that's quite a sight. You think it's wise keepin' it here?"

"Not really," Steve said as he picked up the MK-153. "It's a lot lighter than I would have thought." He handed it to Abdul. "I haven't been able to hardly sleep since I brought it here. Every time I hear a car outside, I go to the window. I need to hide it somewhere."

Abdul tried to calm his shaking hands as he raised the SMAW to his shoulder. "I remember this baby well." He handed the SMAW back to Steve. "We could hide it out at Ray's place." He waited for Steve's reaction.

Steve frowned and then squished his lips to the side, closing one eye. "I don't want Ray to know we've got it until I'm sure I'm in the clear."

"I could take it and hide it at Ray's without him knowin'."

"How you gonna do that on a motorcycle?"

"I'd have to borrow your truck."

"I can't take your motorcycle to work. Besides I never rode a motorcycle before."

"Ray wants to go the Amory Bar to watch NASCAR this afternoon I'm supposed to go back after church to go with him." He couldn't keep his eyes off the SMAW and the rockets. "I could go back with your truck and make some excuse about being sick— bad case of stomach flu. That's why you loaned me the truck because I was afraid the jostle of the motorcycle would cause me to shit myself."

Steve stepped back and scrunched his face. "Eww, that's a nasty story." He shook his head. "I don't know how you come up with such stuff." He laughed. "I guess that will work, but what about my truck?"

"I'll bring it back after I hide the SMAW.' Abdul smiled and hit Steve gently on the shoulder. "I'll tell Ray that the Imodium worked, and I felt well enough to return your truck, so you didn't have to bum a ride to work."

"Okay." Steve grabbed the big duffle and started loading the SMAW. "We still goin' to church?"

"Yes, I think we should."

After church Abdul's palms were sweating as they walked up the steps to Steve's apartment. He wondered if the opportune time to kill Steve was now. He didn't want to. Maybe leaving Steve alive as a possible fall guy was a better option. He found it hard to believe that the stolen SMAW wouldn't be missed. Could he convince Steve that he had to leave for a few days without raising Steve's suspicion?

They walked into the apartment. "You want a beer or ice tea 'fore you take off?" Steve asked. "That sermon produced a powerful thirst."

"Okay, a tea would be nice."

Steve went to the refrigerator took out the pitcher of ice tea and filled two glasses with ice cubes that sounded like ball bearing dropping before pouring in the tea. Abdul abhorred ice filled drinks, but new it was what most Americans drank. He thanked Steve and sipped the tea. No one in Yemen would ever drink iced tea.

"Where you gonna hide the MK-153," Steve asked.

"I thought I'd burry it in the dirt at the rifle range. The soil is all chewed up and no one would notice that something was buried there."

"Yeah, that's a good idea. Anywhere else would stand out like a sore thumb."

Abdul walked to the kitchen and poured some of his tea in the sink. He eyed the wooden block of assorted knives. He could easily snatch one and cut Steve's throat. He had come all this way and was within reach of his goal of creating an act the Americans could not ignore. He moved to the knife block.

"Whatcha doin'?" Steve called from his position on the couch. "You need more ice? Just stick the side of your glass against the lever."

Abdul hesitated momentarily, but then went to the refrigerator and added ice to his tea. He returned and sat down. He wouldn't kill Steve just yet. He drank the tea quickly and stood. "I better get goin' before Ray gets anxious. He loves his NASCAR."

"Yeah, I'm not crazy about it, myself. Goin' round and round a track is not my idea of entertainment, but I'll probably watch it so I can talk about it with the guys. Ray likes the damn crashes. They scare me."

"Yeah, I don't like the crashes either." Abdul grabbed the olive drab duffle bag and hoisted it onto his shoulder. "I'll be back later with your truck. It will take me awhile to bury this. I need to make the hole pretty deep."

"You're a good friend, Sidney. I'm sure glad you came to Colorado Springs. I can't wait to try that MK-153 out. You think we could shoot it at Ray's?"

"No... I think we'd need to go someplace much more secluded. The rocket makes a big explosion."

"Fuck, I hadn't thought about that. Where could we do it?"

"I don't know. You're more familiar with the area. You think about it and see if you can come up with a good secluded place to try it out." He marveled at how naïve Steve was. He wasn't going to try the SMAW out. The SMAW rocket's explosion could expose him needlessly. He would fire it at his target with the expectation that it would work and that would be that.

"Hey, Sidney, about time," Ray said as he looked up from his gun owner magazine and tipped back up his recliner as Abdul entered the trailer. "I didn't hear your motorcycle. Is Steve comin' with us?"

"No, I got the stomach flu or somethin' I ate. I got the shits at Steve's. I was afraid to drive my motorcycle with all the vibrations. Didn't want to shit myself. So I borrowed Steve's truck. I'm gonna have to beg off goin' to the Amory."

"Fuck." Ray stood and looked out the window. "I don't think Steve's ever rode a motorcycle."

"I'll take some Imodium and lie down. If I feel better later, I'll return the truck. If not, Steve said he could get a ride to work in the mornin'."

"Damn," Ray said as he slammed the magazine on the kitchen table. "I sure hope you don't shit my spare bed."

"I think I'm pretty well cleaned out. I had to stop on the way at a gas station. I think some Imodium will do the trick. Don't worry I won't shit up your spare bed."

Ray hung his head. "Sorry, about bein' so nasty." He walked to Abdul and placed his hands on Abdul's shoulders and massaged them. "Does your gut ache?"

"It's not too bad now."

"Good, well, I hope you feel better. I'll see you later." Ray picked up his truck keys and made for the door. "Take care. I may go out with the guys for dinner. I'll might not see you 'til the morning. I can follow you to Steve's in the mornin', so you can drop off his truck and get your bike if you don't feel better tonight."

"Thanks, enjoy yourself."

When he heard Ray's truck leave. Abdul went out and retrieved the duffel bag. He went online and searched for information on the MK-153. It was amazing what someone could find out about weapons on the internet. He loaded and unloaded the MK-153 until he was confident that he could use the weapon. With seven rockets he could destroy Tech Area 54 completely. He was ready to leave, but what to do about Steve?

CHAPTER 22

Fred slipped off the bed of the Santa Fe hotel, making sure not to wake Maggie. He quietly left the room and hurried down to the first floor. He chose an area away from the hustle and bustle of the lobby behind the atrium where some couches and chairs were arranged around a grand fireplace. No one was sitting there. He sat down and called Sunu.

"Hello, Fred, did you get my email?" Sunu abruptly answered.

"No, I'm on vacation here in Santa Fe. I called to invite you to come up for lunch."

"Vacation? Come on Fred, don't give me your bullshit. You're here looking for Hans, aren't you?"

"No, my boss thought I was obsessed with Hans and told me to take a vacation. I'm here with a lady friend, Margret Cummins, honest." He didn't want to admit that Sunu was mostly correct.

"You sure you didn't read my email?"

"No, what did it say. As soon as I hang up, I'll read it."

"Jesus, your sixth sense is working overtime," Sunu said. "A man looking like Hans with his normal brown hair and no mustache was seen here in Albuquerque at a Nuclear Watch meeting in the company of a beautiful blond, who is known to be a regular attendant at the Nuclear Watch meetings. She's a medical student at UNM. The pictures never captured Hans or should I say

Abdul well. The informant, who infiltrated the group, tried to get a good picture of the man, but the informant said the man, Abdul, a Yemeni, who caused quite a stir after the meeting, seemed to have eyes in the back of his head, sensed when the informant was about to take a photograph, and turned aside. The informant got some good photos of the woman, Cindy Clayton. What a beauty."

"My god, Sunu, let me look at your email, and I'll call you right back." Fred scanned the emails on his phone and opened Sunu's email. He read the email and the attached photos. "Fuck," he said under his breath. He was sure the photos were of Hans or should he say Abdul even though none showed his full face. A Yemeni, who would have thought. He called Sunu back.

"We need to alert the Los Alamos Lab. My gut reacted when I visited Los Alamos today. I think the Lab is his target. Can you print out the photos and pick me up in the morning and we'll go to the Lab and talk to Security there? Can you call ahead and set it up?"

"Will do. See you around 8:30. You are amazing, Fred. That's one serious gut you've got."

Sunu's laugh was not amusing to Fred. Things had gotten extremely serious. They needed to find Abdul.

"Can you put surveillance on Cindy in case Hans, I mean Abdul, shows up to see her."

"Already done. We've got her covered 24 hours. She's at her house now. Abdul hasn't been seen again. Cindy went to undergraduate at Berkeley. We've notified our office there, and they're looking for a Yemini named Abdul as a possible student. You may want to call your boss. When I called him after I didn't get a reply from you, he told me he thought you'd gone to the Caribbean on vacation. I sent him a copy of the email. He was sending another agent out, someone named Harry Ragg.

"I saw that I have several emails from my boss. Thanks Sunu. When's Harry arriving?"

"Don't know. He's not been in contact with me."

"Okay, see you in the morning."

Fred read the emails from his boss and telephoned him. When his boss learned he was in Santa Fe, he was vocally angry, but as the call progressed admitted he was glad Fred was there. Fred brought him up to speed on his plans to meet the Los Alamos Security and alert them to Abdul. His boss admitted that he was surprised that Hans was really an Arab. He certainly didn't look like one. Harry would be in arriving in Albuquerque at 2:30 PM.

Fred rubbed his thinning hair. Harry Ragg was a wet behind the ears recent addition to the New York Office. Why his boss would send him amazed him. He was glad Harry wouldn't be in Albuquerque until the afternoon. Harry had a loose mouth and could foul-up his meeting with the Lab. He knew Sunu would let him do the talking. "Have Harry go to the Albuquerque office and wait my return. I'll meet him there after our meeting with Lab security."

Fred walked back upstairs to his room, his gut quivering big time. He felt like driving immediately to Los Alamos, but knew he had to wait until morning. He hoped when he broke the news about Abdul, Maggie wouldn't be mad. There went their vacation.

"Fred, there you are," Maggie said, reclining on the bed, reading a tourist magazine. "I woke up and you were gone."

"I went downstairs to make some calls. I didn't want to wake you."

"You could have left a note."

"I didn't think I'd be gone so long."

"Our reservation at Geronimo is at seven. You look as if you've seen a ghost. Who were you talking to?"

"I called Sunu and my Boss."

"Oh... I've seen how your Boss can discombobulate you." She laughed and stretched her arms above her head, closing her eyes, before pulling her arms in, her eyes wide with a slight grin. "You want to take a shower together first?"

"Sure." He'd wait until after dinner to break the news about Abdul.

CHAPTER 23

Abdul drove Steve's truck slowly across town, his mind racing with an assortment of scenarios for dealing with the stolen SMAW and Steve. He turned off a few blocks before Steve's apartment and pulled the truck to the curb in order to sort out his options. His best option, he decided, was to steal a SUV, switch license plates, and leave the SUV with the SMAW inside before returning Steve's truck. Then he could return for the SUV and leave for Santa Fe, but what was he going to do about Steve still troubled his mind.

After driving the truck to a residential area a mile from Steve's, he looked for a SUV on the street. Finding a black Toyota 4Runner a good distance from a street light, he parked several blocks away and walked back to the 4Runner SUV. After jimmying the door, and hotwiring the ignition, he drove it behind Steve's parked truck and transferred the SMAW to the 4Runner, leaving it parked. As he drove Steve's truck to the apartment, the crickets were singing and the air smelt like rain. No matter what he decided to do with Steve, he would need to get in and out of Steve's quickly and get on the road.

When the buzzer for the downstairs door sounded, Abdul hurried up the stairs. Steve was waiting with the door open. Abdul consciously slowed his gait and smiled as he moved inside. Steve stepped past Abdul. Abdul stared at Steve's back as he slipped his hand in his pocket and grasped the knife. Now would be an opportune time. Abdul withdrew his knife, flicked it open, and stepped toward Steve. When he was close, Steve turned around and Abdul hesitated.

"What's up with the knife?" Steve asked, his eyes wide.

"I got a splinter digging." Abdul replied, poking the knife into his palm, probing for an imaginary splinter. Steve relaxed his face somewhat.

"You should've worn gloves." Steve turned around and headed for the couch. "How'd it go?"

"I wrapped the duffel in plastic and buried it with no problem. Piece of cake." Maybe leaving Steve as a fall guy was a better option. He folded the knife and placed it back in his pocket, causing Steve to relax further as he sat down on the couch.

Steve stared at Abdul a few seconds as if he was solving a puzzle. "I've been thinkin' of where we could try the SMAW out." Steve's demeanor was back to its normal nervous composure. "What do you think of hikin' with it up into the mountains?"

"That might work if we found a very remote clearing." Abdul was still at a loss on the best path for dealing with Steve and hoped his consternation wasn't visible in his face. Perhaps a story about having to leave for a few days might be better than taking the risk of trying to hide Steve's dead body. "I got a call from my old lady in Montana tonight. She was in a car accident. I need to go up there for a few days and help her out... get her settled at a friend of hers. She broke her leg. I hate to do it, but I do owe her."

"I'm sorry to hear that. It's the Christian thing to do, Sidney. You wanna take my truck?"

"No, I'll take the motorcycle. While I'm gone maybe you can check out suitable locations for firin' the MK-153 in the mountains." He could imagine the fool driving into the mountains and hiking to remote spots, thinking they'd be good for testing the SMAW.

"Yeah, I'll check some maps and maybe take a trip after work. You think you'll be gone just a few days?"

"I think so. Her friend should be able to take care of her if I give her some money."

"Okay then." Steve went to his kitchen. "You want a beer?"

"Nah... I should take off 'fore the rain starts. It sure smelt like it could rain on the way over."

"I don't envy you drivin' a motorcycle in the rain. You drive safely. You're the only one who knows where the MK-153 is buried." Steve's nervous laugh solidified Abdul's reservations about killing Steve.

"Here, I wrote out the directions from the target area to the burial site for you." Abdul handed the paper with the fake directions he had created at Ray's. Had he known all along he wouldn't kill Steve? Was he even capable of killing? If he succeeded in taking the SMAW to Tech Area 54, would he have the nerve to carry out the attack? What an absurd thought. Of course he would carry out the attack. He needed to ditch his doubts. Things were going well and unless some unforeseen development stopped him, he would be successful

Steve accepted the paper and studied the directions. "Damn, you think of everything." He slapped the paper on his palm. "See ya when you get back. Don't hurry on my account. We got plenty of time to find a good site to try out that MK-153."

Abdul said his goodbye and left. He drove his motorcycle past the 4Runner making sure no one was around. He ditched the motorcycle several blocks away, walked back to the 4Runner, and drove away. He was glad he hadn't killed the hapless Steve. Steve would support Abdul's story about leaving. He drove most of the night to Santa Fe and rented a room at the El Rey Motel on Cerrillos Road.

Abdul telephoned Ray in the morning after buying a prepaid phone at a cellphone store. "Hey, Ray. I'm in Hammond. My old lady had a car accident...."

"I know all about it," Ray interrupted. "I called Steve last night when you didn't come back. I was worried." There was a prolonged pause. "How come your phone has a New Mexico area code?"

"I'm usin' a phone of a friend of my old lady, who's visiting from Albuquerque."

"Jesus, Sidney. Get your own damn phone."

Abdul laughed. "I'll be back in a few days."

"I'll hide the spare keys out at the second pole on the left in case I'm gone when you come back."

Abdul thanked Ray and hung up. Everything seemed to be in place. Steve and Ray had swallowed Abdul's story about helping his old lady. Steve hadn't told Ray anything about the SMAW. No one had a clue of what he was planning. He smiled to himself as he walked to a New Mexican restaurant a few blocks away. He ate his huevos rancheros slowly, savoring the green and red chili that brought to mind Cindy, who had introduced him to traditional New Mexico cuisine.

He lingered in the restaurant over his coffee. He had nothing to do until the evening, so he took a leisurely stroll for several hours after leaving the restaurant. When he returned to his motel room, the room had been cleaned, and he would not be disturbed. He watched TV news and tried to take an afternoon nap, but his turbulent mind kept him awake.

Abdul gave up on his nap and got out his laptop to work on the Declaration he would send to the *Albuquerque Journal* if he was successful with the SMAW. He spent hours composing and recomposing the Declaration, wanting the Declaration to be succinct and comprehensive enough to expose the US for the history of destructive actions in the Middle East and explain why he released the cloud of death in Los Alamos. When he felt he had done his best, he loaded the Declaration on a thumb drive and went to a copy place where he printed three copies. He would send one to the newspaper, leave one in the 4Runner when he abandoned it, and keep one in his pocket.

He could have used Cindy's help with the Declaration. She was much better with words. He would love to see her again if only for a brief moment. The thought of never seeing her again pained him, but contacting her again would be incredibly stupid. He should have never reached out to her in the first place, but if he hadn't he wouldn't have come up with his plan. He would always be indebted to her, but her knowing him would be so harmful to her. He wished he could apologize to her. The authorities would learn who he was after the explosions and the publishing of his Declaration. Anyone associated with him would be dragged into the investigations and the publicity would create havoc in their lives.

He took a stroll near sunset in hopes of settling his nervousness by watching the beautiful colors of the sinking sun. He had always liked the sunset in California especially when he was on the beach and the sinking sun displayed the many dramatic colors of the rainbow. His Yemen village was on the eastside of the mountains, and the sunrise was the spectacular display of colors he remembered from his childhood. When he returned to his room, he did some stretching exercises, took a hot shower, and dressed in a black, cotton hoodie, black jeans, and black boots. He cut up his other IDs, keeping the Sidney Wallace driver's license and Hans Zimmer passport, and flushed the pieces down the toilet.

He took out a thousand dollars, placed it in an envelope and addressed it to Cindy. He would still have four thousand dollars to make his way back to Yemen. As he sat holding the envelope, he shook his head. What was he thinking? Sending Cindy money would implicate her more than she already was. He removed the money, tore up the envelope, and flushed the pieces down the toilet.

Feeling disoriented with his discursive thoughts, he laid down on the bed. Slowly, his breathing became deeper as he recalled the images of the destruction he saw in Yemen. He sat bolt upright and clenched his fists. Any recalcitrant doubts he harbored were foolish.

He waited until eight before leaving his motel room, knowing that the moon would be up soon when he got to Los Alamos and traffic would be light. He drove the 45 minutes up to Los Alamos, taking the split toward White Rock. He pulled the SUV off the road in the same place he had stopped last time on the motorcycle. The night was calm with just a gentle breeze and the sky was clear, the multitude of stars winking in the dark. The moon just rising over the mountains would make walking easy without a flashlight.

He got out and started to unload the duffel bag when an oncoming vehicle caused him to wait. When he recognized the vehicle as a State Trooper, he shoved the duffle back inside, jumped in the car, and drove to White Rock, consciously keeping himself from speeding away. When he pulled into the gas station, he was shaking and condensed perspiration ran into his eyes. He grabbed his neck and massaged his taunt muscles as he stretched his face skyward.

Should he go back? The trooper saw his vehicle. What if the trooper recorded and called in the plate? The license plate wouldn't match the vehicle. He needed to get out of the area. He'd leave it for tonight and return again tomorrow night. He turned around and drove the speed limit back to the Santa Fe motel.

After arriving at the motel, he stayed in the car until the family carrying suitcases into their room disappeared. What was the reason they were arriving so late? The happy children gave him pause. Was he crazy to kill so many innocent civilians? Was he no better than the Saudis and their bombing of children? Something had to be done to stop the madness in Yemen. Would his statement make a difference in this irrevent country with a lying dictator wannabe as President? He shook his head and told himself when the people of the US read his Declaration, they would know the truth of his words. He had come too far to turn back now. He placed the duffel in the back under a tarp and trudged to his room. He was too agitated to sleep. He took a long hot shower, a luxury most Yemenis would never experience.

As he walked out of the steaming bathroom, he felt a little more relaxed, but still felt like a child who had been discovered in a forbidden act. He laid down on the bed, listening to the clinking sound of the other air conditioners and the traffic out on Cerrillos Road. He took out one of the marijuana cigarettes Cindy had given him and savored the smoke as the relaxing high slipped from his head to his toes. He'd smoke another joint tomorrow night before he left the motel to relax.

He had drastically overreacted after seeing the State Trooper. Tomorrow night would be different. He would not let anything dissuade him from the attack. He would be patient and fire the rockets, insuring the launch of a sizable cloud of deadly radiation.

CHAPTER 24

Sunu pulled up to the security kiosk, presented the letter authorizing their entry into Los Alamos National Laboratory, and showed their FBI IDs. He drove slowly to the main administrative building, parked in the multi-story garage, and stepped out of the car. "Here we go," Sunu said over the roof of the car. "I hope your gut knows what it's doing." He laughed nervously. "You're going to put this place on high alert. If you're wrong and Abdul strikes somewhere else, we'll look like fools."

"Sunu, you are a born cynic," Fred said as he joined him, and they walked across the road and down the sidewalk as the day was heating up. Many people with ID badges either around their neck or clipped to their belt were coming and going. Fred wished he had worn a short sleeve shirt under his sports jacket, feeling his increasing perspiration. Sunu was right, he was risking his reputation.

They walked up the steps to the Security Director's office. The receptionist asked them to take a seat. Before Fred could sit, a man with a blue sport coat, grey trousers, and red tie strode from his office. He had a vigorous hand shake and towered over Fred as he introduced himself, Sam Singleton, and thanked them for coming. His grey hair was cut short and his bearing spoke of a military background. He ushered them into his office, indicated the chairs around the circular table, and took his seat.

"I've already increased security to high alert and have cancelled all vacations and leave for security personnel," Singleton said with enthusiasm.

Fred slid the pictures of Abdul forward. "I know you have already seen these pictures and know about the man, Abdul, we suspect is planning some kind of incident here at the Lab."

"Yes, his picture has already been circulated to security personnel. The man would play hell trying to get into any of the Lab facilities." He angled back in his chair. "What I don't know is what evidence you have that his man is planning at attack on the Lab."

Sunu looked imploringly at Fred.

"Mr. Singleton," Fred began

"Call me Sam and I'll call you Fred," Singleton announced. "You reputation precedes you. That was a hell of a job foiling that bomb factory in New York."

"Thanks, Sam." Fred grasped his chin. "The problem is we don't have a lot of evidence other than we know Abdul has been to a Nuclear Watch meeting in Albuquerque. He entered the US on a German passport, but we believe he is a Yemeni. I saw him at the Empire State Building talking to Rasheed, a leader of a terrorist cell in New York. We're trying to find out if he attended University with the woman he was with at the Nuclear Watch Meeting. I thought since Los Alamos was the birthplace of the atomic bomb that an incident here would be the most dramatic."

"I see. Couldn't he be targeting Sandia Lab or something else?"

"Of course, Sam. We thought it prudent to take all actions possible. Sandia has been put on alert as well as the Airport, Kirtland, State, and local police."

"I understand. Better safe than sorry." Sam stopped talking as his attractive, dark-haired assistant brought in a tray of coffee and Danish pastries. "Just set them here, Liza." Sam grasped the carafe and poured out the coffee. "Help yourself to the pastries, cream, and sugar."

Sunu grabbed a small plate, slipped a Danish pastry onto the plate, and loaded his coffee with sugar and cream. He looked up with a smile and savored his coffee, causing Fred to smile and Sam to laugh.

"You didn't need to drive up here just to meet," Sam said. "We could have done this over the phone." He pushed forward in his chair. "I'm honored that you came. Did you want a tour of our facilities? That is the ones you both have security clearance for. Some facilities are off limits except for those with top security clearance, which I checked neither of you has."

"I'd like to peruse your map, get an understanding of the extent of the Lab, and learn what the various facilities are used for," Fred said as he gazed at the aerial view of the Lab on Sam's wall. "I don't need a statesman tour. I'd just want to get a feel for the Lab and its environs."

Sam rose and walked to the aerial map, followed by Fred and Sunu. Sam started describing the various Tech Areas on the aerial map, what went on in the various facilities, and the security requirements at the entrances to the Lab and the various Tech Areas.

"We're also closing free access to the truck route and across the bridge," Sam added. "Only personnel with Lab ID will be able to drive up the truck route or across the bridge. "Did you come across the bridge?"

"Yes," Sunu answered.

"You must have just made it before we set up the barricade. That about does it unless you want more specifics."

"How hard would it be to alter a Lab ID with another picture?" Fred asked.

Sam blew air out between his lips. "It wouldn't be easy, but with the right equipment it could be done." He looked out his window as he narrowed his eyes. "You think this Abdul character has this expertise?"

"Yes, I believe so," Fred answered. "Plus he's known to have used disguises successfully."

"I'll get another alert out to security personnel to be on the lookout for Abdul with an altered ID and possibly a disguise." Sam licked his lips and let out an audible exhale. "I'm sure glad you brought that up," he said forcefully. "I hadn't thought about that."

"I think that should do it, Sam," Fred said. "Do you know the local police chief?"

"Of course."

"I would like to have permission to look at some of the camera footage from places in town. Could you contact him for us and explain our quest."

"You got it." Sam moved to his desk, picked up the phone, and punched in the numbers. "Chief, it's Sam Singleton. I've got two FBI agents in my office discussing the terrorist alert. They want to look at camera footage the local businesses might have." He listened for a short time. "Great, I'll send them over."

The first place Fred wanted to look at camera footage was the Starbucks coffee house. The police chief accompanied Fred and Sunu to coffee house, and explained their request to the manager. The manager brought out several DVDs, and Fred and Sunu sat down, ordered another coffee, and began viewing the DVDs on Fred's laptop. After about thirty minutes, Fred stopped the DVD and streamed back a few minutes before playing it forward in slow motion. He saw someone entered the shop, who was the same build as Abdul. The man ordered a coffee and sat in the corner with his back to the camera as he worked on his laptop. After nearly an hour, the man got up pulled a stocking cap on his head, kept his head down, and walked out of the shop. Fred noticed a reflection in the window as he passed, but couldn't make out the face. He went through the footage again. He could feel his gut quivering. He felt sure the man was Abdul.

Fred asked Sunu to take the DVD back to the FBI office and see if the blurred reflection could be enhanced. He was convinced that the image was Abdul, which solidified his suspicion that Abdul was planning an incident involving the Los Alamos Lab. Abdul would probably need to steal an ID, switch the picture, and try to gain access. Singleton had told them there were 9,000 employees and 650 contractors at the Lab. That was a lot of possibilities that Abdul could exploit. He hoped Sam's security people were vigilant in their inspection of personnel trying to enter the Lab. Hans's passport photo was a good likeness, and Sam seemed to have things in hand.

Fred was pleased he had come up and actually talked to Sam. He definitely felt better, but still worried that Abdul would find a way around the Lab security. He had done all the due diligence he could think of. Would Abdul recognize the enhanced security and move off to some other target? Perhaps, but Fred felt Abdul was still in the area and would not give up easily. He phoned Sam and told him about the image at Starbucks.

Fred fretted all the way back to Santa Fe. Sunu continued on to Albuquerque with the DVD. When Fred entered his hotel room, Maggie was sitting on the bed, reading a magazine.

"How'd it go?" Maggie asked.

"The security director was on the ball. They've done all that can be done. If Abdul tries to enter the Lab with fake identification, they should be able to apprehend him unless his disguise is superb. That's what worries me. He has shown himself to be wily and determined. I feel better having talked to the Security Director. I'm sure a man fitting Abdul's height and size was filmed at the Starbucks in Los Alamos, a month ago, but he purposely made sure the camera never saw his face." He sat down on the bed and exhaled loudly.

Maggie scooted to him and rubbed his shoulders that were tight as a drum. "I watched the news. Why didn't you have his picture published?"

"I want to catch him, not alarm him. He's demonstrated his resolve. If we spook him, he'll move off to some other location. He'll not be able to leave the US on any regular transportation. Border security, every FBI office, and local and State police have his picture."

"Sounds like you've got the bases covered. Would you like to take a nap?"

"I'd love a nap. It feels like I haven't slept in weeks."

Fred's phone pinged. He looked at the incoming email and recited the information out loud. "Abdul

Salaamed, is an engineering student at University of California Berkeley and is scheduled to resume studies in September for his final year in electrical engineering. He is from a small village in the mountains of Yemen, and his father works for the Yemen government as an accountant. Abdul left California in May from San Francisco and flew to Frankfurt, Germany. We're having the authorities in Germany search for where Abdul went from Frankfurt. There is no record of him returning to the US."

"You've been right all along," Maggie said and wrapped her arms around his muscular frame. "You are an amazing FBI agent, Fred Samson. I'm sure glad to know you and salute your diligence even though you brought me out here and abandoned me." She laughed and gave him a shove.

"Thank you, Maggie." He fell back with her and pulled her to him and gave her a long kiss. "You want to have some lunch here at the hotel."

"I thought you'd never ask?"

"I'm not that hungry. I had several cups of coffee and a pastry besides breakfast, but I bet you're hungry."

"Yes." She rose and went in the bathroom. She turned back. "I'll just freshen up a little and we can go."

CHAPTER 25

Abdul sat up in the middle of the night, trying to remember the dream that had awakened him. He was surprised that it wasn't his reoccurring dream. He remembered disparate snatches of the dream—something about his childhood. Were his parents in the dream? He laid back down, hoping to fall asleep again, but his disturbed mind kept him awake the rest of the night.

When morning arrived, he rose and ventured out for breakfast, longing for a cup of coffee. After breakfast, he walked around the area, watching people leave for work and getting their children to school. How would they react to what he was about to do? Would they understand his Declaration and sympathize with his actions or hate what he did? What did it matter now? He would complete his mission. Nothing would stop him.

He stayed in his motel room, watching the news except for additional walking excursions for lunch and an early dinner. He tried to laugh about his abandonment last night. It didn't matter. He would be resolute tonight. The State Trooper apparently did not check the 4Runner's license plate, and Steve's theft of the MK-153 had not been discovered, since there was nothing about the vehicle or the theft on the news. Not killing Steve had turned out to be the right move.

He tried to dispel his agitation as he waited, anxious for the arrival of night. He was ready to send the cloud of death over White Rock and Los Alamos. He laid back on the bed and closed his eyes.

Abdul was walking in the vineyard imbued with the love of his family when he heard the plane and turned to see the explosion. He tried to run to the house engulfed in the black cloud, but was impeded by some unknown force. Coming out of the black smoke, he saw his father with half his face gone as blood dripped from the raw flesh. His mom followed, holding the hands of his brother and sister. His Mom's beautiful face was intact, but in her chest was a gaping hole from which a slurry of blood spewed. His sister was missing the top of her head and his brother hopped on one leg, his eye dangling from its socket. His father spoke solemnly, "I wanted to speak to you before we left you for good, my dutiful Son. We will always love and remember you. Go forth and keep us in your heart."

Abdul awoke with a start, the memory of the ghastly dream clinging to his mind like a bat on a cave ceiling. He stood up as his tears dripped to the floor. Raising his arms above his head, he announced softly with great force, "I will never forget you!" Slumping back onto the bed, he hid his head in the pillow, crying softly. His father had spoken to him from the grave. Although the dream image was horrid, he believed it reinforced the righteousness of his mission.

He rose with renewed determination as the sun was setting and washed his face in the bathroom, recognizing the accumulated stress while studying his face in the mirror. He told himself his quest would soon be over. He dressed, collected his bag, and strode out to the 4Runner with renewed determination. The heat of the day was quickly dissipating and the evening star was visible in the Western sky. He drove off.

When he reached the Los Alamos and White Rock road split, his nervous energy rose like a soaring helium balloon. A County police unit passing him going toward Los Alamos spiked his danger quotient, but he felt no misgivings about continuing toward White Rock. When he came to a stop at the traffic light at the intersection of the truck route to the Lab, he saw the barricade 30 meters from the intersection, manned by two security personnel.

Why was the Lab on heightened security? Had someone figured out what he was planning? Had Steve been found out and confessed to stealing the SMAW? He counselled himself to calm down. Yes, there was something ominous about the heightened security, but even if Steve had confessed about the SMAW theft, Steve had no idea what he was planning.

The traffic light change seemed to take forever. When the light turned green, he exhaled and drove forward, continuing on toward White Rock. Whatever the Lab knew, he wasn't going to stop now. If they were lying in wait for him, so be it. He pulled off onto the shoulder at the same location as the previous evening, made sure no vehicles were approaching, and quickly hid the duffel on the other side of the barbwire fence before jumping back in the car.

After arriving in White Rock, he stopped at a strip mall away from the main highway and parked. No one seemed to be out and about except a man filling his car at the gas station across the street. When Abdul got out of the car, he stood listening for any helicopters. The sky was quiet. If the authorities had discovered that he had a SMAW, they surely would have had helicopters out. There had to be another reason for the barricade at the truck route. Whatever the reason, he would not let it dissuade him.

He left the SUV and walked leisurely across the intersection, thankful for the lack of witnesses. The moon hadn't risen yet and his trek to the hillside would be hard to follow even if a helicopter appeared. Behind the gas station, he applied black face and pulled up his hoodie before striking out at a fast pace. When he was near the dropped-off duffel, he stopped and crouched down, watching and listening for any oncoming vehicles. The highway was quiet, the crickets chirping in the background. He hurried to the duffel, slung it onto his shoulder, and marched off, his hoodie becoming damp from his exertion.

When he arrived at the hill north of Tech Area 54, he positioned himself behind a pinon tree. Taking out of the duffel the MK-153, he loaded a rocket and took a series of deep breaths to center himself. He waited until the moon rose over the mountains, then surveyed the area for any security personnel besides those at the security entrance on Pajarito Road. The white tents stood out in the moonlight. He watched the men at the security station a few minutes. They were either talking amongst themselves or sitting quietly in their kiosks. They had no idea he was on the hill.

He got to one knee and sighted the MK-153 before dropping it down. It was now or never. He whispered, "Mom and Dad forgive me for what I'm about to do." He opened and closed his eyes to dissipate the tears forming, then lifted the SMAW to his shoulder, sighting the white tents. He took a deep breath, slowly exhaled, held his breath, and then squeezed the trigger. He watched the trajectory as it slammed into one of the tents producing a big explosion and fire ball. He puffed out his chest in triumph and loaded another rocket, sighting one of the other buildings. Another trajectory and another huge explosion and fire ball. The security guards at the station were out of their kiosks and on their cell phones. He loaded another rocket, aimed at the middle of the security station and fired. He saw what was left of a vehicle slam down on the pavement as it came down from the air. He loaded another rocket, targeted the plume of smoke where the tents had been, and fired. The billowing smoke rose higher in the sky. He had done it. His elation of his success rose like a spurting geyser. He told himself he needed to go, but he saw a security vehicle, lights flashing, coming down Pajarito Road. Time for one more. He loaded another rocket, took aim, and hit the racing vehicle. He was done. Abandoning the MK-153 and additional rockets on the hill, he started back at a run through the pinon forest.

When he was close to White Rock, he crouched down and studied the area. A number of people were standing outside at the two gas stations opposite each other at the intersection, staring at the rising smoke in the distance. The Fire Station was in pandemonium as the firefighters prepared to depart for the explosion. When the fire trucks sped away, he hurried past the visitor center, strolled across the highway and down the connecting street for several blocks before circling back to his SUV. Some people were out on the street near his vehicle. He should have parked farther away. He casually walked to his SUV, keeping his eyes on the people. No one seemed to pay him any attention. They were intent on watching the black smoke rising in the distance and the speeding away fire engines. He slipped into the SUV, started the engine, and pulled out slowly, heading away from the highway. Snaking through White Rock back to the highway as far west as possible, he headed off down the highway, watching the rear view mirror. No vehicles were behind him or oncoming.

He drove along the serpentine Highway 4, keeping to the speed limit. As he passed the turn off to Bandelier, he remembered the pleasant time he and Cindy had had visiting the ancient Native American site. He would be dead to Cindy now. She would hate what he had just done. The horrific nature of what he had done was just hitting him. Even his parents if they were alive would be appalled by his destruction of innocent people. Did the workers at the Lab deserve their death for helping the Masters of War? He was at war against the US, and Americans should suffer the same agony for the death of innocents as did the Yemenis.

He continued on Highway 4 past the immense caldera that was visible in the moonlight, trying to imagine the size of the volcano that had collapsed there. He drove through Jemez Springs and met Highway 550 to Bernalillo, then down I-25 to Albuquerque, wishing he knew what had caused the heightened security at the Lab. Something had happened and the authorities could be looking for him as Hans, Sidney, or Abdul. They could even be looking for the stolen 4Runner. He'd ditch it in Albuquerque and steal another, a passenger vehicle.

After he pulled off the interstate south of the big intersection with I-40, he drove to a residential area and turned onto a side street. A white Chevrolet caught his eye as he continued past and parked the 4Runner. He gathered his bag and walked back to the Chevrolet.

After jimmying the door, he hot-wired the ignition, and drove off, not bothering to change the plates, needing to get as far away as fast as possible. He pulled back on I-25 and sped off.

He felt guilty for what he had done and wondered if it had been a terrible mistake. He stiffened and slammed the steering wheel. He needed to drop his contrition. The number of innocents, who would die because of him, was small compared to the innocents dying in Yemen from the bombing, the famine, and disease. He almost wanted to get caught and pay for the horrendous crime. If there was sufficient nuclear radiation released by the explosions many people would die an agonizing death. He had seen documentaries of the people of Hiroshima after the atomic bomb.

He drove through the night and reached El Paso early in the morning. The light from the rising sun was bright and the haze from the traffic fumes was illuminated like a thin cloud. He left the car a few blocks from the border, found a mail box, and mailed his Declaration to the *Albuquerque Journal.* He had left one Declaration in the 4Runner in Albuquerque and had the other in his pocket. He started walking to the border crossing. When the crossing was in sight, he hesitated. It appeared that there was hectic activity at the border. He wondered if the activity was because of the explosions at Los Alamos or were they specifically looking for him. The heightened security at Los Alamos was established for a reason. Maybe he should check the news.

He went to a gas station toilet and pulled out his fake beard and stocking cap. He walked down the street until he found a coffee shop with some early patrons that had a TV and settled at a table with a cup of coffee. Sure enough a passport picture of him as Hans Zimmer was flashed across the screen and was identified as Abdul Salaamed. The commentator said he was wanted for questioning about the explosions at the Los Alamos National Laboratory that had released a cloud of nuclear radiation over the Lab and the city. The towns of Los Alamos, White Rock, Pojoaque and Espanola were being evacuated to makeshift shelters in Dixon. People were advised that the roads north out of Santa Fe and south out of Dixon were closed as well as the other roads toward Los Alamos.

How had they had already identified him as Abdul and Hans? Crossing with his German passport would be impossible. He was thankful that he had hesitated. He might be able to cross the border with his Colorado Driver's license as Sidney Wallace. There had been no mention of Sidney Wallace. Should he chance a crossing now as Sidney or wait and find an alternate way across the border?

CHAPTER 26

"This is pleasant overlooking the Plaza," Maggie said as they lounged on the balcony of the second floor pizza restaurant. The Plaza looked inviting in the moonlight. The sky was clear and the conversation of the people sitting or crossing the Plaza floated up to the balcony and joined the conversation of the other patrons enjoying their food and drinks. The smell of parmesan cheese and wood smoke infused the air. "Shall we go back to the room or would you like to take a stroll."

Fred continued to stare off into the distance. "Fred." Maggie touched his shoulder. "Are you done? You want that last slice. I can't eat it." Fred looked at her, blank-faced. "Fred you've done all you can do. It's in the hands of the Lab security. You said the Director of Security seemed on the ball."

Until they caught Abdul, Fred knew he'd be a wreck. "Let's get the check and go."

Maggie paid the bill and took Fred's arm. They strolled down the stairs and out onto Water Street, which was named for a river that flowed there long ago. "I've enjoyed coming to Santa Fe, despite the ramped up hunt for Abdul," Maggie said as she gripped Fred's arm even tighter. "The city seems to have a different atmosphere. It's a tourist town, but a unique experience unlike anywhere else in America." She laid her head on Fred's shoulder. "Don't feel bad about obsessing over Abdul. What you are doing is extremely important. Being with you has given me a better understanding of the significance you and your people have in keeping the US safe."

"I'm afraid that I've failed," Fred said, hanging his head as he shambled forward.

"Why do you say that?"

"My gut tells me that Abdul has figured out how to access the Lab and will complete his mission. He's fooled us too many times. Despite the heightened security measures there are ways around them. The Lab is spread out, and I can imagine many ways Abdul could gain access around the security." Fred stopped their walk near the hotel and faced Maggie, the angst and fear apparent in his face. "God, I hope I'm wrong."

Fred and Maggie were watching a movie on TV when Fred's phone rang. Fred reached for the phone and sat up in bed as soon as he saw the call was from Sam Singleton.

"Sampson here."

"Fred, all hell has broken loose. The nuclear storage area at Tech Area 54 has exploded and released a cloud of radiation."

Fred stretched his face in surprise, gritting his teeth, then clutched his face. "My God!"

"Readings are very dangerous," Sam continued. "Multiple explosions. How the hell your boy got past our security I've no idea. My family and I are evacuating to Dixon. Los Alamos, White Rock, Pojoaque, and, Espanola are all being ordered to evacuate to Dixon. We're setting up temporary shelters and a treatment center there. The prevailing wind is carrying the radiation north and east. Santa Fe is judged to be safe for now."

"How'd it happen?" Fred's face had lost all color as if his body had been drained of blood. "What's the damage?"

"We have to wait for the hazmat teams to suit up. We had to turn the fire engines back. It's just too hot with radiation. I've got to go. I'll call you when I know more."

Fred laid the phone down and turned to Maggie, his face in agony and disbelief as if he had been shot. "Turn on the news."

Maggie slid off the bed and switched the TV to the news. The commentator stopped reading the news. He announced there was breaking news, looking like he had a severe headache. The screen switched to another scene where a group of individuals and police officers were standing behind the Governor of New Mexico.

The Governor looked out over the gathering of news people. "Thank you all for coming. Unfortunately, I have a grave announcement. Ladies and gentlemen, there's been an accident at the Los Alamos National Laboratory and a release of radiation. Residents currently in the towns of Los Alamos, White Rock, Pojoaque, Espanola, and points near and in between are asked to evacuate to the town of Dixon where shelters and medical assistance will be provided. Buses will be provided for transportation. Do not drive your own vehicle. Emergency personnel will direct you. Emergency personnel will be wearing protective suits as an extra precaution, but there is no reason for alarm. Do not gather possessions. Take what is only necessary for a few days. Please evacuate in a safe and orderly manner. Further information will be forthcoming as it becomes available. I understand this is a great upheaval for those of you asked to evacuate. Please comply promptly."

"Oh my god, Fred," Maggie said. "What's going on?"

"There were multiple explosions at the Tech Area 54 where they store spent nuclear waste. They think somehow Abdul was able to plant bombs there. A large amount of nuclear radiation was released in the explosions." Fred hung his head. "God damn it, this is horrible."

"Are we safe here in Santa Fe? Should we leave?"

"Apparently the prevailing wind was pushing the radiation northeast. Singleton said Santa Fe was safe."

"How would they know?"

"They probably took Geiger countered readings to determine the extent of the radiation spread. Evacuating all those towns is probably more than necessary. It's mayhem."

"I'd feel better if we left," Maggie said.

"Okay, let's pack up and we'll go to Albuquerque." Fred stood. "I should probably go to the office in Albuquerque anyway."

When they walked downstairs with their bags, the lobby was filled with people clamoring to check out. Fred pulled Maggie back from the crowd. "Let's go outside and walk around to the garage. Forget about trying to check out."

"My god, Fred," Maggie said. "They're panicking here even though it is judged safe in Santa Fe. I can't imagine what is happening in the towns asked to evacuate."

Fred pushed Maggie ahead of him. "Go, Maggie. We need to get on the road before all the other people start heading out of town."

They hurried from the hotel and rolled their bags around to the underground garage, loaded the bags into their rental car, and started for the exit. Maggie was driving so that Fred could talk on his phone. When Maggie reached the garage booth, the gate was up and she drove out, following the GPS directions to I-25. The traffic was picking up as people, having heard the news, decided that Santa Fe might be too close to Los Alamos.

Fred dialed Sunu. "Sunu have you heard?"

"Yeah, was it Abdul?"

"I'd say so. How he got past the heightened security in unknown."

"What now?"

"We're on our way to Albuquerque. I'll get a room at the same hotel downtown as last time. As soon as I get Maggie settled, I'll come to the office. Put out an all-points on Abdul. Get it on the local and national news."

"How do you know he didn't die in the explosion?"

"I don't. It'll be days or possibly weeks before they'll know if his remains are at the explosion site." Fred paused and lowered the phone from his ear as he stared at the road before pulling the phone back up. "My gut tells me if he was smart enough to pull this off, he's smart enough to have gotten away."

"How much radiation was released?"

"They don't know."

"Seems it must have been a massive amount to evacuate all those towns."

"They may have overreacted. When Singleton called, he was panicking. He was in the process of evacuating his family to Dixon. Once they start testing the towns thoroughly and the evacuees, they'll have a better understanding of how bad the radiation release was." Fred realized he was speaking much too fast and took a deep breath. "We'll let the radiation experts' deal with the explosion and aftermath. Our job is to find and stop Abdul."

"Fuck, you think he might be planning more attacks?"

"I don't know. He might be. We need to find him. Where are you?"

"On my way to the office. Just pulled into the parking garage. I'll get the all-points out immediately."

Fred sat in the Albuquerque office, tapping his pen on the desk the morning after the explosions. He wondered if Abdul would seek additional attacks at other facilities like Sandia National Laboratory or would he try to escape the country. He was leaning toward Abdul wanting to escape.

He had talked earlier to his boss, who was beside himself. His boss had shouted that Fred needed to catch Abdul one way or another—the reputation of the FBI was at stake. Whatever he needed. Fred had carte blanche. The Whitehouse was up in arms. Everyone wanted to know how the terrorist was able to cause such havoc. Fred had to admit Abdul had planned his attack with deadly aplomb.

"Sunu, what would you do if you pulled off one of the most deadly terrorist attacks? Would you want to do more attacks or escape?"

"Shit, Fred, he's your boy. How the hell you knew he would do something in Los Alamos was beyond belief." Sunu paused and rubbed the back of his head. "Me, I'd get the hell out and try to get someplace safe. I'd rest on my laurels."

Fred didn't like that people were referring to Abdul as his boy. Sunu was probably right. Abdul would want to get out of the US and back to Yemen. He'd probably seen the all-points bulletin and his face on the news. He hadn't tried to fly out on his Hans Zimmer passport. Maybe he had another fake passport with a disguised photo.

"Sunu get your crew to do so work-up photos of Abdul with disguises—mustache, beards, long hair, and get them out on the wire. I think you're right. He's going to want to get out of the country. How would someone get into Mexico from here? It's the closest border."

"There's several crossings in El Paso, Texas, and a crossing at Santa Teresa, New Mexico. There's a bunch in Arizona and Texas."

"Let's contact them all and tell them to be on the alert for a disguised Abdul. When the work-ups are ready, get them to border security, all our offices, police, Mexican authorities, Interpol and all the news people."

"If he had other ID, he could already be over the border."

"My boss confirmed that the Mexican and Canadian authorities have already been alerted. But you're right, he may have already escaped across the border." Fred leaned back and closed his eyes. Abdul had been very clever and careful so far. He wouldn't risk being stopped at a border crossing unless he was able to get across before the all-points. Even then if he was able to get to the border quickly, he would be prudent and make sure they weren't looking for him. He'd wait and maybe try to find another way across the border. "Sunu, I bet he's looking for a way to be smuggled into Mexico. What do you think?"

"Might be a good way to escape. They don't really check vehicles and trucks as rigidly going into Mexico. Fuck... good thinking."

"Christ, I should have thought about this before. Get a bulletin to the border agents to carefully check vehicles and trucks returning to Mexico."

Fred picked up his phone and saw the call was from Singleton. "Hey Sam, what's the latest."

"The radiation spread wasn't as bad as we thought. Some people in Los Alamos got a high dose including myself. My family should be okay. Our house is on the west side of town and the whole family was inside and didn't go outside until we left for Dixon. We'll keep everybody here in Dixon for the night and tomorrow at least. We'll probably need to arrange more comfortable housing for many, who can't return to their homes, after they're cleared for radiation. Hazmat teams are checking the towns. The radiation level in Espanola is not too bad. The closer to White Rock and Los Alamos the worse the fallout is. At Tech Area 54, they found ten bodies and five more on the road at the security station." Sam paused for a moment and spoke to someone. "Any news or sighting of Abdul?"

"No. We think he might be planning to cross into Mexico. Border crossings all have photographs of Abdul and we're working on photographs of him in various disguises."

"You better catch this fucker, Fred. There's a bunch of us that are probably going to die of cancer because of this. Some of my security people are coughing up blood and will probably die soon an agonizing death." Singleton stopped talking as a voice in the in the background spoke to him. "I need to go. They're ready to give me a transfusion. Talk to you later."

"That was Singleton," Fred said, turning to Sunu. "He was exposed. His family is apparently okay. Fifteen dead so far. Some of Sam's security people got a high dose of radiation. Some are throwing up blood."

"That's a bad sign," Sunu said.

"Yeah, they'll probably die. Not a lot they can do for them. Sam's getting a transfusion. His chances for cancer are probably pretty high."

"What about the towns."

"Espanola apparently doesn't have high levels of radiation. Los Alamos, White Rock, and the Lab will be shut down for a while until they can be cleaned up, if they can be cleaned up. They may have to be left abandoned like the areas around Chernobyl. I imagine parts of White Rock near Tech Area 54 may be pretty bad. Shit, we need to find Abdul. I feel like going to El Paso."

"What would you be able to do there?"

"I don't know. Just sitting here is driving me crazy. I'm going to go back to the hotel and get Maggie set up on a plane in the morning. I'll be back later. Call me if anything comes up."

Fred eased the door open to his hotel room in case Maggie was asleep. She instead was sitting up in bed watching the news. "Jesus, Fred, what a disaster. There were some pictures on the news of people in Dixon that look really sick. What's the news on Abdul?"

"He's disappeared. I think he's trying to get out of the country. He's probably seen his pictures on the news. I think the easiest and safest way he could leave the country is to have someone smuggle him into Mexico. He's probably afraid to use fake credentials if he has any besides Hans Zimmer. He must have had some kind of other ID to move around like he did."

"How'd he get into the Lab?"

"You have to promise to keep anything I tell you absolutely secret."

"Of course. If you can't tell me, that's okay."

"They don't know yet. He may have gotten a Lab badge somewhere and added his picture or snuck in around security somehow. He may be one of the dead bodies found at the scene of the explosions." He paused and sat next to her on the bed. "I've got you on a flight at 8:00 AM back to New York."

"Are you coming?"

"No I'm thinking of going to El Paso. That's where I think he is if he isn't dead or hasn't already crossed the border."

"Your gut again? Please tell me you're not going there alone."

"No, Harry Ragg, a rookie agent, will be going with me, and I'll meet up with other agents there."

"Will you take me to the airport?"

"You'll need to take a taxi. I'm hoping to leave for El Paso tonight."

CHAPTER 27

Abdul watched the border crossing at the Bridge of the Americas. It had been over a week since his attack. The backup of vehicles going to Mexico was staggering. He was pleased he had caused such chaos.

In the first few days of his arrival after witnessing the increased activity at the border crossing, he had made the rounds of several Tex-Mexican bars looking for contacts to smuggle him across the border. He had established some viable prospects, but the increasing slow lines crossing into Mexico worried him. It seemed the border agents were searching the vehicles going into Mexico much more thoroughly than when he had first arrived in town. He hadn't planned his escape carefully. He should have visited El Paso earlier before the attack and arranged for someone to smuggle him across. He could have made it across easily before the heightened security and the plastering of his face all over the news.

They even had likenesses posted of him in various disguises. He didn't know what his best option was now. Maybe he should go somewhere to hang out until his pursuit died down. The heightened security at the border was affecting commerce— the all-mighty dollar— and probably couldn't last. Unfortunately, the longer he waited, the more his face would be plastered all over the news, and the chance of someone recognizing him would increase.

Maybe he should steal another vehicle and try for the Canadian Border. He could possibly find some way to cross into Canada. He didn't know if smuggling goods or people into Canada was much of an enterprise. Time was of the essence. He expected the FBI would find and trace the SMAW and figure out where and how he got it fairly quickly if they hadn't already. If he had buried it and the rockets in the woods after his attack, it would have given him more time to make his escape. He had made many mistakes, but he also had created immense havoc.

He was disappointed that his Declaration statement hadn't been published. He was naïve to think it would be published. Undoubtedly the FBI must have stopped its publication. Maybe being caught was his destiny, and the only way to get his message out. He had little to live for anymore. His entire family was gone, and Cindy would be eventually linked to him and would never want to see him again.

He'd give it a few more days and see how the border crossings into Mexico were going. He expected getting a false passport in Mexico would probably be much easier than in Canada. He had read stories of Mexican and Central American illegal immigrants sneaking into Canada from the US after Trump's crack down on immigrants. He'd do some research. For now he was a few steps ahead of the FBI, but they could be closing in fast.

He went back to his dilapidated motel where he had registered under the name of Javier Gonzales in his bushy fake mustache, dyed black hair, dark contacts, darkened face, and cowboy hat that the Mexicans seemed to favor. They hadn't asked for any ID.

He turned on the TV news and learned that his rocket attack had released a great deal of radiation. He was glad that the radiation would probably close the Los Alamos City of Death, but was sorry that it had affected innocent inhabitants and especially children. He was surprised that there was no news about the SMAW. Maybe they weren't releasing the information hoping that he would use his Sidney Wallace ID.

He expected that once they traced the SMAW to Steve and questioned him he would cave and tell them he had given the SMAW to Sidney Wallace to bury at Ray's. He bet the FBI would eventually be all over the Freedom Militia. They would probably dig the hell out of Ray's firing range. He was glad that the assholes would be implicated.

The heightened searches at the border continued as he daily watched the various crossings. The number of black SUVs in town and helicopters flying overhead seemed to be increasing. Waiting for an opportunity to get smuggled into Mexico was futile. He decided his best bet was to obtain a fake driver's license and head for the Canadian Border. He had made contact with a man, Hidalgo, whom he had met when looking for contacts to smuggle him into Mexico at a Tex-mex bar. Hidalgo had told Abdul he could get him a fake Texas driver's license.

That night he went back to the Tex-mex bar and waited at the long bar for Hidalgo. When he saw Hidalgo enter he watched him take his seat at a table after Hidalgo shook hands with a number of the clients. The music, a type of polka, was loud and the dance floor was full of couples.

Abdul strolled to Hidalgo's table. "Ola, Hidalgo."

"Javier, my friend. Sit down." Abdul took a seat. "What can I do for you?"

Abdul leaned across the table and said softly, "I'm interested in the driver's license you mentioned when we first met."

"Oh yes," Hidalgo said as he stretched back in his seat and raised his hand. The waitress sped over. "What will you have, Señor?"

"A beer would be good." Abdul smiled at the attractive waitress.

"Two Modelo Especial." Hidalgo scooted forward. "It's five hundred for the license and I'll throw in a social security card. Are you looking for a job? My organization may have need for additional personnel."

"No, I'm not looking for a job. I just want to be able to move around freely. Maybe in the future I might be interested in a job. I can manage the $500. I took some pictures for the license." Abdul slipped the photographs to Hidalgo he had taken and printed at a copy place. "When will the license be ready?"

"Come back in two days, my friend." The waitress arrived with the beers. Hidalgo raised his beer bottle. "Salud."

"Salud," Abdul returned. He drank his beer quickly, but not too fast to cause suspicion.

"My friend, where are you thinking of going? Do you have relatives in America?"

"No, I have no relatives here." Abdul wondered if Hidalgo was just making conversation or was pumping him for information for some alternative reason. "I just want to see more of this country." He held up his beer and finished it off. "Thanks for the beer. I'll see you in two days, Hidalgo." He rose and pushed his chair in.

"Javier, what's your hurry," Hidalgo said in his sing song manner. "Let's have another. The night is young."

"I have a women I need to meet. She's not the kind to keep waiting."

"Okay, my friend."

Abdul left the bar and walked away before doubling back to wait across the street from the bar behind a truck. When he saw Hidalgo leave the bar after midnight, he followed him on his stolen motorcycle. Hidalgo drove his fairly new massive, black Dodge Ram pickup to a house where a heavy set Hispanic woman greeted him. There was swing set in the yard and a plastic child's pedal tricycle. Abdul judged the man was probably legitimate and not an FBI informant. Probably worked with the coyote smugglers in Mexico. Everyone at the bar had seemed to know the man. Abdul felt his practiced Hispanic English accent and his disguise had worked, and Hidalgo believed he was Mexican. He thanked his mother for teaching him to mimic.

CHAPTER 28

Fred arrived in El Paso early in the morning. They had spent the night because Harry's flight had been delayed, leaving before sunrise. He was glad Harry Ragg hadn't been too talkative on the drive. Gave him time to think and catch a little shut-eye. His sleep had been fitful and full of dreams of Abdul. As they pulled up to the FBI office, Fred's cell phone rang.

"Your boy used a SMAW, shoulder-mounted, aerial weapon, rocket launcher," Singleton said. "He left it on the hill north of Tech Area 54. How in the hell he got his hands on a weapon like that is beyond me. Anyway, we're tracing the SMAW. It's a MK-153 Mod 2. Must have come from a military base. Any news on Abdul?"

"No," Fred replied. "We think he might be trying to cross into Mexico. I've just arrived in El Paso, which seems a likely spot he might try to cross. Since he's all over the news, I doubt he'll try to cross with any fake ID, unless he already crossed very soon after the incident. Border surveillance is on high alert. There are helicopters in the sky and we're having border security thoroughly check vehicles and trucks crossing into Mexico. Mock up pictures of Abdul with various disguises have gone out." Fred paused and wet his lips. "How's it going up there?"

"It's a cluster fuck. Jesus, I haven't had a wink of sleep." Singleton spoke with angry force and noticeable weariness. "There's a bunch of sick people. White Rock, Los Alamos and the Lab is hotter than hell with radiation. Most of the other towns aren't too bad. We were lucky it wasn't a windy night." He stopped and breathed in deeply as if he just surfaced from a deep dive. "We may be able to let people return to their homes in a few days except for Los Alamos and White Rock. The National Guard has stepped up and are helping us. You need to catch this sick fucker and anybody else in on this. He needs to die for what he's done."

"I'll do my best, Sam. I'm so sorry I couldn't stop him."

"Don't beat yourself up. You gave us plenty of warning. If anybody dropped the ball it was me."

"Hey, you did your best, Sam. Talk to you later."

Fred felt like crying. Those affected by the radiation would suffer for years. He had failed miserably in preventing the attack. If he had known earlier that Abdul was from Yemen, would it have made a difference in his investigation? He doubted it. He had suspected all along that Abdul as Hans was working with Islamic terrorists. He'd have plenty of time to reevaluate his pursuit of Abdul. Now he needed to concentrate fully on finding and arresting him.

Fred dialed Sunu. "Did you hear about the MK-153 SMAW they found?"

"Just reading the email now," Sunu said.

"Singleton was working on finding the origin, but utmost on his mind is his personal exposure and worry about the future. Would you try to ramrod finding where Abdul got his hands on a weapon like this?"

"I'll get right on it, Fred. Anything going on in El Paso?"

"I just arrived. There's a bunch of helicopters in the sky. I'll keep you informed of any developments. Find where Abdul got that damn rocket launcher."

Fred hoped discovering how Abdul got his hands on the weapon would lead to the Abdul's other identity for which he must have a fake ID and might be a way of finding him.

When Fred and Harry walked into the FBI office, the place was abuzz. They were rushed into the section chief's office.

"Fred Sampson," the man behind the desk exclaimed. "Glad you could make it." He came from behind his desk and grabbed Fred's hand and almost shook it off. "Agent Bonner. Call me Bob." He still had hold of Fred's hand, which Fred eased from his grasp with his other hand. "I got a call from the Director. I'm to give you whatever you want."

"Thank you, Bob." Fred turned to Harry. "This is agent Harry Ragg."

Bob Bonner couldn't help himself and laughed, but caught himself quickly. "Glad to meet you, Harry. Welcome."

"Thanks," Harry said. "Don't worry, I get that reaction wherever I go. I should change my first name."

Bob indicated the chairs around a long table. "We've got coffee and donuts." He waved his hand at the array of donuts and coffee urn. He poured himself a cup and held the coffee urn toward Fred. Fred and Harry nodded. Bob poured the other two coffees. "We've had no sighting in town or at the border of your boy, Abdul. The back-up of vehicles trying to get into Mexico is creating havoc, but they're checking them thoroughly. I've got some of my men stationed there as well. He'll not easily get smuggled into Mexico." He took a sip of his coffee and licked his lips. "Are you pretty sure he didn't already cross? We've looked at the footage of the cameras, and apparently he didn't cross on foot."

Fred stiffened at the 'your boy'. "Good. I've no idea if he has already crossed. I suspect not. He's been a very careful person." Fred took a sip of his coffee while Harry loaded his coffee with cream and sugar. "He may have setup a means to be smuggled into Mexico before the attack. He's moved around fairly easily. If so he would have already crossed." His gut told him Abdul was still in the US, but he had no evidence to back it up. One of the reasons he wanted to come to El Paso was to get a feel for the town and envision how Abdul would react. "It sounds like you've got everything in hand. Is there a desk I can use to check the internet?"

"You bet," Bob answered. "Those two vacant desks just outside my office are for you two."

"If you don't mind, I'll check my mail and make some calls." Fred poured himself another cup of coffee, passed on the donuts, and stood.

"Go for it," Bob said and stood as well.

Fred went to the vacant desk and logged into the FBI website. There were no new messages of any importance. He called Sunu. "Seems they're searching vehicles thoroughly going into Mexico. They've checked camera footage of the foot crossings and haven't found any images of Abdul. I may check the footage myself." He took another sip of coffee. "What's going on with the search for the origin of the MK-153?"

"Seems there's number of bases with the weapon. So far there's no record of a stolen or missing MK-153."

"Can you buy one on the black market?"

"Overseas, you could, but they don't think someone could in the States. Bazookas, recoilless rifles, and old antitank weapons are available, but we've found no evidence of anyone selling the MK-153. Have you checked it out? It's a powerful weapon."

"Keep on it. I would suspect he obtained it in New Mexico or a neighboring State." He didn't need to check out the MK-153. The destruction it caused testified to its power. "Has there been any contact with his friend, Cindy."

"No."

"Have you pulled her in for questioning? What about any other friends he had at Berkeley."

"Yes, they're questioning her now. She's admitted to meeting him in Albuquerque and going out on dates with him. Sounds like she was in love with the guy. She doesn't believe he could have blown up the Los Alamos Lab site. She's a pacifist and thinks Abdul is one also. When she last saw him, he told her he was going to a graduate school interview at Arizona University and would return. We checked. It was a lie. Besides her, she doesn't know if he had many other friends. He was kind of a loner."

"Maybe he got the MK-153 in Arizona."

"We're checking. Nothing yet. We've got agents visiting every military base that have the weapon."

"Call me as soon as you have something."

"Did you get any sleep on the way? You and your gut need to be in top form."

"I caught a few winks. I'm good."

Fred would have liked to talk to Cindy and get a better feel for Abdul. He'd have Sunu send him a video of the interview. There was nothing important in any emails. He'd seen all except for a few on his cell phone on the way down. What would Abdul do if he judged the Mexican border crossing was too dangerous? He could wait. If the crossing to Mexico was creating havoc, how long would industry allow it to go on?

Fred swallowed the last of his coffee and stood up. "Harry, want to take a drive and have a look at the border crossings?"

Harry looked back at him like he had two heads. "Come on. Check with Bonner and get a local agent to come along and show us around." He was in no mood to be subjected to Bonner's sunny personality again.

CHAPTER 29

Abdul went to the Tex-mex bar with $800. If Hidalgo tried to milk him for more, he'd be ready to pay a little more. If they attacked him and tried to steal his money, they wouldn't get much. He wanted to get on the road to Canada and didn't want to dicker with Hidalgo. He had his knife in his pocket and another in the cowboy boots he had bought. After parking his stolen motorcycle down the street from the bar so he could make a quick getaway, he approached the parking lot, the sound of Tex-mex music drowning out the chirp of the night crickets. He searched for Hidalgo's pick-up to make sure he was inside. The light of the blue and yellow neon 'El Rito' sign and dim outdoor lights washed over the parked vehicles, giving the parking lot a fairy tale appearance. He ignored the moths, dancing in the dim light, and the group of smokers near the front entrance as he searched for Hidalgo's truck. After finding the black pickup around the side of the bar, he loosened the valve stem on one of tires, went around back, and entered through the kitchen, bullying his way through as the workers tried to stop him.

As soon as Abdul stepped out into the crowded bar, he noticed Hidalgo seated at a table with another Hispanic gentleman, who looked big and menacing like a grizzly. Abdul had practiced martial arts in Yemen, but he didn't know if he could defeat both the big man and Hidalgo if it came to that. He'd have to risk it. He walked slowly through the crowded bar around the edge of couples dancing a looping two-step to the blaring music.

"Buenas noches," Abdul said and pulled out a chair, but remained standing.

"Hello, my friend," Hidalgo said. "Sit down."

Abdul nodded at the other man. "Can we be alone?"

"This is my friend, Mañuel." Hidalgo said with a crunched brow and downturned lower lip. "You can trust him, Amigo."

Abdul sat down, but kept his hands in his lap. "Do you have the documents?"

"Oh, yes, my friend. Let's have a drink first." Hidalgo raised his hand. "Guadalupe, three shots of tequila."

"Can I see the documents?" Abdul asked.

"Of course. You have the money?"

"Yes." Abdul placed an envelope on the table, but kept his hand on top of it.

Hidalgo placed an envelope on the table and shoved it toward Abdul. Abdul let go of his envelope, giving it a shove across the table, and picked up Hidalgo's envelope.

Abdul glanced inside where a Texas driver's license for a Juan Martinez with his picture and a social security card resided. "Gracias, Amigo."

Abdul started to rise, but Mañuel put a hand on his shoulder. "It would be rude of you to leave before drinking your tequila." His voice was deep and sonorous as if it emerged from a deep cave.

"Si, Señor," Abdul answered. He didn't like the vibe and stiffened, gauging how he would attack the two if required. A blow to Mañuel's throat would stop him momentarily, while he dealt a kick to Hidalgo, then he would try to finish off the big man, and draw his knife to keep others at bay.

When the waitress set the three tequilas and limes on the table. Abdul moved a shot glass in front of him, never taking his eyes off the two. "Salud." He licked the back of his hand, sprinkled salt on the wet area, licked the salt, downed the shot of tequila, and sucked on the lime. "Bueno." He started to stand but Mañuel placed his hand on his shoulder again and pushed him down. Mañuel had immense strength.

"Let's have another," Mañuel said.

Abdul pushed Mañuel's hand off and stood, staring staidly at Mañuel. He placed his right hand in his pocket and pushed the envelope in his left pocket. "I don't want any trouble, but if you do, I am ready," he said forcefully.

Mañuel laughed. "We're just being friendly. Relax."

"I'm not the relaxing type. Are we good?"

"Sure, my friend," Hidalgo said. "We're good. But you know you have the strangest accent. Where are you from, Amigo?"

Abdul backed away slowly, making sure no one was coming at him from behind. "Adios."

When he was near the kitchen door. He slipped inside, ran through the kitchen, and sprinted for his motorcycle. As he jumped on, he looked back and saw Mañuel and Hidalgo running to Hidalgo's truck. Abdul kicked over the motorcycle, pulled on his helmet, and was off before the truck even started up. They'd not catch him. He sped through the streets, turning often, and then went to his motel. He watched his room from a distance to make sure he hadn't been found. He hurried to his room, fetched his bag, placed it on the back of the motorcycle, and headed for the interstate.

He'd steal a vehicle in Las Cruces. He didn't think Hidalgo was with ICE or the FBI. They probably wanted to rob him. Or maybe they recognized him and wanted a reward. If they recognized him and went to the police, the driver's license would be worthless. They didn't seem the type that would want anything to do with the police. Just to be safe, he'd steal a student ID in Las Cruces and switch the picture with his to use as a back-up ID for checking into motels. He'd use the driver's license only if he was stopped on the road by the police.

Abdul finally stopped in Salt Lake City in the afternoon and got a motel room using the student ID, George Franklin, he had stolen in Las Cruces at the University. He had checked in with his hair still dark but he had removed the fake mustache and the darkening agent on his face and neck at a gas station on the way. He was exhausted from his nearly 17 hours on the road in the stolen Honda Civic. He had written a fake vehicle license number on the motel registration since he hadn't bothered to change the license plate. He left the motel soon after checking in and drove the Honda a few blocks away, so the desk clerk could not check the license plate. He had stopped only for gas and was hardly able to keep his eyes open. He went to his room, flung off his clothes, and slipped into bed. He lay under the covers, his mind racing, until his fatigue took over and he fell asleep.

CHAPTER 30

Fred returned to the El Paso office after his excursion to the border crossings in town. They looked to be pretty solid with the increased personnel and activity at the stations and sky-bound helicopters. He didn't think Abdul would risk crossing at an official station or sneaking across the Rio Grande.

Back at the FBI office, Fred watched the video of the interview with Abdul's girlfriend, Cindy. He thought Cindy genuinely didn't believe Abdul capable of causing the heinous explosions at the Los Alamos Lab. Something had happened to push Abdul to undertake such a deadly terrorist attack. Interpol was trying to trace his movements after he landed in Frankfurt in May, but he had somehow disappeared in Germany. Fred suspected he had somehow returned to Yemen where he must have been radicalized. Cindy had insisted the Abdul was not interested in religion and hated the schism between the Sunnis and the Shias. He had grown up as a Muslim, but didn't practice the faith. His father was a Sunni and his mother a Zaydi Shia.

The spreading fatigue from the intense but futile search for Abdul had Fred's gut in complete disarray. He logged off the computer and reluctantly knocked on Bonner's door before entering. "I'm in need of some rest," Fred announced. "Did you get rooms for Harry and me?"

"Yeah, at the Hilton Double Tree."

"Thanks. Harry and I will check in and probably take a nap and get something to eat. Don't hesitate to call if there's any new developments— any developments at all."

Fred had spent nearly a week at the El Paso Office and was feeling dejected. Maybe Abdul had left town. He listened to Cindy's interview again, but had no idea where Abdul was. He was about to call Sunu when his cell phone rang. It was Sunu. "Sampson."

"They found the origin of the MK-153. A supply Specialist at Fort Carson in Colorado Springs stole the MK-153 and seven rockets. The Specialist, Steve Moore, who's in the Colorado Freedom Militia gave the MK-153 to Abdul, who was using the name Sidney Wallace, to hide it for him. Apparently Abdul as Sidney Wallace was staying with another militia member, Ray Osborn, at Ray's trailer for weeks and joined the Freedom Militia. I've put out an amended all points saying Abdul may be using the alias, Sidney Wallace. It should be up on the news by now.

"Well done," Fred replied. "Where are these two Militia members held?"

The Colorado Springs office have Steve Moore and Ray Osborn in custody. Steve has been very cooperative. Ray has been less cooperative, but did admit Sidney Wallace had stayed with him for many weeks at his trailer. Ray claimed he knew nothing about the MK-153." Sunu laughed. "Kevin Smith, who interrogated the two, thinks Ray and Steve may be in on the plot with Abdul."

"They sound like a right pair."

"Ray claimed that he thought Sidney Wallace was an American patriot and never would have guessed he was a Yemeni terrorist. These two and the Freedom Militia group appear to be unbelievable idiots or are lying through their teeth." Sunu paused as if he expected Fred to speak, but when Fred was silent, he continued. "The Army wants Steve back to charge him with the theft of the MK-153 and aiding a terrorist. We haven't charged Ray with anything yet."

Fred heard Sunu take a drink. "We've got agents searching their homes," Sunu continued. "Agents spoke to the Militia Commander, who admitted approving Sidney Wallace's application for the Militia. The Commander claimed he had no idea Sidney was an Arab named Abdul. He provided a list of the other Militia members for the Office to interview." Sunu exhaled and took a deep breath. "A team is in route to search the Commander's ranch, and they are going to interview the rest of the Freedom Militia."

"Good work, Sunu." Despite Sunu's minimal fitness and clumsiness, he had turned out to be an excellent desk jockey. "I still think Abdul might be in El Paso. We're checking all the motels and other possible places here for Abdul. I may fly out to Colorado Springs and talk myself to these Freedom Militia guys if all our actions here come up empty. Are you looking for the real Sidney Wallace?"

"Yes, but nothing yet."

Fred left Harry in El Paso several days after his call with Sunu when nothing for Sidney Wallace had turned up and flew to Colorado Springs. Steve had been turned over to the Army and Ray was let go, pending possible future charges. The search of Steve's apartment and Ray's trailer had not turned up much. Ray had some illegal automatic weapons that were confiscated.

In Colorado Springs, Fred rented a car and drove to the Fort Carson Confinement Facility to interview Steve

Moore. When Fred walked into the interview room, Steve was shackled to the table and looked like he was scared half to death. Fred causally walked to the table, keeping his eyes on Steve. He smiled and sat down. "Hello, Steve, I'm Fred Sampson with the FBI and would like to ask you some questions."

"Sir, I've already talked to I don't know how many police, FBI, and MPs. I've told them all I know about Sidney Wallace." Steve looked like a deer in the headlights. He was shaking and wouldn't look Fred in the eye.

"I understand, Steve." Fred said and placed his hands on the table. "Whose idea was it to steal the MK-153?"

"Well, I guess it was Sidney's. He and I became pretty good friends... or so I thought. I never suspected he was a Muslim terrorist, otherwise I never would have stolen the SMAW and given it to him." Steve spoke softly, looking like he could erupt in tears at any moment. "I'm real sorry about all the people at that Los Alamos Lab that was killed. Heck, I would have turned Sidney in if I'd known who he really was."

"Did he come right out and ask you if you could steal a MK-153."

"Sort of. He was real cagey. He talked about how he had fired SMAWs in Afghanistan." Steve glanced quickly at Fred, then looked away. "He told us he was a Ranger there. He had us all fooled. We thought he was one of us. He talked like us an' everything. He didn't look like no Arab."

"And who is us?"

"Freedom Militia."

"How long have you been a member of the Freedom Militia and why did you join?"

"I've been in the Militia a couple of years. We think there's going to be an uprising with all the blacks, Mexicans and sorts. We train to be ready for the revolution and stand up for the Country. Sidney said one of them SMAWs would come in handy when fightin' broke out."

"I see." Fred peered away from Steve, grasping his chin. He waited in silence as Steve fidgeted in his seat, looking at the walls and back to Fred as if the silence was a prelude to some devastating action. Fred turned back to Steve abruptly and asked, "You never thought that Sidney would use the MK-153 in a terrorist act?"

Steve, noticeably disturbed by the question, shouted loudly, "No Sir." He seemed embarrassed by his shouting and lowered his voice. "I thought we'd have fun tryin' the MK-153 out. I was supposed to find a place in the mountains where we could fire it. Sidney said they was a lot of fun to fire."

Fred leaned back and studied Steve. He wondered if Steve had a learning disability. He didn't think he was putting on an act. "What do you think of Ray Osborn?"

"Ray's a stand-up guy. Sidney had Ray fooled as well."

"So you don't think Ray was in cahoots with Sidney?"

"Hell, no. Excuse the language, Sir."

"In your written statement, you said Sidney had a Colorado driver's license. Do you know how he obtained one?" It was obvious the question hit a nerve with Steve and his eyes darted around the room.

"No, Sir."

Fred stared at Steve for a prolonged interval without speaking. Steve was noticeably becoming more nervous. "Did you or Ray obtain the license for Sidney?"

"No, Sir."

"It seems to me that somebody, who was friends with Sidney, helped him obtain the license. He wouldn't have been able to obtain it without help."

"Yeah...well I didn't help him."

"But you did steal a MK-153 SMAW for him." Fred paused until Steve was about to answer, then asked, "Or did you want it for other purposes?"

"What do you mean, Sir?" Steve started to tear up and twist in his chair, his eyes roving everywhere except at Fred.

"Perhaps you and your cohorts in the Freedom Militia wanted the SMAW for your own attack."

"No, Sir." Steve started rocking back and forth. "We weren't gonna attack nobody. We just thought it would be fun to have and would come in handy for the revolution. Honest."

"Perhaps you wanted the SMAW to start the revolution."

"No, Sir. That's not true. We wanted it to be able to protect ourselves."

"Yet in your statement you said only Sidney knew you had stolen the SMAW."

"Yes, that's right. I trusted Sidney." Steve tilted forward and almost came out of his chair. "He betrayed me, the damn Arab."

"So you knew he was an Arab."

"No...no. I didn't find out Sidney was an Arab until the FBI told me."

"Okay, Steve." Fred leaned back and watched Steve in silence as Steve hung his head. He didn't think additional questioning would be worthwhile. "Thank you for your time, Steve, and for answering my questions." He stood, nodded to the MP guard and left the room.

He didn't know what to make of Steve Moore as he drove out of the Army base. Either Abdul had been incredibly lucky in finding such an impressionable and willing individual, or Steve was a participant in the terrorism plot. If Steve was lying, he was putting on a five star act. Maybe it was Ray Osborn, who got the driver's license for Abdul as Sidney Wallace and was the mastermind behind the attack. Whoever obtained the driver's license for Abdul may have gotten a second license with another name.

He needed to talk to Ray Osborn. He doubted he'd be home in the middle of the day, but called anyway. Ray was at home, and Fred arranged for an interview

When Fred pulled up to the secluded trailer on the outskirts of town, Ray came out and stood by Fred's rental car. "Hello," Fred said as he opened his door and stepped out to face Ray. "I'm Fed Sampson. You must be Ray Osborn."

Ray grasped Fred's extended hand, squeezing extremely strongly— his face scrunched like he was cracking a nut with his teeth. Fred had to grit his teeth to stop from calling out in distress. Ray was dressed in jeans and a baggy, beige, untucked work shirt. He had a five day growth of salt and pepper beard, and smelled rank, like a high school locker room.

"Come on in," Ray said. He turned his back, and stomped up the stairs, opening the door to the trailer before looking back at Fred.

Fred had waited to see Ray's reaction at not following him. Ray's handshake had irritated him as he suspected was Ray's intent—wanting to demonstrate he was a tough guy and not to be messed with. He would mess with him, but needed to be careful and alert with this one. He noticed a quick sneer when Ray gazed back at Fred.

"Are you comin'?" Ray shouted with a grimace.

"Yes. Just admiring the scenery." Fred waved his hand in front and across his body as if he was wiping the landscape. "You've got a nice place here." He ascended the stairs and followed Ray into the trailer.

Ray moved to the refrigerator. "You want a beer? Oh... of course you're on duty." He laughed and with a smirk popped open a beer, taking a big swig, followed by a belch.

"A glass of water would be welcome," Fred said as he stood in the living room area of the trailer. Gun magazines were scattered on the coffee table. He wasn't sure why Ray was being rude. "I was surprised you were at home. Are you on vacation?"

"I've been fired," Ray vehemently shouted. "I told them I hadn't been charged with a crime, but the fuckers fired me anyway." Ray spoke with such force that his spittle nearly flew across the room. He filled a glass with ice and water and handed it to Fred. "Sit down, and take the load off."

"Thank you." Fred took a seat on the sofa and glanced at the empty gun cabinet.

Ray settled in his recliner chair and took a few gulps of beer. "They took my rifles. Am I ever gonna get 'em back?"

"You'll have to talk to the local FBI office about them. As I understand it there were a few illegal, fully automatic weapons. You won't be getting those back." Fred waited in silence expecting Ray to complain or ask another question. "I came to see you to talk about Abdul, who you knew as Sidney Wallace."

"I've talked about Sidney Wallace until I'm blue in the face. I hope I never have to talk about the son of a bitch ever again. That damn Arab had us all fooled. If I could get my hands on the fucker, I'd ring his neck."

"I understand why you would feel that way," Fred said sympathetically. "How would you describe Abdul as Sidney?"

"He knew a lot about militias, said he was in the Montana Militia before he came to Colorado Springs. We thought he'd be a good addition to our Militia group."

"Yes, I've read your statement." Fred leaned forward. "Did Sidney have any other friends in Colorado or other places that he might have mentioned?"

"Said his ole lady lived in Hammond, Montana."

Fred had already contacted the Hammond Sheriff, who knew nothing about a Sidney Wallace or anyone meeting Abdul's description. "Yes, that was in your statement. Anybody else?"

"No."

"Did he ever mention a woman named, Cindy?"

"No."

"He apparently obtained a fake Colorado driver's license in the name of Sidney Wallace. You have any idea where he may have gotten the license?"

"No sir, I know nothin' about that."

Fred sensed that Ray's answer had been much too quick and vehement. He was convinced that Ray was somehow involved in getting the fake license for Abdul. He'd alert the local office and let them follow up. "Did you know that Steve was going to steal a MK-153 SMAW for the Freedom Militia?"

"No way. We wouldn't need something like that. He tricked Steve into sneakin' out the damn thing. I knew nothin' about it."

"I thought you and Steve were good friends."

"We are."

"Are you sure you didn't mention to Steve how getting a MK-153 SMAW would be desirable?"

"Hell, no. Are you insinuating that I was involved in the theft of that damn weapon?" Ray's face was screwed tight as he stared at Fred with grit teeth, looking like he wanted to attack Fred.

Fred settled back against the couch in case he needed to draw his weapon. He didn't like Ray's demeanor. "No Ray, I'm not. I'm just trying to learn all I can about Abdul so we can catch him."

"I hope you do and execute that damn killer. I hate him."

"I understand, Ray. We're trying our best to find Abdul Salaamed." Fred waited and watched Ray as Ray relaxed somewhat. "I understand that the Militia Chapter Commander had a recoilless rifle at his ranch that belongs to your Militia group. What was the need for it?"

"Shit, I don't know. I don't know how the Militia got the damn thing."

"Have you seen it?"

"I did once."

"And where did this take place?"

"Out at the Commander's ranch."

"Was the Freedom Militia planning an attack on the government?"

"Fuck, no" Ray almost came out of his seat, squishing his eyes half shut. "What are you implyin'?"

"Just asking questions." Fred smiled and waited to see if Ray would say anything else. "From you statement I understand you met Abdul at a bar called the Amory."

"Yeah."

"Did you think it odd that a stranger wanted to befriend you?"

"When he first came to my table, I was suspicious, but after talking to him for a while, I thought he would be a good candidate to join our Militia."

"And why would that be? Are you always on the lookout for new Militia members?" Fred waited until Ray was about to speak. "When did you suspect Sidney was a Muslim?"

"What in the fuck is the matter with you?" Ray growled, his face contorted. "I never knew the son of a bitch was a Muslim."

"I see. Abdul sounds like a very adept impersonator. Did any other members of the Militia suspect he was a Muslim?"

"Hell no. I told ya he spoke just like an American. He didn't have any kind of accent."

"What kind of qualities would you look for when seeking new members for your Militia group?"

"Our Militia is small. We're always open to recruiting new members. We look for patriots that feel the same way we do about the Country."

"And what way is that?"

"That immigrants are dangerous and should be sent back to their own countries like our President is tryin' to do. Immigrants attacked us on 9/11. They come into the country, live off welfare, and commit crimes. They're worse than Niggers and Jews."

"Do you advocate violence against the people you don't like?"

"No, I've had blacks workin' for me. If I had my druthers, I wouldn't hire them, but I don't pick on them."

"Do you believe there is a revolution coming?"

"Could be. Trump's tryin' his best to prevent it. If he don't get re-elected, we may need to support him."

"And you and your Militia cohorts would start the revolution?"

"No, the Blacks, Mexicans, and Muslims would start it, funded by the Jews."

"Why would they do that?"

"To take control of the country."

"And you and the Militia would fight them?"

"You damn right, we would." Ray finished the last of his beer and crushed the can before tossing it across the room. At the sound of the beer can crashing into the metal trash can, he raised his hand in a snarl.

Fred was amazed how these militia idiots got such insidious thoughts. He doubted talking any further with Ray would give him any clues as to where Abdul was hiding. "Thank you for taking the time to answer my questions" Fred stood. He had had enough of this angry racist. He felt sad that his own President catered to and encouraged these white nationalists. He was worried for the country. "If you remember anything else about Abdul, no matter how small or trivial, please call me." He handed Ray his card, and Ray stood.

Ray followed Fred to the door. Fred said his goodbye, shook hands, and left.

He drove away, thinking they needed to arrest Ray Osborn. The man wasn't being truthful. Maybe the Freedom Militia was in cahoots with Abdul—both Ray and Steve were definitely lying.

CHAPTER 31

"I'm glad you're here," Sunu said as soon a Fred walked into the Albuquerque office. "Abdul sent a letter of Declaration to the Albuquerque Journal."

"When?"

"They received it several days ago. It was mailed from El Paso. Your gut was spot on about El Paso. I played hell to stop the paper from publishing it." Sunu was holding up a sheet of paper.

Fred hurried to Sunu's desk and snatched the Declaration before plopping down in the adjacent chair and reading.

Declaration of Revenge

I, Abdul Salaamed, have taken revenge against the United States for their destruction of my beloved Yemen.

The United States has worked tirelessly to destroy the Middle East. First with the CIA induced overthrow of the democratically elected government of Iran in 1953. In 1980 the US encouraged and backed Sadam Hussein to start the Iranian-Iraq war that changed nothing and resulted in 500,000 needless deaths. Then in 1990 the US turned on Sadam after encouraging him to invade Kuwait, decimating his forces and slaughtering his retreating troops with the "Highway of Death'.

After the 9/11 Al-Qaeda airplane attacks on the twin towers in 2001, for which the upper echelons of the US government had advance warning, but allowed the attack to unfold in order to fool the populace in giving them broad war powers, the US attacked Afghanistan to go after Osama bin Laden and Al-Qaeda even though they had supported Al-Qaeda as the Mujahedeen against the Soviets, and despite the Taliban agreeing to hand Osama over to them.

Then Bush and Cheney decided they weren't done with Iraq with its abundance of oil, so they attacked Iraq in 2003 on false accusations that Iraq had nuclear, chemical and biological weapons even though the UN Inspectors verified they didn't. The United States thirst for oil and power is insatiable.

The Saudis and the US supported the rebels in Syria that started the civil war because Bashar al-Sadd would not bend to their will. They supported Al-Qaeda in Yemen that has led to the Saudi and US supported bombing campaign resulting in immense death and destruction— thousands starving and a million suffering from cholera.

The United States supply the Saudis with their weapons, intelligence, and even have troops in Yemen. They are the force behind the Saudis, who destroyed my family and are destroying Yemen. I have struck at the heart and symbol of their war machine, Los Alamos, the home of nuclear weapons. Their criminal destruction has come home to roost.

Fred stood after reading the Declaration, shaking his head in disgust. "I knew that something had happened to turn him to his attack." He began walking back and forth, his face contorted in thought. "He somehow got from Germany to Yemen to see his family and discovered their death— an excellent inducement for revenge. He's undoubtedly wondering why his Declaration hasn't been published. He'll know we had it squashed."

"You learn anything in Colorado Springs?"

"Nothing useful other than Abdul is a superior actor and very good at manipulating people. We need to arrest Ray Osborn as an accessory providing material support to a terrorist. I'd bet money he's the one that got Abdul the fake Colorado license. He and Steve may have helped Abdul, knowing he was planning to attack Los Alamos." Fred rubbed his head, squishing his lips to the side. "Anything from El Paso?"

"No."

"I'm going to check in at the hotel," Fred said as the Declaration played in his head like a broken record. The Declaration solidified Abdul's guilt, but gave him no notion where Abdul was hiding. "Shall we have dinner there tonight?"

"Sounds good. Seven?"

"Yeah." Fred wearily left the office.

When he arrived at his hotel, he went to the mini bar and consumed several miniatures of bourbon whisky as he sat on the edge of the bed listening to the hum of the air conditioner and the sounds of doors closing along the corridor and the floor above. He slipped off his shoes and laid back on the bed, scrunching the pillow underneath his head and closed his eyes. The synthetic smell of his hotel room annoyed him, acrylic rugs and fabrics. He missed his small apartment and Maggie. He was so on edge he felt like he was coming out of his skin.

He replayed the information and sighting of Abdul in his mind like the disjointed scenes in a movie, wondering where he had made his mistakes, searching for clues that could lead to Abdul's whereabouts. He would be known forever as the agent, who allowed the madman to release the cloud of radiation. What induces a man like Abdul to commit such a horrific act? He initially was going to work with Rasheed, and, from the little evidence they had obtained, the terrorist were going to explode a bomb at or near Times Square. How had Abdul figured in that plot? Somehow Abdul either realized that Rasheed was being followed or had other plans when he left New York for Chicago. Perhaps his plan was to go to Chicago for some other reason all along. Did he have contacts in Chicago? Would he, fearing the heightened security at the Mexican Border, go back to Chicago? Did Abdul travel to Albuquerque to be reunited with his college sweetheart or was Los Alamos his target all along. He was able to fool everyone he came in contact with including her, who knew Abdul better than everyone. She genuinely didn't believe, he was sure, that Abdul was capable of the explosion of nuclear waste. When she accepts the realization that Abdul did the heinous act, she will be devastated. Abdul knows this. He won't contact her again.

Fred rose and retrieved another miniature from the minibar. He'd have to watch it, he was close to turning into an alcoholic. He retrieved his cell phone and dialed his boss.

"Yeah, Fred. What have you got?"

"I talked to the Army Specialist, Steve, who stole the MK-153 SMAW for Abdul and the Freedom Militia. I believe Abdul had Steve totally fooled. Steve might be somewhat learning disabled. I also spoke to Ray Osborn, who as you know Abdul stayed with for weeks. I think he was probably involved in getting Abdul the Colorado driver's license and may have been in on getting Steve to steal the MK-153. We should have him arrested. I didn't like the vibe from the guy. He was very belligerent. I think we should get an informant in the Colorado Springs Freedom Militia too. I don't know if they were in collusion with Abdul, but it's possible. Nevertheless, I think the group could be capable of domestic terrorist acts."

"Where do you think Abdul is?"

"I'm stumped, Boss. We know from the mailing of the Declaration he went to El Paso, but we haven't found any evidence that he is still there. He may have already crossed the border. You may want to check-in with the Mexican authorities again. Did you get a copy of Abdul's Declaration?"

"Yes and I've been onto Interpol to try and light a fire under them to find out how Abdul got in and out of Yemen. If he did make it to Mexico, he'll probably use the same route through Germany to Yemen."

"Good thinking, Boss. I'll hole up here in Albuquerque. We've got surveillance and phone tap on his girlfriend, Cindy. Although I doubt he'll contact her again. She doesn't believe Abdul is responsible for the explosions at Los Alamos. He had her fooled too."

"Stay on it, Fred. I'm counting on you."

Fred thanked his boss and hung up. He laid back down and closed his eyes as images of Abdul swam around his brain.

Two days later his boss called to say Abdul had been sighted at a Tex-mex bar in El Paso where an undercover agent was staked out because the bar had been linked to a Mexican smuggling ring.

"Abdul received a fake Texas driver's license and social security card from a man named Hidalgo, who we suspect was head of a smuggling ring on the US side," his boss explained. "Hidalgo admitted he had supplied Abdul, who he thought was a Mexican named Javier, the driver's license with the name Juan Martinez. They put out an all points on Martinez, but nothing has come back. Apparently, there was a near altercation, and Abdul had to hightail out of there on a motorcycle."

"Jesus, Abdul is always two steps ahead of us. He may be leery of using the ID, suspecting this Hidalgo chap might have turned him in." Fred stood, held the phone out and turned his head up to the ceiling. "Where in the hell are you, Abdul," he said under his breath and sat back down, closing his eyes.

"Fred, talk to me. What do you think he's up to?"

"I bet he's given up on trying to get into Mexico in El Paso. He could be going somewhere else to try and cross, but he knows the border security is tight. He might be holed up somewhere waiting for the border security to die down. We can't keep this level of security at the border indefinitely."

"Would he try and cross the desert in Arizona to Mexico?" his boss offered.

"Who knows? He might, but that might seem dangerous to him with the heightened security and the numerous helicopters."

"What's your next move?"

"I'll stay here in Albuquerque until we figure out where he is. You'd think someone would recognize him. He's been plastered all over the news. Hopefully we will get some word soon. Talk to you later." Fred set the phone down on the bedside table. He walked into the bathroom and thought about taking a shower to relax and think.

In the morning as Fred sat at the desk at the Albuquerque office nursing his morning coffee, Sunu arrived and they exchanged greetings. He hadn't slept well after emptying out most of the whiskey in the mini bar and came to the office very early just to get a change of scene. He was doodling on a scratch pad when his cell phone rang. It was his boss in New York. "Sampson."

"Fred, we had a possible sighting at a motel in Salt Lake City that could be your boy," his boss said.

Fred wanted to yell, 'he's not my boy' but instead said, "Go on."

The man left this morning. He had checked in with a Las Cruces, New Mexico State University ID under the name, George Franklin. They've put out an all points on Franklin."

Fred sat in silence.

"Fred, you still there."

"He's headed for Canada."

"How do you know?"

"I don't, but he's headed north for a reason. Did they broadcast Franklin on the news?"

"Not yet. I wanted to talk to you first."

"Don't do it. He'll be less alert if he thinks we don't know he's in Utah."

"Okay, I'll get an extra alert out to the Canadian authorities."

"Did he know he was recognized?"

"The desk clerk didn't think so. He paid cash for the room and left early in a green Honda Civic. The clerk followed him and saw him drive away, but didn't get a plate. The plate he listed on his registration is a fake number. He was wearing a camouflage baseball cap, had blond hair and a blond goatee."

"Why weren't we notified when he checked in?"

"Different desk clerk in the morning, who thought he recognized him when Abdul dropped the key off and got a cup of coffee."

"Get the helicopters and planes out looking for the Honda. What time did he leave?"

"7:00."

Fred thanked his boss, hung up, slipped the phone in his pocket, and looked at his watch. Abdul had two hours head start. "Come on Sunu were going to the Airport. Call ahead and arrange for a charter jet plane."

"Where to?"

"Just call and get the plane. I'll figure where to on the way."

CHAPTER 32

Abdul awoke with a start and grabbed his head. The dream of his mutilated family had invaded his sleep again. The lingering image of the dream haunted him. He shook his head to dispel the gut-wrenching scene, questioning his previous interpretation of the dream as representing his father's assent for his attack. Maybe his interpretation had been terribly wrong. He was positive his mother would be appalled at the number of deaths he had caused. In anger, he sat up and threw off the covers. He looked at the clock and was surprised he had been asleep less than an hour.

He suddenly felt nauseous and raced to the bathroom, but only spewed up a tiny amount of mucous. He hadn't eaten anything since El Paso. He returned to the bed, wiping away his tears. Maybe he should just give up and turn himself in. Would that be what his father would want him to do— admit his guilt and take his punishment? If he did, would his Declaration be revealed? Probably not. If he made his escape, he would have a better chance of getting his Declaration published. He was going round in circles. He needed to eat— get fuel in his body so he could think straight.

He dressed and walked to a nearby restaurant. He ordered a burger and fries since the menu was the usual American fare and nothing actually appealed to him. He could have gobbled up a Saltah stew like his mother made. When he left the restaurant, he was feeling a little better and thought about leaving, but knew he needed more sleep. He would need to be alert and rested to cross undetected into Canada. The long drive, confrontation with Hidalgo, and the thefts in Las Cruces had drained him. He'd leave before first light.

Back at the hotel, he turned on the TV news, retrieved his laptop, scrunched several pillows against the bed's headboard and brought up a map of the Canadian border. If he could find a forest that continued into Canada, he might be able to sneak across the border. There appeared to be many places along the border that might work, but he didn't know which area would be the easiest or what types of fencing there were if any. The Glacier National Park directly north caught his eye. If he could hike through the forest of Glacier Park, he might be able to continue into the Canadian Wateron Lakes National Park that was contiguous to the American Park. Glacier Park would get many visitors this time of year. His Honda Civic would blend in nicely. It would be worth a try.

Abdul abruptly sat up as the newscaster announced there had been a sighting of Abdul Salaamed in El Paso disguised as a Hispanic possibly using the alias Juan Martinez. They displayed the photograph he had given Hidalgo with his dark hair, Poncho Villa mustache, and dark contacts, asking anyone sighting the man to contact their local police. The newscaster warned that Abdul was dangerous and people should not confront him under any circumstances, but should leave apprehension to local police. Fucking Hidalgo had turned him in.

He was glad he hadn't used the driver's license. He had sensed that Hidalgo couldn't be trusted. Maybe the sighting in El Paso would work to his favor. They'd still be expecting him to attempt a crossing into Mexico. He dyed his hair blond and flushed the dark contacts down the toilet. There was no need to rush. He turned off the TV and crawled under the covers. The central air conditioning in his room was way too cold even though he had turned down the thermostat. These fucking Americans had to have cold rooms so their fat asses could get to sleep.

He awoke at 6:00 AM, feeling surprisingly fresh. He didn't remember dreaming and thanked providence for not having to dispel the mental anguish of his reoccurring dreams. He had wanted to leave while it was still dark in order to avoid the morning traffic. It didn't matter. The authorities wouldn't have any idea he was traveling north to Canada.

He leisurely showered, applied a blond goatee and went downstairs. The lobby was empty except for the clerk behind the counter, who only looked up briefly at Abdul when he laid his key card on the desk counter. He poured coffee in his traveling mug, slipped on a baseball style camouflage cap, and surreptitiously glanced at the clerk to make sure he had not been recognized. The clerk was reading his newspaper and seemed relaxed and indifferent to Abdul's appearance. He walked out of the lobby, and strolled down the street to the vicinity of the Honda. He stood across the street and waited a few minutes to make sure no one had spotted the stolen car.

He got in, took a deep breath, and drove off. It was almost eleven hours to the border. He'd skip breakfast. Following I-15 north, the traffic in Salt Lake was heavy, but he was able to get out of the city without too much delay. It was cloudy and cold, but the car heater soon made the interior of the car toasty. He felt relaxed as he listened to news on the radio. The radiation in Los

Alamos was still too high to allow entry except in hazmat suits.

He was glad he had closed the City of Death and hoped the Laboratory would never resume its nuclear work. People exposed to radiation were still dying. He didn't know how he felt about the continued dying. No mention of his Declaration. Fortunately, there was nothing on the news about George Franklin or a stolen green Honda Civic. The clouds were building, and it smelled like it could rain. He liked rain and thought it could make a clandestine crossing into Canada easier.

He stopped in Dillon, Montana for gas and something to eat at what looked like a popular restaurant. The landscape was flatter than a pancake. Dillon was a cattle ranching and farming small town. He ate quickly, nonchalantly, scanning the room of Formica topped tables and booths to make sure no one was paying him undue attention. He had barbecued ribs, which seemed to a specialty of the restaurant. He paid no attention to the Moslem prohibition on eating pork and thought it would further enhance the difficulty of identifying him as Abdul. He paid for the meal at the register and purchased a jacket, which displayed the logo of the restaurant, and would come in handy on his trek through the forest to Canada. The waitress, who rang him up at the register, didn't seem to pay him much attention. He was confident she hadn't recognized him.

When he got back on the road, the rain started after a few miles, coming down in sheets that made him slow his speed drastically. He rolled his window down an inch to smell the sweet damp air. He switched the radio station to music and settled back in his seat as he leisurely drove forward in the slashing rain.

CHAPTER 33

Fred found Salt Lake on his phone map while Sunu drove and scrolled the map north. When he found the destination he was looking for, he raised his head and asked Sunu the charter service telephone number. "We're going to Great Falls," Fred told the charter company. "How long will it take? Good, we'll be there in fifteen minutes."

Sunu pulled up to the Albuquerque Sunport Airport. "Get out and I'll go park."

"Forget the parking, leave the car. We'll have somebody come and pick it up."

Sunu got out of the vehicle and started after Fred. When the security guard came forward to say he couldn't leave the vehicle unattended, Sunu flashed his FBI identification. "National emergency. Keys are in it if you want to move it. Somebody from the FBI will be along to collect it."

They went to the charter plane area and flourished their FBI IDs to the woman behind the counter. The woman checked them in and led them to the door to the outside where the Lear Jet sat. The morning sun gleamed off the white paint of the plane and heat waves rose from the asphalt. Fred thanked the woman and hurried to the plane followed by Sunu. Sunu took a seat while Fred walked to the cockpit.

"Are we ready?" Fred said to the pilot. "We need to get going as soon as possible."

"We'll have to get in line. May take a while to get in the air. This is a busy time."

"Call the tower. This is a National Emergency."

"You got it, Sir." The pilot nodded to the copilot.

"Flight 7532 to tower," the copilot radioed. "We have FBI agents on board needing to take off as soon as possible. It is a National Emergency. Repeat, a National Emergency." The copilot waited as he glanced up at Fred before spinning forward. "Okay, roger that." He turned back to Fred. "The runway is clear and we are a go. Please take your seat."

Fred scurried to a seat across from Sunu and buckled up as the plane started rolling.

Sunu bent across the aisle toward Fred. "I hope your gut is on target. What if he takes a different route from Salt Lake?"

"Then we're on a wild goose chase. Have you a better idea?"

"No way."

"Sunu, call ahead to Great Falls and have a chopper ready to go when we arrive." Fred said as they taxied to the runway.

Sunu pulled his cell phone from his pocket and made the call. Fred could only make out snatches of Sunu's conversation over the roar of the jet engines as they revved for takeoff.

Fred pulled out his cell phone, thinking from what he could tell from the snatches of conversation Sunu was getting the run around. He tapped Sunu's arm, pulled his hand across his throat, and then punched in a telephone number on his phone. "Boss, we'll be in the air headed for Great Falls in a few minutes and need a chopper ready to go when we arrive. Can you make sure that happens? Infrared capability would be nice too. Abdul left at 7:00 and it's 11:00 now. It's at least an eight hour drive from Salt Lake to Great Falls and with stops probably nine. Our flight should take a little over two hours. We should arrive well ahead of Abdul if, as I surmise, he is headed up I-15. We'll backtrack in the helicopter and look for him. Has there been any sighting of the green Honda?"

"No, it's raining heavy up north, terrible visibility. The choppers had to land and the planes are useless with the cloud cover. Why I-15?"

"Shit... damn weather." He shook his head with a grimace. "I-15 is the interstate from Salt Lake. He'll want to take the quickest route. It's imperative that I get a chopper pilot that's not afraid to go up in the weather. Make it happen, Boss."

"Any other orders, Fred," his boss said, his sarcasm dripping through the call.

"Sorry, Boss. I'm a little hyped up."

"No kidding. I'll get you the best chopper pilot I can and the infrared. Maybe it will clear up some."

Fred ended the call and checked the weather in Great Falls. Looked like the rain was expected to last the rest of the day and into the night.

"What's up, Fred," Sunu asked.

"It's raining like hell up north. Planes and choppers are grounded. We can't seem to catch a break."

When they landed at Great Falls and taxied to the terminal, Fred rose and went to the cockpit. "Thanks gentleman for the quick flight. You've done us a great service."

Sunu unlatched the door and extended the stairs. Fred followed Sunu down the stairs and hurried through the streaming rain to the terminal.

As soon as they walked inside, a tall Air Force Captain stood. "Agent Sampson, Captain Doug Monteban, at your service. I'll be your chopper pilot, infrared is on board, and we can leave whenever you're ready."

Fred said 'thanks Boss' under his breath as he shook out his coat, spraying water on the floor. "What about the weather?"

"It's not ideal and possibly dangerous. The rain has slowed some, but is still quite heavy, and the gusts are intermittent. I've flown in a lot worse weather. I've been ordered to take you up if you want to go in this weather."

"Let's go then, Captain Monteban."

They followed Captain Monteban out to the Air Force PAVE Hawk helicopter, standing to the side of the small terminal. They climbed aboard, and Monteban started the rotors as Fred and Sunu slipped on the headphones.

"Follow I-15 south," Fred directed. "Be on the lookout for a green Honda Civic." It was 1:30 PM. He pulled up the map of Montana on his phone. Abdul left at 7:00. Give him 30 minutes to get out of Salt Lake. At 70 miles an hour, he would have travelled over 400 miles with stops to eat and gas up. "He should be close to Helena now. We're 90 some miles from Helena. We should find him north of Helena. What do you think Captain?"

"Sounds about right. With this weather we won't be able to go very fast." Monteban lifted the helicopter into the surging rain as the wind gusts moved the helicopter around like a toy. Fred gripped the arms of his seat and glanced at Sunu, who was as white as a sheet. Monteban was able to right the helicopter as they rose, and they sped forward through the river of rain.

Fred consulted his watch. It was 2:30 PM. He pulled up the map of Montana on his phone. "If my calculations are correct, he could be pretty close," Fred said into his headphone.

"Keep them peeled, gentleman," Captain Monteban said as they flew forward, swaying with the wind gusts. The rain dispersed somewhat and the highway came into view.

Fred, excited by the increased visibility, had a twitch in his gut. He prayed his estimations about Abdul's travel plans were correct as he peered out at the flow of vehicles travelling north and south.

After a few minutes Captain Monteban said. "There's a green Honda I think just up ahead.

"Buzz him close, Captain, and see what he does," Fred said.

"Here we go," Captain Monteban said as he swooped down and flew a few feet over the green Honda.

The Honda increased its speed. "That's got to be him," Fred said with obvious jubilation. "We've got the son of a bitch. Land the helicopter up ahead of him across the road and see what he does. Sunu, call it in to the police in case he turns around."

Captain Monteban turned the helicopter, flew about a quarter mile ahead, and landed the helicopter across the road. The green Honda slowed, but kept coming forward. Fred donned a bullet proof vest and grabbed the M-16A4 rifle. The Honda pulled off the road and sat about 50 feet from the helicopter. The other light traffic stopped in place. Fred stepped out of the helicopter onto the road, ignoring the hammering rain. Sunu did the same and joined Fred. Fred and Sunu started walking toward the vehicle, the driving rain making their vision difficult. Some people stopped in their vehicles had their windows down. Sunu, yelled for them to remain in their vehicle.

CHAPTER 34

Abdul felt relaxed as he leisurely drove forward to the rhythmic slap of the windshield wipers. He had destroyed the City of Death, fooled the FBI, and felt certain he would soon make it to Canada. In Canada, he'd make his way to Vancouver and look for ways to obtain a false passport. With a fake passport, he could fly to Germany from which he knew he could easily make his way to Yemen. Back in Yemen, he'd join the Houthi fighters and wage war against the Saudi supported coalition trying to destroy the Houthi. He would be blessed to die in Yemen if it came to that. He had been naïve thinking his Declaration would be published in the *Albuquerque Journal*. So much for America's freedom of the press. Maybe he could get *Der Spiegel* in Germany to publish it.

When he saw the Air Force helicopter flying low in the distance, his heart jumped, and he felt his stomach drop. Could it be just a military exercise—heightened alert after the explosions in Los Alamos? The helicopter was flying desperately low in the heavy rain for an exercise. The helicopter zoomed down over the top of his vehicle way too close for any kind of exercise. He'd been found. He slowed, trying to think of a plan. There would be no escape. He saw the helicopter swoop around and fly northward before settling across the road blocking the traffic. He drove on until he decided he would go no farther and pulled off onto the shoulder. Two men emerged from the helicopter, wearing bullet proof vests and carrying automatic rifles.

It was over. He felt a kind of relief. With any luck, he would be tried in open court and his Declaration would be heard. Conversely, he could be labeled an enemy combatant and subjected to enhanced interrogation—their euphemism for torture. His Declaration would never see the light of day, and he would be known as a deranged, jihadist Muslim. He'd be locked away forever.

Either way he would need to be strong. He asked the spirits of his mother and father to forgive him for the taking of so many innocent lives and to help him survive the chaos awaiting him. He had no illusion that his attack would stop the Saudis and the Americans from trying to destroy his beloved Yemen. His only hope was the fact that he was from Yemen would lead to more coverage of what was happening in Yemen, and eventually the international community would clamor for a peace settlement.

He waited in the car with his hands up as the two men approached with their FBI emblazoned vests.

CHAPTER 35

Sunu moved toward the left side of the vehicle as Fred moved to the right. "The hands up may be a ploy," Sunu shouted against the rain. "He might have a pistol in his lap or side."

"I don't think so," Fred replied. "He's done." Fred pointed his rifle at the driver's window. "Come out slowly and keep your hands up."

Abdul opened the door and stepped out onto the shoulder, squinting against the rain.

"Abdul Salaamed, I am arresting you for the terrorism explosions and murder in Los Alamos, New Mexico," Fred announced. Sunu had come up to stand next to Fred. "Turn around, Abdul, with your hands behind your back." Abdul complied. Fred nodded to Sunu, who hand-cuffed Abdul. "You have the right to remain silent. Anything you say may be taken down and used against you in a court of law. You have a right to an attorney. If you cannot afford an attorney, one will be appointed to you by the court. As a foreign national, you may consult your country's consulate before answering any questions. Do you understand your rights as I have informed you?"

"Yes," Abdul said.

Fred was surprised by Abdul's calmness. It almost seemed as if Abdul was relieved to be caught.

Sunu held up his cell phone. "I'm recording."

"Do you have anything to say?" Fred asked as he took hold of Abdul's arm and led him toward the helicopter.

"How did you know where I'd be?"

"You were recognized in Salt Lake City."

"Ah," Abdul said weakly.

"Anything else you'd like to know or say?"

"No. I'll wait to talk to an attorney."

"Are we going to wait for the police?" Sunu asked.

"No let's fly him back in the helicopter before the police get here", Fred said. "The press will be coming with the police. We don't need a media circus."

They had Abdul in a room at the Air Force base that Captain Monteban had arranged for them. The press and the police were probably foaming at the mouth that they couldn't get into the base. Sunu had arranged with Monteban for an Air Force plane to take them to Albuquerque. The press knew they had arrested someone.

"We'll be leaving for Albuquerque in a few minutes," Fred said. "I read your Declaration. I don't agree with my government supporting the Saudis. What's happening in Yemen is a travesty in my opinion. The slaughter of innocent civilians in the manner you did makes you as guilty as the Saudis. Many are going to die an agonizing death. You think what you did is going to help Yemen?"

Abdul shrugged his shoulders, but said nothing.

"It may cause the opposite," Fred said. "Look what 9/11 did."

Abdul just stared at Fred.

Captain Monteban knocked and opened the door. "We're ready to go. I'll be your pilot. There's a crowd at the gate. The Governor called the Base Commander and wanted to know what the hell was going on. The sooner we leave the better.”

“Let’s go then.”

Fred escorted Abdul to the airplane and led him up the stairs to a bench seat mid-plane.

“Shall I shackle his legs to the bench?” Sunu asked.

“No, he’s not going anywhere,” Fred answered as he stared at Abdul, amazed by Abdul’s calmness and resignation. Fred’s pulse was still resounding in his head. He wondered what was going through Abdul’s mind.

Captain Monteban walked from the cockpit back to check on his passengers accompanied by a younger man. “This is Lieutenant Marshall. He’ll be my copilot.”

Lieutenant Marshall shook hands with Fred and Sunu. “Pleased to meet you. My congratulations on capturing the terrorist.” He sneered at Abdul.

Fred thanked the copilot before glancing at Abdul. Abdul stared up at the copilot with tired scrunched eyes and then looked at the floor. Fred sensed that the term terrorist had annoyed Abdul. He was sure Abdul was not prepared for what was to come. He hoped the President wouldn’t make an example of Abdul and send him to Guantanamo as he had promised he’d do to the ‘bad dudes’. He wanted Abdul to have his day in court to publicize the travesty that was going on in Yemen.

“Are we set?” Monteban asked. “Might be a bit bumpy until we get above the clouds. The rain has picked up.” He stepped closer to Fred. “We could wait a while and see if the rain dies down some.”

“If we can, Captain, I’d like to leave as soon as possible.” Fred wanted to arrive in Albuquerque before the national press figured out what was going on and had a chance to set up there.

"Understood." Monteban clapped Marshal on the back. "Let's get this bird airborne."

When the plane touched down, Fred awoke with a start. He hadn't realized he had dozed off soon after the bone shaking takeoff. The adrenalin of the chase had exhausted him and the brief nap hadn't helped much. When he looked up, Abdul was studying him. Was Abdul trying to figure out where he had slipped up? If Abdul hadn't been sighted in Salt Lake or if he had kept going, catching snatches of sleep in rest areas with the truckers, Fred expected Abdul would have made his escape to Canada. For once, luck had been on their side.

After they taxied to the hangar at Kirkland, Fred stood and waited for Monteban to emerge. "Captain, you've been an immense help. Without your expert flying, Abdul might have escaped. If you're ever in New York, look me up and we'll have a drink together."

"I'd like that, Agent Sampson." Monteban replied. "Good luck. I'm overjoyed that I was able to play a part in apprehending this crazed terrorist." He turned to look at Abdul, who returned his gaze with a straight face of defiance

Fred shook hands with Monteban "Thanks again."

Monteban came to attention and saluted. "Take care, Agent Sampson."

Sunu shook hands with the Monteban. "Thanks, Captain." He moved to Abdul and motioned for Abdul to stand. Abdul stood and shifted his eyes from Sunu, to Monteban and then lingered on Fred. Sunu grabbed

Abdul's arm and escorted him forward, following Fred down the stairs to the waiting black Escalade SUV. The sun was out and the azure sky welcomed them. Sunu pushed Abdul in the back seat and entered after him while Fred got into the front seat.

As they drove out through the front gate of Kirtland Air Force base there was a small group of news vans filming their departure. At the FBI office, a bigger group of reporters swarmed toward them, hurling questions as they escorted Abdul inside. Fred was relieved that the news crowd was relatively small, and they had little trouble taking Abdul inside. They escorted him to the interrogation room. Abdul sat down and wearily stared at the table in front of him.

"Anything you would like to say, Abdul?" Fred asked.

Abdul shook his head. "No."

"They'll take you in a few minutes to the City Jail where you'll be housed until your arraignment," Fred said. He hoped he was speaking the truth. He was still worried that Abdul could be snatched from them. So far no one had mentioned enemy combatant. What Abdul had done was despicable, but he was a human being and should be treated accordingly. Guantanamo was no place for anyone. He believed it should be closed as Obama had wanted to.

Fred stood near the security entrance to the Albuquerque Airport and held out his hand. "Sunu thanks for all your help. I couldn't have done it without you."

Sunu grabbed Fred's hand and shook it vigorously. "Fred, I'm privileged to have worked with you. Without your intuition and unbelievable tenacity, I don't think we would have caught Abdul. He'd have made it to Canada."

"He was a quite an intelligent and cunning terrorist. We were lucky, but I doubt the people in Los Alamos feel the same. I should have checked the security camera footage at the Los Alamos coffee shop when I was first there. I don't know. I think I might be too old for this game."

"I know you hate that you didn't stop him. There was not much more you could have done. You alerted the Lab. Too bad we didn't know about the stolen rocket launcher. If we had known, I bet the Lab would have had helicopters out in force. Actually I'm rather surprised they didn't have any helicopters out. If anyone dropped the ball it was them." Sunu placed his hand on Fred's shoulder. "Say hello to the lovely Margret. I'll see you back here for the trial."

"I'm glad you think there will be a trial."

"I doubt the military will seize him now. If they were going to, they would have already done it."

"Let's hope you're right."

CHAPTER 36

Abdul was kept in isolation at the Albuquerque City Jail. He had not yet met with an attorney and hated the idea that tiny cells would be his world until he was put to death. The FBI had questioned him several times, but he hadn't answered many of their questions. When they brought up Steve Moore and Ray Osborn, he admitted he knew them, but offered nothing else. He hoped his association with Steve and Ray would ruin their lives and cause the Freedom Militia great displeasure and difficulty. When they asked about Cindy, he acknowledged he knew her at Berkeley and had talked to her in Albuquerque, but ignored their other questions.

He was profoundly sorry that in his weakness he had involved Cindy by contacting her in Albuquerque. He wouldn't blame her if she hated him and wished she had never met him. When he asked about his appointed attorney at another questioning, they said one would be forthcoming soon. He declared he would say no more until he met with an attorney.

Several days later, Abdul was placed in room at a table, his arms and legs shackled and told an attorney wanted to speak with him. When the distinguished looking American, wearing a very expensive tailored, dark gray suit with a red and blue striped tie, entered, Abdul was surprised that the court had appointed such an obviously successful lawyer for him. He thought he'd end up with an overworked public defender in a cheap wrinkled suit, who would want to get things over with quickly. He was relieved that he hadn't been shipped off to Guantanamo.

The man sported a pair of black framed glasses that had a slight grey tint. His blond hair with graying temples was combed back off his forehead. He was quite handsome and had a proud air about him.

"Good day, Mr. Salaamed," the man said matter-of-factly as if he was out for stroll and set his briefcase on the metal table. "Thank you for agreeing to see me. My name is Marvin Gladden, and I would like to represent you."

Abdul had not agreed to see this attorney. He was given no choice, but was glad to see a successful attorney wanting to talk to him. Actually he was glad that anyone besides the FBI wanted to talk to him.

"Mr. Salaamed as you probably know you have been charged with terrorism murder of as yet unnamed number of people, the unlawful use of a 153-MK SMAW, rocket launcher, the release of toxic radioactive debris, and interstate flight. From what I been able to learn, you will be arraigned in federal court, possibly next week, and be asked to plead guilty or not guilty."

Marvin opened the briefcase he had set on the table and withdrew a typed single page. "This is a short agreement designating that you accept me as your attorney. The notoriety of the explosions in Los Alamos may cause other lawyers to seek your representation. This agreement will stop any other lawyers trying to bother you." He slid the agreement to Abdul. "Write your name in the blank at the top and sign it at the bottom. That is if you want me to represent you. I assure you I am an experienced criminal law attorney with an excellent record of acquittals."

"Why do you want to take my case?"

"I believe your trial will be one of the most important cases in many years. I am against the country's handling of the so called war on terror, and vehemently against the support of Saudi Arabia's bombing of Yemen. I also, most selfishly, want to represent you for the furtherance of my career. I have earned good money in my legal career and feel taking your case on a pro bono basis will elevate me as one of the top criminal lawyers in the country." He paused and watched Abdul. "So I have idealistic and selfish reasons for wanting to represent you."

"Thank you for your honesty." Abdul signed the agreement and slid it to Marvin.

"How would you like to plead?" Marvin asked.

"I did it," Abdul said.

Marvin held up his hand to stop Abdul from saying more. "I'm not convinced the evidence the government has is very solid for proving that you executed the attack. From what I've read so far, all they have is circumstantial evidence linking you to the attack. You could plead not guilty, and we could fight conviction on their inability to prove you are guilty beyond a reasonable doubt."

"Did you read my Declaration that I tried to get published in the *Albuquerque Journal*."

"No. Who is in possession of the Declaration?"

"I would suspect the FBI. I mailed a copy of the Declaration to the Albuquerque Journal, but it was never published. I left a copy on the seat in the stolen 4Runner SUV I abandoned in Albuquerque, and I had a copy on me when I was arrested."

"That's unfortunate. Why did you write this Declaration?"

"To explain why I blew up the nuclear waste at Los Alamos."

Gladden frowned and sucked in his lips. "Can you paraphrase the Declaration for me? I must say your English is very good." He took out his fountain pen, a legal pad, and looked up at Abdul. "Go ahead."

Abdul studied Marvin but said nothing. When Marvin furrowed his brow and was about to speak, Abdul slid his cuffed hands out. "It might be easier if I tried to write out the Declaration."

"By all means," Marvin said and slid the legal pad across the table, rose, walked to the door, and knocked.

The guard opened the door. "Are you leaving?"

"No," Marvin replied. The guard's expression changed to bewilderment. Marvin smiled at the guard. "Please take the cuffs off my client so he can write properly."

"No, Sir." The guard puffed out his chest. "It is not allowed for dangerous prisoners."

"I'm his lawyer. I don't think he'll be dangerous toward me."

"Against the rules, Sir. Sorry, Sir."

"I'll be able to write," Abdul called.

"Okay, guard, you may go," Marvin said. The guard closed the door as Marvin walked back and took his seat. He watched Abdul write a semblance of the original Declaration. Abdul raised his head and solemnly slid the pad to Marvin.

Marvin leaned back and massaged his chin as he read. "This is quite damning against you, but we might use it to establish mitigating circumstances." He squished his lips together and looked up at the ceiling. "I'm just thinking aloud here. Since your family was killed, we could try an insanity defense. They will probably ask for the death penalty. Of course we'll try for a change of venue. Getting an impartial jury in Albuquerque would be difficult. For that matter an impartial jury anywhere will be difficult to find."

Marvin paused and stared at Abdul. "Maybe it's better to keep the trial here. This is a much smaller city than we would probably be transferred to." He squinted as he hummed softly, raising his head toward the ceiling. "I assume, since you tried to get your Declaration published, that you would like the Declaration to be a central point of your defense as well as the US support and supply of the weapons for the bombing of Yemen."

"Yes, I certainly would." Abdul felt for the first time that his reasons for what he did might come out. He still worried that he would be labeled as an enemy combatant and treated with techniques to break him as they had Jose Padilla— even if he had an attorney.

"Then, I think it would be best to plead not guilty."

"But I am guilty of firing the rockets at the spent nuclear storage." Abdul could smell the stink of himself. He had been spoiled by his adoption of the American proclivity for frequent showers.

Marvin held up his hand. "That's between you and me." Marvin pressed his hands on the table and straightened his back. He looked around the room in a slow search of the ceiling and walls.

Abdul watched Marvin's roving inspection of the room at the ceiling level and judged that Marvin suspected they were being monitored. There were no apparent listening devices, but they could be cleverly hidden. He believed that it was most likely they were being recorded even though he knew it was illegal. Any recorded conversations with his lawyer could not be used against him, but would be valuable information for the prosecution as to what his defense was planning.

"A not-guilty plea will allow us more room to mount a defense," Marvin said. "I need to think about this." He placed his legal pad into his briefcase. "I'll need to rent an office here and make some calls." He closed his brief case. "I'm based in New York City and need to move my operation out here." He stood. "Thank you Mr. Salaamed for accepting my representation. I believe we will get on very well. I'll be back tomorrow to discuss things in more detail. My assistant is on her way out here. I'll need to hire a local attorney to help as well." He smiled and placed his hands on the table palms up. "I would shake hands, but I've already been warned that any physical contact with you is prohibited."

Abdul stood and nodded. "Thanks, Mr. Gladden. I welcome your help."

CHAPTER 37

Fred was relieved when he walked into his apartment, feeling like he'd been stomped on. He breathed in the familiar smells— no acrylic carpeting or stale cheap musty air-conditioning. It felt good to be home. The flight had been delayed, his bag, which had apparently burst from handling, was held together with rope, and the taxi driver from the airport had his grating Turkish pop music turned up very loud. All of which had irritated him to no end on the taxi ride. His accumulated anger slowly started to dissipate as he set his damaged bag down near the door and went into the bright kitchen with its light blue tile and white walls to fetch his bottle of Irish whiskey. As he shaded his eyes, thinking he needed to reduce the wattage of the bulbs in the lights or get a dimmer switch, he poured a glass half full of whiskey, sucked it down, and released a long sigh. He inhaled deeply and exhaled with a prolonged whoosh, looking longingly toward his bedroom. He would welcome crawling into bed, but first he needed to call Maggie. He walked with his whiskey out to the brown leather couch, sat down, and retrieved his phone.

The mellifluous voice of Maggie answering her phone was a soothing balm. He smiled to himself. "I'm back. I know it's late, but I wanted to apologize for abandoning you in Albuquerque."

"Fred, there's no reason to apologize," Maggie responded, heightening Fred's smile. "I understand completely. You got him. That's what's important. You stopped him from any other horrible acts."

"He was done. He wanted to strike back at the US that he thought was ultimately responsible for the death of his family, the devastation of Yemen, and bring to light what the US is doing by supporting the Saudis." Fred walked with the phone to the kitchen and poured another glass of whiskey. "Such a horrible act. I doubt he knew the extent of the deaths he would cause. I can understand his motivation, but not his act. I'm afraid his actions will cause the opposite of what he intended. I would imagine that we'll step up our support for the Saudis and may even invade Yemen after the trial, and what he did is more publicized. A perfect opening for our President to increase his flagging support. We'll be out for retaliation blood."

"You want to come over? You sound really down."

"No." He would have loved to see her smiling face and feel her warm embrace, but, in his present condition, it wouldn't be fair to her. "I need to go to bed. I'm exhausted and the trip back was fraught with mishaps." Realizing he sounded like a moaning child, he tried to jolly his voice. "I'd like to join you for breakfast though. Shall we meet at that French café near your place, say 8:30?"

"Okay, that would be nice. Are you intending to take the day off? You deserve some time off."

"No, I'll need to go into the office and talk to my Boss and meet with my team. I imagine I'll be going back and forth to Albuquerque a lot."

"See you tomorrow 8:30. Sleep tight, my love."

"Will do, bye."

He was surprised by the 'my love'. She'd never used that expression before. He decided he liked it and smiled to himself.

When Fred walked into the French Café, Maggie was already seated looking gorgeous in her cerulean silk shirt. Those hazel eyes that appeared almost green today were like beacons. He smiled, waved, and made his way to the table. He was so happy that he had someone to come home to and hoped he didn't look too wrung out. He wore a blue blazer and open collar blue shirt with dark gray trousers that had been in his closet and didn't bare the wrinkles of travel. "Maggie, you are a sight for sore eyes."

Maggie sprang up, hugged him tightly, and kissed his cheek. She sat down and picked up the carafe of coffee and poured him a cup. "I like the casual look, but am surprised you'd go to the office without a tie."

Fred pulled a tie from his pocket.

"I see the casual look is just for me. I approve. Drink your coffee. You look like you need it."

"Yeah, I think I overdid the Irish whiskey to hasten my sleep last night."

"I offered to help."

Fred held up his cup. "I wouldn't have been good company by any means, but I appreciated the offer."

Fred walked into the office feeling much better than he felt upon first waking. The breakfast with Maggie had grounded him, and he felt he could handle the onslaught to come.

Jeff stood up when he saw Fred coming. "They've been replaying you and Sunu marching Abdul in the FBI office in Albuquerque over and over," Jeff said. "You're famous now."

"Yeah, famous for not stopping the worst terrorist attack since 9/11," Fred replied with a grimace.

"There is that," Jeff said. "Just kidding, Fred. You did all you could do. No one could have stopped him from what I've read. Without knowing he had a rocket launcher, the measures the Lab took were extensive. He was a smart cookie. I'll give him that."

Mary came up to Fred and gave him a hug. "You did your best, Fred." She patted his arm. "The boss has come out of his office several times looking for you. You better go on in and relieve him before he comes apart at the seams."

"Yep." Fred nodded, ambled to the boss's door, and knocked before entering.

"Fred," the boss exclaimed and hurried from his desk to shake hands. "You got him. Thank you." He patted him on the back. "If you hadn't I'd probably would have been out of a job."

"I doubt that, Boss."

"You wouldn't believe the crap I took from the Director. He wanted me to send every agent I could muster to Albuquerque. I told him you were the best agent we had. I would let you do your thing and give you any and all the support you asked for."

"Thanks, Boss."

"Sit down." The boss walked to the small table in his office. "There's coffee if you need it. Thanks for coming in. You could have taken the day off to gather your strength. I imagine the stress of trying to find that horrible terrorist was extreme. The search for Abdul cleaned my clock. I didn't get a good night's sleep until you caught him."

"I wanted to bring you up to date," Fred said. "You've seen Abdul's Declaration. When I questioned him, he wouldn't answer many questions without a lawyer. He did admit knowing those Freedom Militia idiots in Colorado Springs. Have we arrested Ray Osborn for providing material support to a terrorist yet?"

"Yes, he's in jail in Colorado Springs. He was belligerent and shoved the officers arresting him. We charged him with resisting arrest as well as supporting terrorism. He had a concealed loaded pistol without a permit on him when he was arrested as well and was charged for that also. You think this Steve Moore and Ray were in on it and knew about the planned attack?"

"Could be. I doubt they knew Abdul was a foreigner. Abdul can speak without a trace of a foreign accent. Ray was belligerent when I interviewed him. He's full of hate. I'm glad no one was hurt in the arrest." Fred rubbed his cheek as he looked up briefly. "That's about it. I expect once Abdul is arraigned, I'll need to go back and talk to the federal attorney assigned to the case. I will be back and forth quite a bit. I thought it would be best to turn team leadership over to Jeff."

"Of course."

"I'll talk to the team and get up to speed and announce Jeff's leadership role until the trial is over. If you don't mind, I'll take some time off and get some rest. I haven't been able to sleep very well with all the traveling."

"By all means."

Fred was lounging at home, resting before his dinner and theater date with Maggie. He'd been back two weeks and was starting to feel like his old self. Maggie had been a big help. He still had dreams of Abdul escaping out of the county, but expected they would wane. He avoided watching the news and reading the papers. People recognized him on the street to his dismay and congratulated him on catching Abdul. When his cell phone rang, he picked it up and saw it was from Sunu.

With a frown, he answered, "Sampson."

"Fred, you won't believe who's taking Abdul's case. Marvin Gladden."

"What," Fred replied and blinked. "Marvin Gladden is a New York City criminal defense attorney. He commands an unbelievable price. Abdul doesn't have that kind of money. Who's bankrolling this?"

"According to Gladden, he's taking this case pro-bono. Abdul pled not guilty at his arraignment. The prosecution is seeking the death penalty. The assistant District US attorney, Jim Johnson is the prosecuting attorney. He's good, has an excellent court room demeanor and record. Thought I'd give you a heads up before they contact you."

"I should have known an ambitious attorney would want to take the case. I thought Abdul would plead guilty, and it would be a quick trial."

"No such luck. The judge, Henry Basset is a no-nonsense judge. He'll move things along as fast as possible. So you know Marvin Gladden?"

"Know of him. He's gotten some supposed racketeers off, defended demonstrators charged with interfering with police actions, conducted some successful environmental suits, and made a lot of money. He's considered a smooth operator. The trial is going to be an even bigger media circus than I had imagined." He shook his head. "Shit... thanks for the heads up."

"I expect I'll see you soon. You coming for the jury selection that starts next week?"

"I thought I'd skip that. There's nothing I could do to help with that. Seems like they're proceeding fast."

"What did you expect? It's the most famous trial since I don't when, especially for New Mexico. You wouldn't believe the number of news people in town. You want me to find you an apartment to rent. All hotels will probably be full."

"Good idea, Sunu. See if you can find a place in a quiet neighborhood."

Fred and Sunu walked into the New Mexico Federal District Attorney Office. Fred had returned at the request of the prosecuting attorney. They were shown into the assistant district attorney's office where Jim Johnson sat behind a large mahogany desk. The floor was carpeted in dark blue wool and the off-white walls exhibited New Mexico landscape paintings. Jim Johnson rose to greet them and led them to the long mahogany table that could easily seat twelve. "Can I get you anything, coffee, iced tea? It's a little hotter than normal today." He was shorter than Fred and had an angular face with a stern expression. His thick brown hair was parted on the side and perfectly combed. He exuded confidence.

"I've read your reports, Agent Sampson" Jim began. "I must say that was an excellent job of apprehending Abdul before he got to Canada. I thought when I read

Abdul's Declaration we had an open and shut case. However, we don't have any evidence that Abdul fired the rockets at Tech Area 54 besides the Declaration. There were no finger prints on the launcher. Only Specialist Moore's finger prints were on the rockets left with the launcher. We have Moore's deposition that he gave the SMAW to Abdul. The fact that Moore stole the weapon doesn't make him a very good witness. Plus the guy's a wreck. He's scared witless."

Jim Johnson poured himself a glass of water and took a long drink. "We haven't deposed Abdul yet. I've scheduled his disposition for tomorrow morning. I suspect Gladden won't let him answer many questions. We've had Ray Osborn, transferred to the jail here as well as Moore. Osborn denies providing material support to Abdul, but admits Abdul stayed at his trailer for weeks. He eventually admitted to getting Abdul a Colorado Driver's license from a friend of his at the Department of Motor Vehicles after Steve Moore stopped lying and admitted that Ray had gotten the license for Abdul as Sidney Wallace. Ray denied it to the end until we produced the signed confession of his buddy at Motor Vehicle. He refutes that the Freedom Militia was planning any attacks against government facilities. He gave us the standard Freedom Militia mission statement of working politically and training in the advent there is a civil war."

Jim took another drink and stretched his neck. "We've deposed the Commander of the Militia Chapter. He doesn't know where the Militia Chapter obtained the recoilless rifle we found at his ranch. He had 30 rifles and an assortment of pistols as well." He shook his head. "We'll have to question all the damn Freedom

Militia members to find out where the recoilless rifle came from. They can be bought online. I never knew the extent of weapons people can buy online. Just the fact that the Militia has a weapon like that doesn't show them in a good light. If we didn't have Abdul's Declaration, we'd have a better conspiracy case against the Militia." Jim leaned back and looked from Fred to Sunu. "We've no witnesses, who can place Abdul the night of the attack anywhere near the Lab. He was checked in at a motel in Santa Fe. That's as close we can get him to Los Alamos."

"Abdul was very careful in making sure he was not detected," Fred said. "You don't think the Declaration he wrote is enough?"

"There's no quality finger prints on any of the three copies of his Declaration. The Declaration was typed. Someone else, trying to frame Abdul, could have written the Declaration. His girlfriend even after seeing his Declaration doesn't believe Abdul wrote the Declaration or fired the rockets. She will probably be called as a witness for the defense."

"What about the fact he had a copy on him," Sunu said.

"That helps, but what if he was carrying it to confuse us. Your report stated that you thought Abdul acted alone. What if there were others involved, who shot the rockets, and Abdul's Declaration was part of a plan to sow confusion? We can call Abdul as a witness, but he can invoke the fifth. We could use a witness, who saw him near the Lab. He had to leave the stolen vehicle somewhere in the vicinity and had to return to it to make his escape."

"I would suggest placing several pictures of Abdul and the black 4Runner SUV in the Santa Fe, Espanola, Taos, and Albuquerque papers, asking if anyone saw Abdul or the vehicle on September 25th," Fred said.

"That's an idea. Will you take care of that?"

Sunu glanced at Fred, who nodded. "We'll take care of it. When's jury selection start?"

"Next week."

"What other deaths are there besides the 15 near the site?" Fred asked.

"Two security personnel that were near Tech Area 54 have died in the hospital in Taos," Sunu replied. "Twenty people in the hospital are in poor condition with radiation poisoning. Mostly security and Lab personnel that were outside during the explosions."

"I suspect the number of deaths will mount and then level out," Fred said. "Many with less radiation poisoning may end up with cancer in the coming years." Fred massaged his neck. The talk of the dead and dying reinforced his guilt of not stopping Abdul. The case seemed to be disintegrating. "Can I be present when you depose Abdul?"

"Sure, I'd welcome your input. Tomorrow at ten. Come by here around 9:30 and will drive over to the jail together."

CHAPTER 38

Abdul shuffled into the interrogation room encumbered by leg and wrist shackles, led by the jail guard. Gladden rose, nodded to Abdul, and turned to Johnson. "Counselor, can we dispense with the shackles."

Johnson frowned. "Guard, please remove the shackles."

"Sir...."

"I know what your orders are," Johnson interrupted. "Please go check with your supervisor and tell him the Assistant District Attorney, Jim Johnson, has requested the shackles be removed."

"Yes, Sir." The guard helped Abdul to his seat and left.

"Counselor Gladden, may I introduce Fred Sampson, the FBI Agent, who arrested Abdul."

Fred rose and shook hands with Gladden. "Pleased to meet you, Mr. Gladden."

The guard came in and removed Abdul's shackles while Abdul stared at Fred, and Gladden stared at Johnson, all keeping their faces neutral as if they were riding on a subway.

"Abdul, please tell us your full name, place of birth, and your reason for visiting the United States," Johnson asked.

"My name is Abdul Hussein Salaamed. I was born in the mountains of Yemen in a small village called Asal Ali in 1993. I originally first came to the United States in 2014 to attend the University of California at

Berkeley. I returned to the US in July of this year to complete my University studies."

"When did you leave the United States?" Johnson asked.

"I left May 15, 2018 to visit my family in Yemen."

"When you left the United States, where did you fly to?"

"I flew to Frankfurt Germany from San Francisco."

"How did you get from Germany to Yemen?"

Gladden held up his hand.

"I invoke the 5th Amendment and decline to answer," Abdul said.

"According to your Declaration you family was killed...."

"I abject," Gladden said. "You have no evidence to support that Abdul wrote the Declaration."

"It was found in his possession after he was arrested and searched."

"Did you advise him of his rights before he was searched?"

"Yes," Fred answered. "We have a recording of the recitation of his Miranda rights."

Gladden smiled and placed his hand out. "Thank you, please continue."

"Was your family killed in Yemen by a bomb dropped by a Saudi Arabia plane?"

Abdul's face hardened as he turned to Gladden, who shook his head. "I decline to answer in accordance with my 5th Amendment rights."

"Where were you on the night of September 25, 2018?" Johnson asked.

"In a room at the El Rey motel in Santa Fe, New Mexico."

"And what were you doing there?"

"Sleeping for the night."

"Why did you check-in under the name of Sidney Wallace rather than your real name?"

"I invoke my 5th Amendment right not to answer."

Fred leaned forward after nodding to Johnson. "We have evidence that your entered the United States on July 18, 2018 using a German passport with the name, Hans Zimmer. Seems strange you would enter on a false passport when you had a student visa in your Abdul Salaamed, Yemen passport." When Abdul started to answer, Fred said. "I know you are going to invoke your 5th Amendment rights. Save your breath." Fred leaned even closer "After I arrested you, I told you that I believed your reasons for blowing up the nuclear waste at Tech Area 54 were undertaken for what you thought was a noble purpose. I said that your actions would probably lead to results contrary to your purpose. Do you remember this? This denial defense seems contrary to your wish to bring attention to the US support of the bombing of Yemen by Saudi Arabia and the United Emirates."

Gladden clapped his hands. "Very good, Agent Samson. That was quite a speech, but completely wasted on me or my client. Shall we get on with questioning?"

Fred saw the confusion in Abdul's face despite Abdul's attempt to keep his face expressionless. Abdul was going along with his attorney's defense that the government's case lacked any real evidence against Abdul. He doubted that Abdul wanted in his heart to be found innocent. Nevertheless, without some additional evidence the case against Abdul looked shaky to say the least.

Fred called Maggie soon after he arrived at his New York apartment from his return flight from Albuquerque. "Hi Maggie, I'm back. Do you have plans tonight?"

"No... aren't you tired from your flight?"

"Tired is not the half of it. I need to unload my thoughts. I know this is selfish of me. I thought I'd get some Chinese take away. Will you come over?"

"Oh, Fred you sound awful. Of course I'll come over."

Fred felt relief when the buzzer rang and rushed to hit the relay to open the downstairs lobby entrance door. He needed to get his thoughts off his chest. Maggie had the innate ability to listen to him and open new ways of looking at things. He didn't know why first seeing Abdul with Rasheed had thrown him for such a loop. There was something about the handsome man that stirred his interest the first moment he had laid eyes on him.

In his long career no other case or incident gripped his psyche so strongly. Of course no other case was as horrific. The results of the radiation release would cause many deaths over many years to come. What could he have done differently to stop Abdul? If Mary had come with him that day at the Empire State Building, she could have followed Abdul? If they had tracked Abdul's movements, they could have arrested him before the attack. Having Mary stay and watch Rasheed's apartment had been a fatal mistake.

Fred heard the elevator and opened his door. He smiled as he watched Maggie approach, feeling blessed that he had met her, and that they had grown so close in such a short time. He was in love. "I'm so happy you could come."

Maggie looked ravishing in her sleeveless forest green V-neck dress and matching shoes. Her green eye shadow highlighted the green tint of her hazel eyes. The sway of her ample hips reminded him of the feel of those hips against his. His excitement rose like the soaring temperature of a noon-day desert.

She was silent as she stepped close to him and kissed him. "Glad you're back. I smell the Chinese from here." She hooked her arm in his and pulled him into the apartment, pushing her rear to close the door and kissing him again. "Tell me all about it."

Fred placed his arm around her back and escorted her to the brown leather couch where the coffee table hosted an ice bucket with a bottle of Pinot Gris. He poured each a glass of wine, and they clinked glasses. "Cheers. I don't know where to begin." He took another sip of wine. "The meeting with Jim Johnson, Assistant District Federal Attorney, was awful. The case against Abdul looks very flimsy with no hard evidence that Abdul is the person, who fired the rockets at Tech Area 54. When I arrested Abdul, I sensed he was relieved to be caught. He's going along with his attorney, Marvin Gladden, who seems intent on sowing enough doubt that Abdul didn't fire the rockets to get him acquitted." He placed his wine glass on the table and leaned back.

"I think Gladden is going to insinuate that the Freedom Militia members were the perpetrators of the rocket firing."

"But you have his Declaration."

"That's about the only evidence. Unfortunately there are no viable finger prints on the three copies of the Declaration."

"What about his attempt to go to Mexico or Canada?"

"All circumstantial."

Fred ran through the lack of evidence, and how he had confronted Abdul in the deposition to no avail. They ate the Chinese food at his dining table. Fred asked about her work and if she'd been out to any movies or plays. She hadn't. Going to events without him seemed unfulfilling, she told him. After dinner and a small glass of cognac, they retired to the bedroom. Their coupling was passionate and they held each other until Maggie fell asleep with a beatific smile on her lips. Fred watched her chest rise and fall as he gazed at her full breasts. He had not thought of any sterling new ideas on how he could insure Abdul was convicted. He did feel more relaxed after talking the situation over with Maggie and feeling the warmth of her body against him. If only he could get Abdul to confess.

CHAPTER 39

"Ladies and gentlemen of the jury," Jim Johnson began his opening remarks as he approached the jury box to stand erect, unsmiling. "The prosecution will prove beyond a shadow of doubt that the accused, Abdul Salaamed, did plan and willfully attack the Los Alamos National Laboratory Tech Area 54 on September 25, 2018 with rockets from a 153-MK SMAW Mod 2, shoulder-mounted multipurpose assault weapon, killing 15 people immediately, releasing stored spent nuclear waste debris that sickened untold more with radiation, and fleeing arrest with interstate flight. Five more people have died subsequent to the attack from radiation poisoning, and more are in critical condition. The accused was possibly aided in the attack by Steve Moore and Ray Osborn, members of the Colorado Springs Freedom Militia, who both have been charged with providing material support to a terrorist."

Johnson paused a few seconds to let his statement sink in. "The prosecution is seeking the death penalty for Abdul Salaamed." He walked down the length of the jury box, making eye contact with each juror, and returned to the center. "I am confident that once you hear the evidence against Abdul Salaamed, you will find the accused guilty on all charges. Thank you."

Abdul watched the jury's reaction to Johnson's statement. They all looked serious and several glanced over at Abdul as Johnson was talking. The statement was short and concise. He wondered how Gladden would counteract such a damning opening statement.

Marvin Gladden, dressed in his tailored blue suit, flecked with gray, looking like a male model, approached the jury box and stood a few feet away in silence, surveying the six men and six women, three of whom, one male and two female, were African American, and four, two male and two female were Hispanic.

Abdul watched Gladden, knowing that Gladden believed he had been quite successful in the jury selection. He had told Abdul that he would have preferred more women on the jury and knew several of the men were more conservative than he would have liked, but overall Gladden thought this was a jury he could influence. Abdul liked Gladden's air of confidence and hoped the airing of Abdul's history would eventually result in the Americans stopping their support for the Saudi bombing campaign in Yemen, but had no illusions about acquittal, expecting his conviction was just a matter of time.

"Ladies and gentlemen of the jury, you have a solemn duty to listen carefully to the evidence— real evidence and not sensational rhetoric— and decide whether Abdul Salaamed is guilty of the charges against him," Gladden began his opening speech in his strong stentorian voice. "You heard Assistant Federal District Attorney, Jim Johnson, proclaim that he would prove beyond a shadow of a doubt that my client, Abdul Salaamed, a native-born Yemen citizen, is guilty of the charges brought against him." Gladden walked slowly a third of the way down in front of the jury box railing, then slowly pivoted to the jury. "Abdul has pleaded not guilty to the charges." He paused, walked another third down the jury box, and then swept his eyes from one end of the jury box to the other. "The case against Abdul is circumstantial at best. The prosecution has no real evidence that Abdul committed the heinous acts for which he is charged."

Gladden paused, then raised his voice. "Yes... no real evidence." He continued walking in front of the jury box to the end of the jury box, then turned and moved back to the middle. "The defense will show that Abdul Salaamed is being used as a scapegoat because he is a Muslim from Yemen. We all know what the current climate in the United States of America is toward Muslims." He nodded his head, adopting a solemn expression of slightly scrunched face. "Abdul Salaamed is not guilty of the charges against him." He stepped back keeping his intense gaze on the jury. "Please bear in mind that the prosecution must prove the charges against Abdul Salaamed beyond a reasonable doubt."

Gladden stepped closer to the railing and leaned forward. "Beyond a reasonable doubt— beyond— a reasonable— doubt." He stood straight. "The doubts in this case are massive." He raised his hands in front of him, palms facing each other his long arms outstretched, and gave them a shake. "Massive!" He then stepped back from the railing. "I am confident that you will find Abdul Salaamed not guilty of the charges against him. Thank you."

Abdul thought Gladden's opening remarks had made quite an impression on the jury. Gladden's regal bearing and well-chosen words seemed to hold the jury's interest. They followed his peregrinations with rapt attention, watching his performance, seemingly mesmerized. For the first time Abdul thought Gladden might be able to sow enough doubt that he could be acquitted. Did he really want to be acquitted?

Johnson called Fred Sampson as his first witness. Fred in a navy blue suit took his seat in the witness chair and was sworn in. "Agent Fred Sampson, you arrested Abdul Salaamed on October 16, 2018." Johnson announced. "Please tell the court how this came about."

Fred explained the arrival of Abdul as Hans Zimmer in New York City, the various possible sightings on security cameras across the country, the attendance of Hans Zimmer at the Nuclear Watch meeting in Albuquerque that revealed his real name, resulting in the raising of security precautions at nuclear facilities in New Mexico and initiating the intensified hunt for Abdul. After the explosions in Los Alamos at Tech Area 54, the FBI hunt for Abdul became the most important goal for the Agency and himself.

When the FBI learned of the discovery of the abandoned MK-153 SMAW and the Declaration mailed from El Paso, the hunt for Abdul was concentrated on the Mexican border. A possible sighting of Abdul disguised as a Mexican in El Paso and the counterfeit driver's license purchase solidified their expectation that Abdul was trying to leave the US. When Fred was notified of the sighting of Abdul in Salt Lake City, he suspected that Abdul was heading for the Canadian border.

He and Agent Sunu chartered a flight to Great Falls, and took a helicopter flight back down I-15 hoping to find Abdul. When they discovered Abdul driving the stolen Honda Civic, they stopped and arrested him, discovering a copy of the Declaration in his pocket.

After Fred's lengthy statement, Johnson looked at the jury with a satisfied smile. "Thank you Agent

Sampson," Johnson said as he stepped out from his table "May I approach the bench, Your Honor.?"

With the ascent of the Judge, Jim Johnson walked to the Bench, carrying a sheaf of paper, and the SMAW. "Your Honor, I would like to enter into evidence all the photographs that Agent Samson has referenced in his testimony, the three copies of the Declaration, and the MK 153 Mod 2 SMAW and two rockets." Johnson handed the paper evidence exhibits to the Judge and placed the SMAW and rockets on the table in front of the Judge's bench.

The Judge accepted the papers, enumerated all the evidential exhibits and entered them into evidence.

"Thank you again, Agent Sampson," Johnson said. "I've no further questions."

As Gladden stood to cross examine, the Judge spoke, "Considering the time and amount of evidence entered, I am adjourning the court for today. Counselor Gladden you will have your chance for cross examination tomorrow." He turned to Fred. "Agent Sampson you are excused."

Fred left the stand and walked to his seat behind Jim Johnson.

The Judge banged his gavel. "The court is adjourned until 9:00AM tomorrow."

Abdul thought Agent Sampson had laid out the evidence succinctly and well. He expected the jury believed the Agent's testimony. He admired the Agent's dedication, remembering well the day in the pouring rain he was apprehended. He wondered if the Agent was instrumental in Abdul being tried in open court rather than being shipped off to Guantanamo or kept in prison as an enemy combatant. For that he was profoundly thankful.

After the Judge left the courtroom, Gladden shook Abdul's hand. "I would say that the first day has gone exceedingly well. I know being isolated in jail is no fun, but keep up your spirits. Tomorrow is a new day." Abdul thanked Gladden and was led away.

Outside the sun was bright, and Abdul enjoyed the warmth on his face as he was ushered out of the court building. There seemed to be even more people milling about than in the morning when he had arrived. The mood of the crowd appeared to have an almost carnival air. He had a guard on each arm, two guards in front and two behind, each heavily armed in bullet proof vests and helmets. When he came down the steps, the media people rushed toward him, their spokespersons calling their questions and thrusting their microphones at him. He hurried along, ignoring their questions, and was relieved once he was inside the van.

He was glad of the media circus, exulting that the news of the trial was entering the living rooms of most Americans and highlighting what was happening in Yemen. He doubted that the coverage would quickly lead to the US stopping support for the Saudi bombing, but one could hope.

CHAPTER 40

After the Judge called the trial to order in the morning, he nodded at Gladden. "Counselor Gladden, would you like to cross examine, Agent Fred Sampson?"

"Most certainly, Your Honor." Gladden stood and slowly surveyed the courtroom while Fred moved to the witness stand. The Judge reminded Fred he was still under oath. Gladden studied Fred in silence, a few moments from the defendant's table before asking the Judge's permission to approach. He walked slowly to the witness box without expression. "Agent Sampson, did you have any evidence when you first saw an unknown man, you photographed talking to Rasheed Malika, at the Empire State Building viewing platform that the man was a possible terrorist?"

"None, other than the fact that he was speaking to Rasheed Malika, who we suspected was leader of a terrorist cell, and we had been following him for months. Rasheed was subsequently arrested for conspiracy to commit an act of terrorism and involvement in an illegal bomb making factory. He has been tried and convicted and is serving a twenty year prison sentence."

"Do any of the photographic exhibits entered into evidence as possibly being Abdul Salaamed, except for the passport photograph of Hans Zimmer, the photograph of the man talking to Rasheed Malika, and the driver's license photograph for Sidney Wallace clearly and categorically depict Abdul Salaamed?"

"No."

"Could they be photographs of other individuals?"

"Possibly."

"Did you find any fingerprints of Abdul Salaamed on the three copies of the Declaration entered into evidence?"

"No."

"Did you find any fingerprints on the MK-153 SMAW or the rockets abandoned on a hill north of Tech Area 54 at the Los Alamos National Laboratory?"

"Yes. We found no prints on the MK-153 SMAW, but we did find fingerprints of Specialist Steve Moore on the rockets abandoned."

"So you found no prints of Abdul Salaamed."

"No."

"Do you have any witnesses that saw Abdul Salaamed on September 25, 2018 in the vicinity of Los Alamos or Tech Area 54 of the Los Alamos National Laboratory?"

"No."

"How then did you feel warranted in arresting Abdul Salaamed for the attack on Tech Area 54?"

"Based on the testimony of Steve Moore that he gave the stolen MK-153 SMAW to a Sidney Wallace, who Abdul Salaamed was posing as, and the discovery of the Declaration that was sent to the Albuquerque Journal newspaper, where a named Abdul Salaamed claimed responsibility in the Declaration for attacking Tech Area 54, we believed we had enough evidence to arrest Abdul Salaamed. The sighting of Abdul Salaamed posing as a Mexican named Javier Valdez trying to buy a counterfeit driver's license in El Paso, added to our suspicions that Abdul Salaamed had fired the rockets at the Los Alamos National Laboratory Tech Area 54."

"Is it possible that someone else wrote the Declaration to implicate Abdul Salaamed?"

Johnson stood up. "I abject. Counselor Gladden is asking the witness to make a conclusion that the witness cannot objectively make."

"Your Honor, Fred Sampson has made quite a few conclusions concerning Abdul Salaamed," Gladden countered. "He is the arresting officer, and I would think he's quite capable of making a conclusion about the Declaration."

"I'll allow it. Agent Sampson, please answer the question."

"I suppose it is possible, but, if so, it seems strange that Abdul would be carrying the Declaration in his pocket when he was arrested."

"So you have answered that it is possible someone else wrote the Declaration and not Abdul Salaamed. Is that correct?" Gladden turned to the jury while he waited for Fred's answer.

"Yes."

"Perhaps there is a perfectly good explanation why Abdul Salaamed would have a Declaration he did not write in his pocket when he was arrested. Would you agree?"

"I don't know what that explanation could be."

"But you would agree that it is possible."

"Perhaps."

"Thank you, Agent Sampson," Gladden said as he turned to the jury with a big smile. "No further questions."

Abdul thought Gladden's cross examination of Fred was masterful. He had gotten Fred to admit he had no evidence that Abdul had fired the SMAW other than Steve Moore's testimony of giving Abdul the SMAW and the Declaration. Abdul was thankful he had wiped the SMAW clean. Abandoning the SMAW had been a colossal error. Had he unconsciously left the SMAW and rockets on the hill on purpose?

Johnson called Steve Moore as his next witness. Steve was a bundle of nerves as Johnson questioned him. Steve's explanation for why he stole the SMAW seemed infantile. Steve came across as a very conflicted, damaged individual. He suspected Gladden would tear him to pieces.

When Johnson finished questioning Steve, Gladden, after asking to approach, walked slowly to the witness box keeping his eyes on Steve with a deadpan expression. "Steve Moore, you testified that you stole the MK-153 SMAW because you thought it would be fun for the Freedom Militia to have and would come in handy for the coming civil war," Gladden said. "Why do you think there is a coming civil war?"

Steve closed his eyes part way and leaned back, shifting his eyes from side to side. He started to speak, but hesitated. He looked down at his hands, clutched together in his lap, before looking up at Gladden with intense worry. "Well... ah... because of the strife between people. Blacks, Mexicans, and Muslims, are arming themselves with the help of the Jews. Christianity is in danger. The country has fallen into ungodliness. We can't even trust the military. The Deep State is trying to get our President impeached. All hell is gonna break lose."

Gladden stepped back from Steve and looked over at the jury with a bemused expression of wide eyes and grin. "I see. That was an ominous and worrying statement. Mr. Moore, I take it you are extremely worried for the country?"

"I am."

Gladden moved closer to Steve. "Wasn't it your idea, Steve, to steal the MK-153 SMAW in order to get ready for the revolution?" he asked forcefully.

"No... it wasn't," Steve exclaimed. "I hadn't even thought about sneakin' out no SMAW 'til Sidney asked about gettin' one." His expression looked like he had been caught at school cheating on an exam.

"Are you and the Freedom Militia trying to frame Abdul? Wasn't it the Freedom Militia's plan to attack the Los Alamos Laboratory with the MK-153 SMAW? The arrival of Abdul, who you and your compatriots figured out was an Arab, gave you the perfect scapegoat."

Steve twisted in his seat, almost as if he was desperate to go to the toilet. "That's not it at all. Sidney was the one, who wanted to steal the SMAW."

"You testified that you stole the 153-MK SMAW and seven rockets, did you not."

"Yes." Steve's eyes were full of tears.

"But you want us to believe it was Abdul as Sidney, who wanted you to steal the MK-153."

"Yes." Steve looked at the Judge as if he expected the Judge to help him.

"Do you often do what other people want?"

"No... but Sidney was one of us."

"By us, you mean Ray and you?"

"Yes, and the rest of the Militia."

"So the rest of the Freedom Militia were all in on the plan to attack the Los Alamos National Laboratory?"

"No... we didn't plan no attack on the Laboratory."

"Oh, did you have another target in mind, but changed it to the Los Alamos Lab?"

"No." Steve jerked forward his face white. "We weren't gonna attack anyone with the SMAW."

"Then why did you steal it?"

"I already told ya, we wanted it for the comin' revolution."

"I see. Do you suffer from PTSD from your combat experience in Iraq? Does your PTSD affect your memory? Have you not told us the complete story? Did you think blowing up nuclear waste at Los Alamos would hasten the revolution?"

"No. You're puttin' words in my mouth" Steve looked imploringly at the Judge. "I do suffer from PTSD, but it don't make my memory no good."

Johnson stood up. "I object, Your Honor. Councilor Gladden is badgering the witness."

"Objection sustained. Counselor Gladden, can we dispense with this barrage of questions. Ask your questions one at a time and let the witness answer."

"No further questions, Your Honor."

Abdul felt rather sorry for Steve. Gladden had tied him in knots. He was thankful that he hadn't killed the unfortunate man. Steve's country had ruined him in Iraq for no other reason than the pursuit of oil and power.

Ray Osborn was called as the prosecution's next witness. Ray walked to the witness stand, his shoulders back as if he was on parade, his balloon stomach sucked in. Johnson had Ray describe how Ray met Abdul as Sidney, and why Ray invited Abdul to stay with him. Ray went on to explain how he obtained a Colorado driver's license from a friend of Ray's, who worked for Department of Motor Vehicles, for a fee of $2,000 for Abdul as Sidney Wallace. He talked about his membership in the Freedom Militia and his reasons why he had joined the Militia. Ray spoke with conviction as he kept staring at Abdul with obvious disdain throughout his testimony.

When it was Gladden's turn to cross examine, he strolled up to the witness box to stand in front of Ray blocking his view of Abdul. He straightened his tie and stood staring intensely at Ray a few seconds. It was obvious from Ray's grimace, he didn't like Gladden's antics.

"Ray Osborn, you testified that Abdul stayed at your trailer for nearly a month," Gladden said. "During this time, you testified that you never suspected Abdul Salaamed as Sidney Wallace was an Arab. Personally, I find it hard to understand how Abdul fooled you. How was he able to fool you?"

Ray narrowed his eyes at Gladden and moved to the edge of his chair. "He talked just like us and all. He don't look like no damn Arab."

"How is it that a young man from Yemen, who spent a scant four years in the United States, could talk like you?"

"I don't know how he did it, but he did it. Maybe he practiced and stuff."

"Do you dislike Arabs and Muslims in general?"

"I do. They're trying to take over the country to impose Sharia law."

Gladden smiled at the jury. "Do you realize there are 3.5 million Muslims of all ages in the US and this is a scant 1.1% of the population? How could such a small population take over the country?"

"They may be a small percentage now, but they breed like rabbits and more want to come. We're lucky we have a President who wants to keep them out. They're a bunch of terrorists." Ray straightened in his chair with a smug expression, obviously happy with his answer.

Gladden nodded and moved to the side so Ray could see Abdul. "Isn't it true that you suspected Sidney Wallace to be a Muslim?"

"No." Ray's response was loud and vehement. "I never knew he was a Muslim. I wouldn't let no Muslim stay with me."

"Was it your idea for Steve Moore to steal the MK-153 SMAW?"

"No, it wasn't." Ray replied loudly, gritting his teeth as he lurched forward, glaring at Gladden.

"The Militia Chapter has an M18 recoilless rifle. Have you ever fired the recoilless rifle?"

Ray settled back, relaxing somewhat. "Yes, once."

"Why would the Militia need such a weapon?"

"To defend ourselves and have fun shooting it." Ray looked over at the jury with a smirk.

"I see... for the coming revolution I suspect," Gladden said softly then raised his voice, placing his hand against the witness box railing and leaning toward Ray.

"Didn't you want a more modern weapon that could compliment the recoilless rifle when the so called revolution began?"

"Hell, no." Ray nearly shouted, grabbing the railing of the witness box with a sneer. "You damn asshole. You better stop tryin' to put words in my mouth and tryin' to confuse me like you did Steve. I don't have to take your shit."

"Mr. Osborn, please just answer the questions and refrain from profanity in my courtroom," the Judge admonished. "Or you will be held in contempt."

Ray stared at the judge, his reddened face contorted. Abdul thought Gladden had been masterful in inducing Ray's anger. Ray settled back in the witness chair with a snarl.

"Mr. Osborn, the FBI confiscated a number of illegal weapons from your trailer. I also learned that you have a rifle range on your property. You like firing weapons it seems."

"Yeah, so what?"

"You were glad when Steve Moore stole the MK-153 SMAW and couldn't wait to shoot it, was it not?"

"I didn't even know Steve stole a SMAW. Hell, I didn't even know what a SMAW was."

"I understand you subscribe to a number of weapon magazines. In your reading, you never came across an article on SMAWs?"

"I may have. I call them rocket launchers."

"Oh. I'll rephrase the question. Were you anxious to shoot the rocket launcher after Steve stole it?"

"Are you deaf?" Ray grabbed the railing, his knuckles white from the pressure. "I didn't know Steve stole a rocket launcher." Ray looked as if he wanted to throw himself at Gladden.

Gladden said he had no more questions and turned his back on Ray. The judge excused Ray and called recess for the day, announcing the court would resume at 9:00 AM.

Johnson began the morning with testimony from David Snyder, the Colorado Springs Militia Commander, establishing that Snyder had been the Commander for three years and had approved Sidney Wallace's application to become a Militia member. The Commander testified that in his few interactions with Sidney Wallace, Sidney did not raise any suspicions that he was anything other than what he purported to be— a patriot seeking camaraderie with other like-minded individuals.

The Commander admitted that the Chapter owned a M18 Korean War recoilless rifle. He wasn't sure where or when the organization obtained the weapon. It was old and finding ammunition for it was difficult. When he joined the Freedom Militia five years ago, the group already had the weapon. After he became Commander, he received the M18 from the previous Commander who had recently died, and had stored the weapon at his ranch. The weapon hadn't been used in over a year and was essentially mothballed. Johnson thanked Snyder and said he had no more questions.

Gladden rose to cross examine. "Mr. Snyder, why do you suspect the Colorado Spring Freedom Militia possessed this M18 recoilless rifle?

"As I've said, I do not know where the Militia obtained the recoilless rifle."

"That was not my question, Mr. Snyder. What purpose could the Freedom Militia possibly have for such a destructive anti-tank weapon?"

Johnson called from his seat, "Objection, calls for a conclusion the witness has no knowledge to answer."

"I'll rephrase," Gladden announced. "Why would the Freedom Militia continue to keep such a destructive weapon?"

"We on past occasions, have fired the M18 weapon for fun at my ranch. We are interested in weapons of all sorts and enjoy shooting them."

"I understand that the FBI found at your ranch not only the recoilless rifle, but also thirty other rifles, many of which were illegal, fully-automatic rifles. This seems like quite an arsenal for just fun. For what purpose have you amassed such an arsenal?"

"I wouldn't call it an arsenal. I collect weapons. It's a hobby of mine."

"So you did not suspect Sidney because of his slightly darker complexion of being Arabic?"

Johnson stood. "I object. The question was asked and answered."

"I'll allow it," the Judge said. "Please answer the question, Mr. Snyder."

"No, I did not suspect Sidney Wallace was Arabic."

"What is the mission of the Colorado Springs Freedom Militia?"

"We are a patriotic group, who work to influence legislation for the protection of the Nation, and we train to counteract any insurrection that would arise."

"Sounds like a private police force."

Johnson stood up. "Objection...."

"Sustained," the Judge announced. "You know better that to make such opinionated statements in my courtroom."

"I beg your forgiveness." Gladden bowed to the Judge before turning back to David Snyder. "Mr. Snyder, are you familiar with the novel, *The Turner Diaries?*"

"Yes."

"Do you believe the book could describe a real future situation in the United States where it would be necessary to eliminate all non-white people?"

"I don't know."

"Does your chapter of the Freedom Militia have any non-white members?"

"Not at present."

"Do you discriminate against non-white members?"

"No."

"Then why do you not have any non-white members?"

"Since I've been Commander of the Chapter, none have applied.

Gladden said he had no more questions of the witness and resumed his seat. The Judge adjourned the court for the lunch break.

In the afternoon Johnson called Hidalgo to testify about the Texas driver's license he obtained for Abdul as Javier. Abdul was surprised that Gladden did not cross examine Hidalgo. He thought Gladden would go after Hidalgo for his illegal activities and for trying to attack Abdul, but realized that any cross examination would offer little in the way of casting a shadow on Abdul's guilt.

Johnson's next witness was the motel clerk from Salt Lake City. The clerk had been very cagey in not showing any sign that he had recognized Abdul. He wondered what he would have done differently if he had known the clerk recognized him. He could have taken a different route, gone west instead of straight north, and searched for a different area to cross into Canada. If so, he might have made his escape. He was again surprised Gladden did not cross examine the witness. Gladden could have questioned the veracity of the clerk's recognition of Abdul. Not that it mattered. The clerk's recognition had no real importance in proving Abdul was guilty of the attack. It only established how they knew he was heading for Canada. He had to hand it to the FBI agent Fred Sampson. He had connected the sighting in Salt Lake to Abdul trying to escape to Canada very quickly and had acted with decisiveness.

"Your Honor, the prosecution rests," Johnson said with a smile for the jury. Abdul thought the smile was forced.

When the Judge adjourned the court for the day, Abdul was relieved. He wanted the trial to be over as soon as possible. Now it would be Gladden's turn. He thought Gladden had expertly sown the seed of doubt with his cross examinations. He began to believe

Gladden just might get him acquitted. If he was acquitted he'd probably be deported back to Yemen. He could then continue to fight for Yemen's independence. Did he want to continue to fight the war? He had succeeded in getting his Declaration disseminated and had struck against the US war machine. There wasn't much else he could achieve if he was freed.

CHAPTER 41

Fred watched Gladden gently slap Abdul on the shoulder after the Judge left the courtroom. "The prosecution has failed miserably in proving the charges against you," Gladden said. "Relax and try to get a good night's sleep. I'll put you on the stand tomorrow and I need you looking calm and collected."

"Okay, Mr. Gladden," Abdul replied with little enthusiasm.

Fred thought Abdul seemed solemn and not as happy as one would expect someone, who thought he could be acquitted. Perhaps he was exhausted. Fred felt wrung out himself, and he wasn't staying in a prison cell. Or perhaps Abdul in his heart did not want to be found not guilty. In any case, Gladden was right— the prosecution's case was not looking good.

"A new suit will be delivered to you at the jail tonight for tomorrow morning," Gladden said. "I want you sharp and confident. You'll be brought to the courthouse at 8:00 AM and we will have some time to go over your testimony again. I'm sure you'll do well."

Abdul thanked Gladden and shook hands before being led away. Fred was worried that Abdul could be acquitted. If so, Fred and the FBI would look like amateurs. He doubted that Abdul had planned it this way, but the circumstances aligned very favorably for Abdul Salaamed. He waited for Johnson, who after packing up his brief case, walked like he wore a 200-pound backpack.

"Jim, I thought you presented the case against Abdul well," Fred said, hoping to encourage Johnson. It wasn't

Johnson's fault that they didn't have more concrete evidence. "Too bad we didn't have fingerprints. You did your best."

"Thanks," Johnson said. "Gladden was good at the cross examination. Abdul sure found some willing idiots in the Freedom Militia. I myself wonder how Abdul fooled these men. I must admit that Abdul must have been extremely masterful in his act as a Militia member. Seems he had them completely fooled. Too bad they weren't better witnesses. It's amazing how Abdul found and infiltrated these imbiciles."

"Yeah, Abdul is a cunning individual," Fred said. "Just imagine what he could have done for Yemen if he had just completed his degree and gone home."

"Let's get a drink," Sunu said. "I'm thirsty as hell and want to put this day behind me."

"Sounds good," Fred said.

"I'll take a rain check," Johnson replied. "I need to work on my summation. That will be my last chance at a conviction. It will need to be damn good."

"I understand, Jim," Fred said. "See you in the morning."

Fred and Sunu walked to the local bar that the court personnel frequented. Sunu went to the packed bar for drinks while Fred went to the last vacant booth.

Sunu placed the drinks down and slid into the booth. He picked up his Manhattan and took a large swallow. "Christ that was difficult to watch. I think we're fucked."

"It's not over yet," Fred said, but his voice lacked conviction.

"No, but the defense has rested with little real evidence against Abdul."

"I think the Declaration is the key."

"Yeah, but there is no concrete evidence that Abdul wrote it." Sunu took another long drink. "Shit we even got the envelope that Abdul sent it in. The only prints were the newspaper staff. Abdul must have worn gloves." Sunu finished his drink. "Jesus, Fred you haven't touched your drink." Sunu pointed to Fred's glass. "Don't blame yourself. Drink up. I'll get another round."

"Sure," Fred said and pulled a twenty from his wallet and slid it across to Sunu. "Make mine a double." Fred clasped his glass of Irish whiskey and downed it in one gulp.

Sunu slipped back against the booth in surprise. "Double it is."

Fred believed the Declaration was the key to convicting Abdul. Abdul had put his heart and soul into the Declaration. He wondered what alternate explanation Gladden was going to use as to why Abdul had the Declaration in his pocket. Gladden had introduced the possibility of a reason that Abdul would have the Declaration in his pocket even though he supposedly hadn't composed the Declaration. He wondered what the reason would be. He had to hand it to Gladden. He was an excellent courtroom actor and played his role well. Leaving the reason hanging was shrewd. The jury would be wondering what the reason was as well. Abdul was lucky that he had Gladden as his attorney.

CHAPTER 42

After the Judge called the court into session, Gladden called Rasheed Malika as his first witness. "Mr. Rasheed Malika," Gladden began, still seated at the table next to Abdul, "do you know the accused, Abdul Salaamed?" He pointed to Abdul.

"I do not know him. We did meet briefly at the viewing platform at the top of the Empire State Building when he kindly picked up a newspaper I had dropped. I asked if he wanted the paper, since I was through with it, and he said yes, thanked me, and left. That was the last and only time I saw the accused."

Gladden rose, asked to approach, and walked to the witness stand. "Did you know Abdul Salaamed as a terrorist?"

"No, I did not know the accused at all."

"Thank you, Mr. Malika. I have no further questions."

Jim Johnson rose to cross examine. "Rasheed Malika, you have been convicted of conspiracy to commit a terrorist act and as an accessory in a bomb making factory. You are currently serving a 20 year sentence in prison. Is that correct?"

"Yes, but I'm innocent."

"Why in light of your conviction should we believe anything you say?" Johnson waved away Rasheed as he started to speak. "I've no further questions, Your Honor." He walked back to his seat.

Gladden called a clerk from the University of California Berkeley as a witness, who testified that Abdul had a spotless record at the University and had

3.9 grade average with only one B in his freshman year. Abdul was on a full scholarship and worked in the Commons Food Hall.

Gladden next called to the stand a student, John Donnelly, who had worked at the Commons Food Hall with Abdul. The student testified that Abdul was a hard worker and friendly. Abdul had never mentioned anything about radical Islam to him and was always polite to students, even those who gave Abdul a hard time.

Johnson had not cross-examined the University clerk, but rose to cross examine the student worker. "Mr. Donnelly, how long did you work with Abdul Salaamed?"

"Three years."

"Did Mr. Salaamed speak with an accent?"

"He did when he first started, but he picked up the vernacular and the way most students talked, and, by the end of the first year, he sounded like an American."

"Do you know any other students who speak with an accent?"

"Yes, several."

"And do these students still speak with an accent."

"Yes."

"Would you say that Abdul's skill in changing his speech patterns and losing his accent was good?"

"Yes."

"Thank you, Mr. Donnelly. No further questions."

Gladden stood. "If I may, Your Honor, I would like to redirect some questions to Mr. Donnelly."

"You have the floor, Counselor Gladden."

"Mr. Donnelly, did Abdul ever confide in you why he changed his speech and did away with his accent?"

"Yes, he said he wanted to fit in and not stand out."

"Did you think his motives were unusual?"

"No, if I had the skills I would have done the same thing. Arabs and Muslims are not exactly welcomed in the US."

Gladden thanked the student and announced he had no more questions. Next, Gladden called Cindy Clayton to the stand. Abdul stiffened. Gladden had not told him he would be calling Cindy as a witness. Abdul felt he had done enough to ruin Cindy's life. Her testimony would open her up to immense scrutiny and probable humiliation on social media and in the news. He wished he could stop Gladden, but knew he would have to endure the agony of her testimony. He wanted to scream.

As soon as Cindy was sworn in and the judge gave permission to approach, Gladden strolled toward the witness, who looked stunning in her tailored dark green suit, her golden hair shinning in the courtroom lights and her upright posture denoting confidence. "Cindy Clayton, how long have you known Abdul Salaamed?"

"Four years."

"Would you explain in your own words how you met Abdul and what your relationship was with Abdul Salaamed?"

"I met Abdul my sophomore year at the University of California at Berkeley." Cindy's calm presence and soothing voice was well received by the jury. "I had seen him working in the Commons Food Hall and had been told he was from Yemen, but had never talked to him.

We met by accident when we bumped into each other at the library, and I dropped my books. He helped me pick up my books and was very apologetic when it was really my fault we bumped together because I wasn't looking where I was going." She laughed slightly, but recovered her calm demeanor quickly. "I thought he was handsome and was intrigued by the fact he was from Yemen. I was very much against our government's support for the Saudi bombing campaign against Yemen and told him of my opposition to the bombing. I invited him to the War Resisters League meeting that evening, which I often attended, thinking he might be interested in learning about the War Resisters League. After the meeting, we had coffee together."

Cindy paused and glanced at Abdul. "I liked Abdul's company and thought he was charming. He didn't seem to have many friends and apparently never went out to entertainment venues. I thought he was missing out on those aspects of college life, so I invited him to come with me the next evening to hear a friend of mine play guitar. He enjoyed the musical evening and thanked me profusely. After that we went to many music venues and plays together. He was an interesting person, and we grew close."

Abdul fought back the tears that wanted to erupt, trying to think of something pleasant to distract him. He envisioned swimming in the Red Sea with his family, but it had little effect in dispelling his sorrow. He squeezed his hands into fists under the table and tried to imagine what would have happened between him and Cindy if the Saudis had never attacked Yemen.

"How would you characterize Abdul as a person?" Gladden asked.

"Abdul is a kind and caring individual, who never espoused violence to me. He was worried for his family in Yemen because of the bombing, starvation, and disease resulting from Saudi Arabian attacks and blockade, but never hinted or ever suggested that he would be interested in terrorism."

"Do you believe Abdul Salaamed could be capable of the charges against him? Do you believe he fired rockets into a nuclear storage facility at the Los Alamos National Laboratory?"

"Definitely not."

"Thank you Miss Clayton. I have no further questions."

Jim Johnson rose and approached Cindy. "Miss Clayton, how would Mr. Salaamed react in your opinion to seeing his family and home blown up by an aerial bomb dropped by a Saudi Arabian airplane?"

"I would imagine he would be devastated and feel great sorrow."

"You do not believe as he wrote in his Declaration that he was out for revenge?"

Gladden jumped up. "I object. The prosecution has not presented any concrete evidence that Abdul Salaamed wrote the Declaration of Revenge."

"I'll rephrase, Your Honor. Miss Clayton considering the Declaration of Revenge that allegedly is attributed to Abdul Salaamed, would you believe it possible that the sentiment in the Declaration would be something Abdul would hold after the bombing of his family?"

"I do not. Much of what is included in the Declaration I believe to be true as far as the US actions in the Middle East, and Abdul might hold similar opinions, but I would never believe Abdul would be responsible for killing innocent people or for that matter anyone. I believe Abdul is a pacifist like myself and abhors violence."

Cindy's statement was like a dagger to Abdul's heart. He had been a pacifist as Cindy purported until that fateful day. No wars were ever stopped by pacifism. How wonderful it would be if someday enough people joined in pacifism to stop the human decent into the evil of war. Could it be possible as John Lennon had sung in *Imagine*?

"Who do you think wrote the Declaration?" Johnson asked.

"I object," Gladden called out as he remained sitting. "Calls for a conclusion from the witness she is not qualified to make."

"Sustained," the Judge announced.

Johnson paused and appeared to be thinking how to proceed. "Witnessing such a horrendous end to one's family could drive many people to revenge. Even a pacifist could want revenge and turn to violence, don't you think?"

Gladden immediately called out, "Objection calls for a conclusion again that the witness is not qualified to make."

"Sustained."

Johnson exhaled audibly and shuffled his feet. "Ms Clayton, if you witnessed someone kill your parents would you want revenge?"

"I would want the perpetrators to be brought to justice, but I would not want to attack the perpetrators.

As a pacifist I would never resort to violence except to protect myself or my friends and family."

"So you would resort to violence?"

"For protection only. I would never initiate violence for revenge."

Abdul was heartened and saddened by Cindy's testimony. He didn't deserve the trust she placed in him. He had profoundly betrayed her. If he hadn't contacted her and attended the Nuclear Watch meeting, the FBI would have never found him.

The last witness called for the defense was Abdul. Abdul dressed in a lustrous gray suit, blue tie, white shirt, and polished black shoes walked to the witness box and was sworn in. His heart sounded like a base drum in his head and his perspiration dripped inside his shirt despite the coolness of the air-conditioned court.

Gladden waited until Abdul was seated a few minutes so the jury could get a good look at the composed handsome man before approaching the witness box. "Abdul, please tell the court why you came to the United States to attend college?"

"My parents and I thought that I would achieve a better education in Europe or the United States than in my country that was already experiencing internal strife." Abdul spoke distinctly with just the hint of an accent. "I dropped out of college in Dharma because of the lack of good teachers, most of whom had fled Yemen. My parents and I looked up to the United States as a country that stood for freedom and equal rights for all people. We were impressed by the election and re-election of President Obama and believed Obama would promote peace around the world."

"Was it your decision then to seek admittance to the University of California at Berkeley?"

"It was a joint decision between my parents and myself. I was somewhat reluctant and worried about going so far away to the United States with the deteriorating situation in Yemen. I thought maybe going to college in Germany or France would be better, but my parents convinced me to go to the United States. The scholarship offered by the University of California at Berkeley was one of the better scholarships offered me."

"Did you like going to the University at Berkeley?"

"Initially I was overwhelmed by being in a country so much different than Yemen. I felt forlorn and missed my home tremendously, but I studied hard and settled in, hoping to make excellent grades and make my family proud."

"You heard Miss Clayton's testimony that she considers you a pacifist like herself. Would you say that was an accurate description?"

Abdul hesitated. He did not want to lie anymore to Cindy, but realized he had to continue the act. "Yes."

"Please describe why you returned to Yemen in May 2018 and how you made the journey."

Abdul explained his growing worry about his family as the situation in Yemen deteriorated, and his decision to go to Yemen to make sure his family was still alive and safe. He described his journey from Sam Francisco to Yemen in detail, and the horrors he saw in the Houthi controlled area. When he finally reached his mountain village and home, he was thankful that his family was alive.

"Abdul, please tell us about the night you saw your home bombed and your family killed."

Abdul grimaced at the question. He knew it was coming, but the mention of that day would always bring up the grief embedded in his heart and mind. He took a deep breath and glanced at the jury before beginning. "I was out in our terraced vineyard in the evening, enjoying the cool mountain air, when I saw a Saudi Arabian plane and heard the descending bomb. My home exploded in a huge fireball. I ran to the house, which was nothing but ruble, and found my Father, Mother, Sister, and Brother dead." Abdul dropped his head into his hands as the tears flooded forth. He saw in his mind his entire decimated family lying in a row after he pulled them from the debris.

Gladden waited a few minutes letting Abdul recover. "What did you do then?"

Abdul raised his head and wiped his tears. "After a funeral ceremony, I buried my family in our vineyard with the help of other villagers and then went to Sana'a. I thought about not returning to the US to complete my degree in electrical engineering, but rather staying to help the people, who were suffering terribly— many starving. I was in a quandary, but ultimately decided my parents would want me to finish my degree and then return to help rebuild Yemen after the war. I purchased an altered German passport with the name Hans Zimmer on the black market in Sana'a. My passport had been destroyed in the bombing. I knew obtaining a replacement passport in my name would be difficult if not impossible. Besides, I knew the Supreme Court had upheld Trump's ban on Yemenis entering the US."

Abdul thought the jury listened to his testimony with great interest. Many of their faces seemed sympathetic. Abdul was beginning to believe that he would be acquitted. He felt happy and sad at the same time. The Freedom Militia would be the next logical perpetrators of the attack. He hated the Militia and would be glad to see many of them go to jail, but worried that the Militia being blamed would detract from his Declaration and his wish to show the American people they needed to stop supporting the Saudis.

"Abdul, why did you stay with Ray Osborn and join the Colorado Springs Chapter of the Freedom Militia?" Gladden asked.

"Militias were something I was interested in. In a country of freedom and prosperity, I found it hard to understand why people joined militias and were training to fight against the government. I did not understand the rationale, and thought by joining them I would learn about the motivation for joining such an organization. I guess you could say it was stupid curiosity." His time with the Militia members had been an anathema, and he still did not fully understand how the Militia members accepted the right-wing lies that led them to such treacherous hateful thoughts.

"When did you expect that they had discovered you were Arabic?"

"It was a gradual suspicion I got. Some of their comments and questions seemed very probing as if they suspected me of something. I came to believe that they had figured out I was an imposter and possibly an Arab. I thought they could get violent so I left."

"How did you leave?"

"I borrowed a vehicle and drove to Santa Fe."

"Why Santa Fe?"

"I had visited Santa Fe with Cindy Clayton one Christmas and had liked the City. It seemed different from most American cities. I loved the surrounding mountains that reminded me of home."

"Why didn't you go directly to Albuquerque to see Cindy?"

"I was planning to go to Albuquerque after I spent a few days in Santa Fe to get my head straight after the ordeal of living amongst the Militia."

"When did you learn about the explosions at the Los Alamos National Laboratory?"

"In Santa Fe, I heard the news on the TV about the explosions in Los Alamos. I thought the Freedom Militia might be the ones, who caused the explosion and worried that they would try to blame the attack on me."

"What did you do then?"

"I decided to try to leave the US by crossing into Mexico in El Paso. In El Paso, I saw on TV that I was being blamed for the explosions. I knew then that my Hans Zimmer passport would be useless, and I had doubts about my Sidney Wallace driver's license. To be able to make a crossing into Mexico, I felt I needed another ID. I paid a man, Hidalgo, who I had met at a bar earlier when I first arrived in El Paso, for a false Texas driver's license in the name Juan Martinez. When I tried to leave the bar with the license, Hidalgo and another man seemed menacing, and I thought they may try to attack and rob me. I made my escape and saw them leave the bar to come after me. I gave up the idea of crossing into Mexico with the Martinez driver's license. I decided to head north and possibly find a way to sneak into Canada. I was stopped and arrested on I-15 in Montana.”

“Why did you have a copy of the Declaration of Revenge, entered into evidence, in your pocket?”

Abdul took several quick breaths. Gladden had come up with the story about why he had the Declaration. He knew it was a brilliant story and would probably drive home to the jury plenty of doubt of his guilt, but for a few seconds he felt ashamed of what he was about to say. “I had found the Declaration hidden in the bottom of my bag when I was packing up to leave Salt Lake City. I knew after reading the Declaration that it was dangerous to me. In my haste to leave and get moving toward Canada, I stuffed the Declaration into my pocket and left.”

“Why didn’t you destroy the Declaration?”

“After reading the Declaration, I was so distraught that I thought I had to leave immediately. If I had been thinking straight, I would have destroyed the Declaration and flushed it down the toilet.”

“What about the copy of the Declaration mailed to the *Albuquerque Journal* and the one found in the abandoned 4Runner vehicle you drove from Colorado Springs to Albuquerque?

“I have no direct knowledge of how the copies ended up in those locations. I suspect someone from the Freedom Militia mailed a copy to the newspaper from El Paso and one of them hid a copy in the 4Runner vehicle before I left.”

CHAPTER 43

Fred had been sitting behind Jim Johnson the entire trial, watching the prosecution of Abdul going down the drain. Gladden had been adept and convincing. Steve and Ray appeared as likely perpetrators of the attack at Los Alamos. Johnson had done a tolerable job, considering what he had to work with. The lack of any fingerprints of Abdul anywhere was unfortunate. The witnesses for the defense had portrayed Abdul in a good light and someone unlikely to stage an attack on the Los Alamos National Laboratory. Cindy Clayton had placed the nail in the coffin for the prosecution and Abdul had driven it home with his calm and believable testimony. Abdul had come across as a likely scapegoat. Some of Abdul's testimony had gaping holes, but there was plenty of doubt that would most likely lead to Abdul's acquittal.

He was sure the jury would acquit Abdul unless Johnson could get Abdul to admit the crime—the only remaining hope. He suspected that Johnson wasn't even going to cross examine Abdul. After Gladden completed his questions of Abdul, Johnson's slumped posture seemed to indicate Johnson's resignation of defeat.

Fred leaned forward and tapped Johnson on the shoulder. "Ask for a 30 minute recess to confer with the arresting agent."

Johnson turned around to stare at Fred. "Why?"

"Just do it," Fred said between grit teeth, his forehead furrowed and his eyes half closed. "If you don't Abdul will walk."

Fred met Johnson in the hall and dragged him to a secluded spot in the long courthouse hallway as the many visitors milled about in groups, the sound of their conversation reverberating off the walls. "Abdul doesn't in his heart want to be acquitted. You need to cross examine him and get him to admit he was the one to fire the rockets."

"And how do you propose I do that? He can call on the 5th Amendment to refuse to answer any meaningful questions. I'm sorry. You and I know he's guilty, but we just didn't have the evidence. Those militia idiots are most likely going to be charged with shooting the rockets. If only we had had one damn Abdul fingerprint." Johnson shook his head and placed his hand on Fred's shoulder. "It's over."

"No way," Fred said vehemently and stepped to Johnson, pushing his face a few inches from Johnson. "You've got to play on his Declaration and his wish for the US to stop supporting the Saudis." Fred realized he was speaking too loudly and lowered his voice. "Abdul wrote that damn Declaration for a reason," he growled. "None of those stupid Freedom Militia are capable of writing such a Declaration." He was shaking with anger. "Read the Declaration out loud. Talk about the horrific situation in Yemen. Play up his use of Cindy. Emphasize how she and his parents would view his despicable cowardly attack." He grabbed Johnson by the shoulders. "If you get him going, he might just confess. Damn it, it's worth a fucking try. You're a capable attorney. You know how to do this. Go for jugular."

Johnson held up his hand. "Okay, Fred." He stepped back away from Fred, inflated his cheeks, and blew out a puff of air. "I'll go with your famous gut and go after Abdul. I guess it can't hurt."

When they all filed back into the courtroom, the Judge returned and called the courtroom to order with a strike of his gavel. "Counselor Johnson you have the floor."

"Your honor, thank you for the recess and my apologies to Abdul. I would like to cross examine Abdul."

"Abdul Salaamed you are recalled to the witness stand and are still under oath," the Judge announced.

Abdul walked calmly to the witness stand, took his seat, and glanced at Fred, who was staring intently at Abdul, before looking away quickly. Fred thought he recognized confusion in Abdul's expression.

"May I approach the witness?" Johnson asked. The Judge agreed and Johnson moved to the witness box. Fred recognized a renewed vigor in Johnson's stride. "Abdul, you seem like an intelligent individual, who would be a great asset to Yemen." Johnson studied Abdul in silence a few seconds. "You and your attorney have presented an alternate reality quite cleverly. You and I know it is a farce. You were rightly upset by the Saudi Arabian bombing of your home and the death of your entire family. Who among us would not feel the same?" Johnson scanned the jury. "It is completely understandable that you wanted revenge for the attack as stated in your alleged Declaration."

Johnson paused expecting Gladden would object. When he gazed back at Gladden, Gladden was smiling smugly. Johnson walked back to his table and picked up the Declaration, squinting with determination at Fred.

Fred straightened and nodded. Johnson walked back to the witness stand and began to read the Declaration.

Gladden stood up and objected. "The Declaration has been admitted into evidence. We don't need for it to be read out by the prosecution. And may I remind the court and jury that the Declaration was alleged to have been written by Abdul, but no concrete evidence has been produced to prove that Abdul wrote the Declaration." He turned to the jury and raised his eyebrows as if he was asking the jury to agree.

The judge frowned at Gladden. "You will have time for your summation, Counselor Gladden. We don't need your conjecture at this time." He turned to Johnson. "Counselor Johnson, for what reason do you want to read out loud the Declaration, which has already been entered into evidence?"

"This is a capital, terrorism murder trial, Your Honor. The prosecution believes the Declaration is central in proving Abdul Salaamed's guilt and asks for the court's indulgence."

"I'll allow it, but can you make your way to a question?"

"Yes, Your Honor." Johnson stepped to the side of Abdul so that Fred would have an unobstructed view of Abdul while Johnson completed the reading of the Declaration.

"Do you believe what the Declaration states that the United States is ultimately responsible for the bombing of Yemen by Saudi Arabia and consequently the death of your family and the destruction of Yemen?" Johnson asked.

Abdul hesitated, seemingly unsure of how he should answer. "I do."

"Do you feel remorse that you involved Cindy, who obviously cares deeply about you, in your defense?"

Abdul's expression appeared sad momentarily before he reverted to his calm expression. Fred intuited that Abdul was near the breaking point and he cheered Johnson on in his mind.

"Gladden rose. "I object. The prosecution is offering his opinion and leading the witness."

"Objection sustained."

"I'll rephrase the question. Are you sorry that you involved Cindy in your defense?"

"Yes, I am." Abdul gazed sorrowfully at Cindy.

Fred saw the anguish in Abdul's face and felt a glimmer of hope that Abdul would admit his guilt. "Go for it, Johnson," he said under his breath.

"Don't you think that this Declaration of Revenge would have greater import if you admitted you wrote it and you alone planned and executed the rocket attack on the Los Alamos National Laboratory?" Johnson asked. "Wouldn't your deceased parents and Cindy expect you tell the truth?"

Abdul looked briefly at Johnson, then to Cindy, and finally to Fred, who was staring unflinchingly at Abdul. Abdul looked down at his hands in his lap, then over at the Judge, who was stoically watching him. He looked back at Fred, then again looked down at his hands, remaining silent.

"Abdul, please answer the question," Johnson said.

Abdul, after a few seconds as the courtroom became eerily quiet, raised his head, took a deep prolonged breath, straightened, and closed his eyes briefly before opening them wide. He glanced at Cindy, then turned to stare sternly at Fred. "I, Abdul Salaamed, did write the Declaration of Revenge, and I alone planned and executed the SMAW rocket attack on the spent nuclear waste at Tech Area 54 of the Los Alamos National Laboratory. The Saudis are attacking Yemen at the behest of the United States, slaughtering my family and my countrymen. It is a war crime that needs to stop. I thought by destroying the Lab of Death I could get Americans to see what their support for the Saudis is doing to Yemen. I was sadly mistaken and am sorry for the innocent deaths I have caused— even though they are small compared to the deaths the Saudi bombings and blockade are causing in Yemen."

Abdul paused and wet his lips. "The United States should lead the way in promoting a peace settlement and stop the disease and starvation in Yemen that is the worst humanitarian crisis on the planet. The United States needs to turn away from the Masters of War, who are only interested in the money their weapon production and use brings and should become a beacon of peace for the world. The US is the only country with the history and world standing that could successfully do so." As soon as he finished his statement, Abdul grasped his head and wept.

Fred bowed toward Abdul and mouthed 'thank you' silently.

Gladden stood and asked the judge for a recess so he could confer with his client.

"This courtroom in in recess until tomorrow morning at 9:00 AM." The judge said and smiled ever so slightly as he struck his gavel.

Fred stepped out of his taxi in front of his apartment building to a gaggle of news reporters, who barraged him with questions as he waded through the gauntlet. He was exceedingly weary of all the publicity, feeling like he had been drained of blood, but happy to be back on home turf.

Abdul had changed his plea to guilty and was convicted, but did not receive the death penalty. Gladden had argued well that the situation in Yemen, death of Abdul's entire family, and Abdul's last minute confession were mitigating factors that made the death penalty uncalled for under the circumstances. Fred was glad that Abdul had not been sentenced to death. He was against the death penalty as a matter of conscience.

He thought perhaps Abdul would have preferred the death penalty over spending the rest of his life in prison. He hoped the number of deaths Abdul caused would turn out to be less than anticipated— people were still dying of radiation sickness—it didn't look hopeful. He realized that spent nuclear waste stored around the US at the various sites that produced it was a significant threat. Storing spent nuclear waste in barrels seemed stupid and dangerous. He hoped Abdul's attack would at least result in safer storage of nuclear waste. He also hoped that the notoriety around the trial would lead to the eventual end of the US support for the bombing of Yemen, and Yemen could recover from the devastation the war had caused. He wanted Abdul's courtroom confession to resound around the country and world.

He hoped with all his heart that Abdul's attack would not lead to an escalation of bombing in Yemen or the sending of more troops to Yemen.

He believed Abdul was right. The US should stop the military actions and wars they were involved in. No country needed to spend 717 billion dollars on so called 'Defense' and have combat troops in over 100 countries around the world. If the US spent a good portion of that 717 billion dollars towards the promotion of peace, the destruction of all nuclear weapons around the world, and the mitigation of global warming before the temperature and sea rise ended human existence, the world would be a much better place. All of which was unlikely in the polarized US society that the wealthy had taken nearly complete control of. What had the United States become?

He washed his hands and face and poured himself a glass of Irish whiskey, settled down on the sofa, and kicked off his shoes. The ordeal was over, but the ramifications would continue. Fred hoped his notoriety would fade quickly. He wasn't looking forward to going back to the office. Undoubtedly the news reporters were camped outside the FBI office waiting for him to return to work. Maybe he should get the hell out of the city and even the country. Take a needed vacation.

He called his boss at home and asked if he could immediately take vacation, so he could relax and put the pursuit of Abdul and the trial behind him. His boss agreed and told him he didn't want to see him for at least three weeks. He poured himself another glass of whiskey and dialed Maggie. "Hello Maggie, I'm back."

"Fred darling, I don't know how you did it, but I'm sure you somehow got Abdul to admit his guilt. You are the most amazing FBI agent in the US. Congratulations, my love."

The 'congratulations, my love' was music to his ears. "Thank you, Maggie, I would like very much to take you on a long vacation to the Cayman Islands or Tahiti or anywhere else you'd like to go." He paused to catch his breath— he had spit out the words out so fast and emphatically. "What do you say?"

"When?"

"As soon as we can make reservations. I'll take a quick shower, and I'll come over, if that's okay, and we can plan it together." He thought after the vacation he would give more thought to retiring. The United States he had spent a lifetime trying to protect was a much different country than the country when he first joined the FBI. Maybe he needed to let the younger agents take their rightful place and try to bring the US back toward its ideals.

"That sounds wonderful." Maggie lowered her voice. "I'll be waiting anxiously with your present."

"Present?"

"Oh yes, this overjoyed woman has a welcome surprise for the amazing Fred Sampson. So don't tarry."

ABOUT THE AUTHOR

Donald Houser is a writer of two previous self-published novels, *Death In The Peru Rainforest* (2019) and *Escape From The Presidio* (2015). He is a retired engineer, who is interested in the plight of the world in the face of the continuing climate crisis and devastating militarism. He enjoys reading informative and captivating books, traveling and learning about other cultures, and hiking in the wonders of nature. He is a long time resident of Santa Fe, New Mexico.